D0612554

ee liked it when they left the [window open]. [Living] on the highest floor, she cou[ld hear the] city below — the cars honking their horns, the birdies singing, sometimes even an airplane flying by. She and Dada would stick their heads out the window and look down at the tiny cars. Before bed, they'd look for stars and check what color the Empire State Building was that night. Ree could stand up in her crib, and see the lights of the buildings out the window in her room. Pretty soon, she was getting a big girl bed.

But right now, she was listening to the sounds out the window, and not to Mommy and Dada fighting in the kitchen. Ree didn't understand why they were fighting. Usually everyone was happy in her house. But everyone gets angry sometimes. Mommy told Dada "you can't do this forever," and he didn't like that. Ree understood. Mommy told her the same thing when she wanted to stay in the bath forever, and when she wanted to eat cookies forever, and when she wanted to hold her doggie forever and not let him go into the washing machine.

Ree never stayed mad. Mommy always made her feel better. But she wasn't making Dada feel better. Dada didn't yell very often, but now he was yelling "of course you don't know what it's like!" Ree didn't want to listen to Dada yell, so she moved closer to the window to listen to the cars. She climbed up on the couch — she was a big girl who could get up all by herself. Now she could hear the cars better, and the birds too.

She stood up on the couch, to get a better view out the window. She heard lots of birdies. One was very loud. "Coo, coo" it said. She knew that the bird was a pigeon, but that was a hard word to say, so she called it Coo. Mommy was telling Dada that "it's going to get harder for you every year, and you're going to have to—". She didn't want to listen to that. She wanted to listen to the birds. The very loud bird was sitting on the windowsill next to her window. If Ree stuck her head out the window, she could see it just a few feet away. She stayed like that for a minute, leaning out the window, feeling the breeze on her face, watching the bird turn its head and scratch at the stone of the window ledge.

Ree wanted to pet the birdie. She liked to pet the cat, and the cat liked it too, but when she tried to pet birds, they always flew away. But this one was so close. And it wasn't flying away. Maybe if Ree just reached a little bit further...

She had one knee on the windowsill, but couldn't quite reach the birdie. So she lifted up her other leg, so both knees were on the windowsill, but she still couldn't quite reach. She stretched her arms, like when everyone reached up to the sky at Circle Time in school. She stretched and stretched, until her fingertips brushed the bird's tail. Then the bird flapped its wings, and everything spun around, and Ree was falling.

She couldn't breathe for a minute. It was windier outside than the windiest day she had ever felt. She could see the windows of all the other apartments flying by. If they were going slower, she could see into everybody's house and see what they were doing, she thought. But they were going too fast. Too fast to count. The wind tore at her clothes and was louder and louder in her ears. She started to get upset. "Too loud!" she tried to yell, but when she opened her mouth, it filled up with wind and no sound came out. She looked down at the street, and everything was getting bigger. The cars didn't look like toys any more, they looked like big, real cars, flying up at her, faster and faster. The street was flying up at her faster and faster, and the sidewalk too. Ree was starting to get scared. Mommy told her nothing would ever hurt her, but she knew when a car hit a person it hurt. So when the whole street hit a person it would hurt even more.

She tried to turn around, tried to move, but she couldn't. The wind had her, pushing up, up, up at her, even as she fell down, down, down. She started crying now, wanting Mommy, wanting Dada, wishing someone would come and help her. Her ears were ringing now with the sound of the wind, and the sidewalk was rushing up at her faster, and faster, and faster. She closed her eyes.

And then the sidewalk hit her. If the wind was loud, it was nothing compared to the sound her body made hitting the sidewalk. Her head hit the ground, and it made a sound so loud inside her head that there wasn't room for anything else. She couldn't think, she couldn't see, there was nothing but the loud sound. It only lasted a second, but it kept echoing in her head.

When the sound died down, she couldn't hear the wind anymore, but people were screaming, and all the cars' alarms were screaming along. Why were they all upset? Why were even the cars upset? Ree stood up and opened her eyes.

The sidewalk was broken. Little rocks were scattered all over, and where Ree was standing, there was no sidewalk at all, just dirt. The people on the sidewalk were dusty, and were all staring at her. "I faw down!", she offered. When she said that, an old lady fell down instead. She had light skin, but it turned even whiter, and she fell to the sidewalk in a heap. Ree laughed. She said fall down, and somebody did! Now that was funny. She tried it again, "I faw down!", but nobody else fell down. They just stood and stared — grownups could never tell when something was funny.

Everyone kept staring at her for a second, but one by one, they started to look up. A man was falling down, the same way Ree had come, but he was falling headfirst, big, muscular arms out in front of him. When he got close to the ground, he slowed down. He flipped over in mid-air, and then put his feet on the ground like he had only jumped down from one foot high.

"Marie." Dada only called her that when she was in trouble. Was Ree in trouble? Uh-oh.

SELFDESTRUCTIBLE

REHAB

I rack my brain trying to remember the name of the guy I'm in bed with, but I can't. So, we're not off to a great start, but there it is. Suffice it to say, there's a guy, and when the voice wakes me up, it takes me a minute to realize I'm in his bed. Box Avenue, the voice in my earpiece says, people inside. 155 Box, two, three people.

People inside. Shit. My head's pounding, the voice keeps nattering away in my ear, and I try to get my bearings in the cluttered, dingy bedroom, hoping I can find my clothes. What's-his-name is snoring away as I find my skirt on the floor and a tank top tangled up with the sheets. No underwear; I guess he gets a souvenir. No boots, either. Not in the bedroom or by the front door. Did I take them off when we were making out on the couch? In the kitchen, when we were drinking? No time to check. I don't want to have that conversation again. Sorry your loved ones burned up, but I had nothing to wear.

Truck is still en route, the voice in my ear is saying. There's a shock. Those boys are getting lazy these days, just waiting around for me to show up and do their jobs for them. I'm surprised they even managed fancy words like en route.

I take off from the front yard, and realize I have no idea where I am. I thought I'd have to go up pretty high and use the lake to get my bearings, but the plume of smoke is already snaking up to the clouds and I'm streaking towards it before I even glance at the street grid.

I always bend my knees before I take off. That's dumb, I

know. It's not like I'm flying because of my incredible leg muscles. It's just an instinct. I could take off from a lying-down position if I wanted to, I could just fold my legs under myself like I was doing yoga and levitate away, but it just feels right to jump, and keep the jump going, higher and higher until I'm soaring.

And I'm soaring. Usually I have to follow the street grid and keep careful track of where I'm going, so it's a joy to just streak through the gray sky, a blur of row houses and red and orange leaves, just a hint of smoke in the air. And then I'm in it, right in the center of the plume, wind dispersing it just enough so I can see my hand in front of my face. I throw a shoulder down and bust through the roof. I'm not usually a kicking-down-doors kind of gal, but flying just gives you so much momentum, I can cannonball through pretty much anything. And a burning house is ready to fly apart at any moment anyway.

This one especially. I crash through a smoke-filled attic, and the floor gives way like it's made of cardboard. The second-floor hallway is narrow, with three white doors, paint peeling, and the rest all that dingy shade of Landlord Off-White shared by every cheap rental in the world. Most of the houses in this neighborhood had the same basic layout, so I already knew which door was the bathroom and which were the bedrooms. The first was a disaster area, clothes piled on the bed, empty food wrappers on the floor, Playstation hooked up to a TV with a crack in the glass. But no people, and nothing on fire.

The second door's handle is red-hot. Grabbing a door handle like that always makes me think of the Nazi guy in Indiana Jones, who picks up the medallion and gets its imprint burned into his hand. I never get burned, of course, but I still flinch. I shouldn't do that either. Flinching wastes time.

2

The funny thing is, the doorknob makes me flinch, but the room on fire doesn't. Two walls are consumed by flames, so it looks like fire is all that's holding up the ceiling, which is also on fire. The floor is on fire. The foot of the bed is on fire, and someone's in the bed. Man? Woman? Young? Old? Alive? Dead? All questions to ask later. Right now, the instincts kick in, and the only thing that matters is getting them out.

My life is a mess, I'm well aware of that. I'm reckless and selfish and shortsighted and a screwup in too many ways to list here. But in that moment, when the instincts kick in? For a few minutes, I don't screw it up. I live up to the potential I'm always squandering. I walk through the flames without flinching to pick up the prone figure in the bed, and for a moment, I'm my mother's daughter. I throw the person over my shoulder, barrel through the window in a cloud of splinters and broken glass, and I'm my father's.

I land in the front yard, awkwardly, winded, and drop the body in a heap on the grass. Now let's see who I saved, and if they're even still alive. It's only now I start to register even the most basic details. It's a girl, maybe high school age, skinny, tall, darker skinned than me, hair straightened with a red streak. More importantly, hair not burned off. She's unconscious, but a ragged cough reassures me she's still alive.

I look up to see a fire truck lumbering down the next block. About time those dudes showed up. I should stay long enough to give them my prognosis, smoke inhalation, give her oxygen then off to the burn ward, but I don't really want to talk to those guys, and I'm sure they're not really interested in my opinion. They know the drill, anyway. I run back onto the burning house to see if anyone else is home.

3

If there is, there's no way they're still alive. The air is pure smoke, and everything solid is in flames. I stop for a minute and just listen to the crackle. It's weirdly soothing, just feeling everything around me burn, feeling the ashy carpet on my bare feet, feeling the intense heat, like one of those summer days when the air is like soup, but times a hundred. I stop a minute and just soak it in.

I wouldn't call it pleasant, exactly — I'm drenched in sweat, I can't really breathe, and I'll be coughing up soot for the rest of the week, but none of it can hurt me, and in some ways it's easier than dealing with the guys outside, trying to predict who's on this truck, how much they resent me, and whether I've slept with any of them. It's my own special twist on the Walk of Shame — leaving a one-night stand and running into an ex while half-dressed and showing him up at his job. Ah, the glamorous superhero life.

At least I'll be half-dressed. I've been wearing fireproof clothes since I learned the hard way how quickly and completely regular clothes burn in this situation. That was a fun flight home.

I'm shaken out of my reverie by a noise from the next room. It's not your typical wood-splintering house-getting-ready-to-collapse noise you tend to hear in these situations. There couldn't be anyone still alive in there. The room's completely engulfed in flames. Then again, I'm in here. Stranger things have happened.

I walk through the doorway just in time to be crushed by a falling beam. Stupid, stupid, stupid. It's a big square slab of oak, came crashing through the ceiling just like in the movies. It doesn't actually hurt, nothing ever does, but I'm pinned under it, which is never fun.

I'm not super strong. I mean, I'm stronger than the average

girl, but not like Dad was. No busting through walls or throwing cars at people or any of that. It's funny, but I don't like for people to know that. I feel weird being embarrassed by only being indestructible and able to fly, like that's not enough, but people expect me to have the whole package, for whatever reason, and it feels like a letdown to say, yeah, I could take you in a fight, but not by bending a steel bar and tying you up with it. I just have a good left hook.

So being trapped under a big wooden beam isn't an impossible situation for me, but it isn't a breeze either. My main worry isn't that I'll be trapped here — either the beam will burn up and I'll just walk away, or the whole house will collapse and I'll have to wait for them to dig me out of the rubble. I just hate for those guys outside to have to save me. I'd never live that one down.

So I struggle to lift the beam. You know how, when you're in danger, your adrenaline kicks in and you get a burst of strength? That's not actually true. You don't get any stronger. The adrenaline makes you forget that you can be hurt by overexerting yourself. And since I can't be hurt by overexerting myself, that's me, all the time. I'm not super strong, but I have that adrenaline burst going every minute of the day. So, again, not super strong, just really strong. That should be enough, but days like this it doesn't feel that way.

I can't move the beam even an inch. One end of it is lodged in the far wall, which is on fire, of course, but still solid enough that the beam isn't going anywhere. I think about just waiting out the wall — it'll go before I do — but then I try rocking the beam back and forth and have some success. It doesn't really go anywhere, but I can wriggle out from under it about half an inch at a time. I'm making slow progress, but I'm making progress.

I start to think that I'm almost home free, when I see the face in the flames.

At first, I think it's my eyes playing tricks, but the longer I look, the clearer the outline becomes. The fire is everywhere, just like before, but in one spot, it's taking the shape of a person. He looks at me for a minute, then starts to move closer. I don't know if it's a guy or a girl or even a person at all, but I think of it as a guy. He looks down at me, and cocks his head to one side, like he's trying to figure out what I'm doing here, or maybe why I'm not on fire like everything else.

He rests his hands on the wooden beam, just a foot from my head. And he clearly has hands — each finger outlined in flames, searing the wood like a branding iron. He looks me in the eye for a minute, and I don't know what to do besides stare back. His face is just a mass of fire, so who knows if he even has eyes, but I still feel like he's staring. Is he pushing the beam down so I can't escape? Thinking about how he can help me? Or am I just high on fumes and hallucinating?

There's a crash, as the kitchen ceiling collapses and the bedroom I dragged the girl out of falls into it. I automatically look to see, and when I turn my head back, he's gone. The only way I can tell he was there in the first place are the grooves where his fingers burned into the beam, eight trails of glowing ember.

I spend a few more minutes trying to wriggle free, and eventually the beam just breaks apart where he had burned it. I get out of the house before anything else falls on me, only to be hit square in the chest with a blast from a fire hose the second I step through the front door. Man, this day's off to a great start.

It only gets better, as it's only when I stagger to my feet, dripping wet, that I realize my hair burned off. Don't get too worried, it's a wig, but it still sucks. I'd look bad enough soaked to the skin, crumpled in a heap on the front lawn, but somehow my having no hair always makes me look like even more of a hot mess. And it emphasizes that I'm different from them.

Hair is made up of dead cells, and none of my cells have ever died. So, no hair. No fingernails, either. That's the one that usually freaks people out, and to be honest, fingernails seem like they'd be super useful. The tradeoff is, I never have to shave my legs, so that's something.

Mom always bitched about shaving her legs. She had to do it like three times as often as a normal person, because her body regenerated so fast. Of course, she could also take a gunshot over breakfast and not have so much as a bruise at lunchtime. So her powers had their tradeoffs too.

She always kept her hair natural, which she played off as black pride, but I knew it was because when she relaxed her hair, it'd just grow out a few days later, so it wasn't worth the effort. Looking at old pictures, as the years went by and she didn't age, the only thing that changed was her hair. She had this rockin' Afro in the 70s, then kept it super short in the 80s, which was about the least-bad hairstyle you could have in the 80s. Lately my go-to hair has been the skinny braids she always had when I was a kid. It's funny, I never wanted to look like her when I was a kid, and I probably wouldn't if she was still around. But now I sometimes find myself doing things and hoping she'll approve.

Usually, I'm pretty sure she wouldn't. Last night I had my party-girl hair on, straight and bright blue with bangs, like a Korean pop star. My getting-into trouble hair. And hey, guess what? I'm in trouble! The hair works!

Remember a few minutes ago when I was worried about running into an ex while half-dressed and showing him up at his job? Now add soaked to the skin and bald, hoping my shirt isn't see-through. That subtle blend of desperately slutty and freakish that brings all the boys to the yard. And of course there's an ex. Not an ex-boyfriend, exactly, just a guy I'd jumped into bed with, didn't call again, and now run into awkwardly every few months. Daniel... something. Starts with a P? Lots of consonants? Well, I doubt he'll remember Rezsnyak either. Dad used to joke that we had one of the easier-to-spell Polish last names, because there are so many long and difficult ones in Buffalo. I'm hoping the firefighter doesn't take it too hard that I don't remember which one his is.

Before you judge, ask yourself what you'd do if you had just been through a thrilling life-and-death experience with a hunky firefighter, couldn't get an STD or get pregnant because you're indestructible, and were as drunk as I was. Maybe you would have high-tailed it to the nearest Sunday school, but that's just not how I operate.

So. Now I have to try my best to act serious and dignified as he comes over to ask me about the girl.

"You look like hell."

"Hey, nice to see you too. I just ran into a burning building while you and your boys were sitting out here scratching your asses. Did you turn the fire hose on me yourself, or ask one of your bros here to do you a solid?"

Okay, off to a great start. Way to turn on the charm. He's pissed now, but not because I'm being a bitch. It's because I'm right. I was in there, and he was out on the lawn, watching me do the dangerous part of his job for him. And what's worse, now his job is to ask me how it went. He bristles before he starts in on the questions, and I suspect he'd rather run into the burning building himself than ask me about it.

"Is there anyone else inside?"

I decide not to tell him about the face I saw in the flames.

"If there were, I'd still be in there. How's the girl? Smoke inhalation? Anything else."

"Nope. That's it."

Yeah, I miss our long talks. While making a grudging stab at conversation, I notice his eyes darting back and forth between my scalp and my breasts. This is fun.

"What happened to your shoes?"

Man, I just don't want to get into this. Do I lash out at him? Try and explain everything? Lie and say they burned up? Then it hits me, I have the perfect rejoinder for every occasion.

This time, I don't bend my knees. I just float up. Away from him, away from the fire, away from the awkwardness. I don't look down, partly because if he has anything else to say I don't want to hear it, and partly because if he's looking up my skirt I really don't want to know. Flying with your legs crossed looks weird, but I do really have to start making a habit of it. Apart from anything else, it only takes one guy with a decent phone, and there'll be pictures of my cooch all over the internet. More pictures, I mean.

I fly into the plume of smoke and out the other side. I follow it for a bit, just to stay out of sight, before I try to get my bearings. Where was I again? Oh, right, Box Street. That's the East Side of Buffalo for you — even the people who name the streets have given up. At least I'm close to home. I need to go put on some clothes.

9

BURNS

I can't believe we don't learn programming until 11th grade. It's utterly stupid. It's, like, the one thing they teach us that's an actual job skill we'll use after high school. But God forbid they should teach us something worthwhile when we can have stupid health class. It's an every-other-day class, and in a whole year you get two days of drugs are bad, m'kay, six days of eat right and exercise, one awkward period of sex ed where they're required by law to tell us not to do it until we're married even though, as far as I can tell, no one actually does that, and the rest of the year is filler.

I usually just read in this class, or do homework for other classes, but today I'm too bored to even do that, so I'm staring into space and, yes, I'm tracing four-letter words on the desk with my finger. That's what I do when I'm really bored. Sue me.

Mrs. H. is in the middle of one of her usual non-sequitur monologues, jumping from one thing to another and cackling at her own jokes, which are never funny and are barely even jokes. I start to smell this woodsy smell, like being around the campfire, and I start daydreaming about summer camp, about how you always hear about people hooking up with girls at camp but it never actually happens to you or any of your friends.

Then I see where the smell is coming from. Burned into the surface of the desk, right under my finger, is a letter F, and the beginning of a U. I swear I just touched the desk with my finger! But I had burned right into the wood. I'm starting to freak out a bit — damaging school property could get me into serious trouble, and I clearly wasn't spelling out "fun". Maybe if I can get through the class without anyone noticing, they might not realize it was me that did it.

So, of course, someone notices immediately. Kevin, the jerkwad who sits behind me. "Ohhhhhhhhh, what'd you do to your desk?" he says, just above a whisper. Everything that ever comes out of his mouth starts with this long "Ohhhhhhhhh" that gradually rises in pitch, like the sound the cafeteria makes when somebody drops a tray, but just coming from one guy. He's one of those guys who only talks to you to point out what you're doing wrong. "You got pen on your hand." "Why do you always have the same thing for lunch?" "You wore that shirt yesterday." "Ohhhhhhhhh, you're gonna be late!" He's a joy to have in class, as the report cards say.

I try to cover up the burned spot on the desk with some papers, but he isn't about to let it go. "Were you writing fuck on your desk? Ohhhhhhhhh, you were writing fuck!"

"Shut up," I whisper.

"You were writing on your deeeesk! I'm tellllling!"

"Telling? What are you, seven?"

"Ohhhhhhhhh, you're gonna be in so much trouble!"

Now, I don't want to give the impression that Kevin is some goody-goody who's in any way concerned with who's following the rules and who isn't. Heck, he's spent so much time in detention he's on a first-name basis with all the ladies in the main office. He's just trying to aggravate me. And it's working.

"Shut up," I hiss at him. I clench my fist around my pencil, and that's when I smell that wood-burning smell again. I drop the pencil, and the middle third of it is blackened and charred. Holy crap, how did I do that?

"Ohhhhhhhhh, you burned your pencil!"

Does it even strike him as weird that I burned it with my bare hands? Did he not notice that part? How did this guy's mind even work, that he was able to block out everything other than attempting to aggravate me? My mind is still reeling from the fact that it had happened at all, and the last thing I needed is this jackass bothering me.

"I'll burn you next if you don't shut up!" I hiss, louder than before.

"Ohhhhhhhhh, you threatened me!"

I turn around, pointing the burned pencil at him like I'm going to stab him with it. Which I know is pretty lame, but you can really only be so tough sitting in health class at 10:30 in the morning.

"Charles."

It's Mrs. H.

"Do you think you could turn around and re—

"Heburnedhisdesk!!!!" Kevin blurts out.

"Shut up!!!" I yell it this time. Mrs. H. comes over, and it's impossible to hide the burned pencil and before I can stop him, Kevin pushes the papers off my desk to reveal the F and part of a U burned into the wood.

"Charles, I'm very disappointed that you'd show such disregard for school property. That's not like you at all."

"I didn't... I mean, I didn't mean to... it just..."

"Charles, give me your lighter, and then see me after class."

For a minute, I don't know what she's talking about. Lighter than what?

"Hand it over. You don't have any business having a lighter in school."

"A... what? I don't have a lighter. I don't know how—"

"Did the desk just burn itself? Because that would be something. Please turn it over."

I hold up my hands, empty. "I don't have a lighter! I don't have anything! I don't know how this happened!"

I can hear the kids around us murmuring — if there's one thing everyone loves, it's someone making a scene.

"Now, I'm not going to just—"

"Look! I don't have anything! I just touched it, and... and..."

What even happened? I didn't know myself. I just need to calm down and try and explain.

"Okay, it's not time for joking around anymore. You have to give me the lighter."

"I keep telling you, I DON'T HAVE A LIGHTER!"

It's bedlam after that. The papers on my desk burst into flame, and the class roars like the crowd at a football game. I jump back from my burning desk, only to realize my clothes are on fire.

"I DON'T KNOW WHY—" I start to try and explain, but Mrs. H screams and runs to the front of the room. Kids are running every which way, someone even opens a window and a few people jump out onto the grass. I feel dizzy, I grab my desk to steady myself, and it starts to seriously burn. I feel woozy, but nothing hurts. It must be like a shark attack, where you block out the pain and don't feel anything until later. Because I'm definitely on fire, and that has to hurt like hell. It just hasn't hit me yet.

I'm still in a daze when the fire extinguisher hits me. It's Ms. Sullivan, the chemistry teacher from next door. She's always

13

level-headed, in sharp contrast to Mrs. H. I almost get knocked down by the shock of the spray when it first hits me, and I'm determined to stand my ground but she just keeps spraying and spraying. I can't breathe for a minute, and I slump down into my chair. Sullivan keeps spraying until the extinguisher's empty.

"Stop!" I finally manage to sputter. I'm trying hard not to start sobbing. I know that makes me a big baby or whatever, but put yourself in my place. I'm covered in foam, I can't stop coughing from the smoke, not to mention the foam she sprayed into my mouth. I must be horribly burned over my whole body. And I have no idea why it even happened.

It takes me a minute to catch my breath and take stock. I wipe some of the foam off myself, and it's only then that I realize I wasn't burnt at all. I don't have a shirt on — it must have burnt up completely, and my chest is completely smooth, where I had expected it to be scarred and disgusting. My socks burnt up too, and my sneakers are two lumps of charred rubber that disintegrate the moment I take a step. Thank goodness jeans are tough — they're blackened, and have holes in them, but at least they still exist. All that's left of my underwear is a melted elastic band I can feel slipping further into my pants.

I finally stop coughing, and look up at Ms. Sullivan.

"What happened?"

"I was going to ask you that question."

The fire alarm's blaring, and little white lights are flashing from across the classroom. The room is empty besides the two of us — everyone else ran out into the hall or out the window.

"Charles, I don't think you're going to be in any trouble. But this isn't something the school's equipped to handle. I'm going to take you to the office, and we're going to call the police."

"You're going to tell my dad?" It's more of a resigned statement than a question, and in hindsight, duh, of course she was. Should we tell Mr. Lesch that his kid just spontaneously combusted? Naw, I'm sure he's got more important things to think about.

"I'd like to get some idea of what to tell him first."

"Should I bring my backpack?" Habit, I guess, but she laughs when I say that. I look behind me, and see why. The back of my chair is a slab of charcoal, and still hanging off of it by one strap is a melted lump of what must have been polyester. I'm sure if I opened it up, there'd be nothing but ashes inside.

I go with her to the office, and on the way try to explain everything — the desk, the pencil, the flames everywhere. It's weird walking through school, half-naked, wet, leaving behind a charred wreck of a desk. But I have a feeling I'm going to have to get used to weird stuff happening.

REHAB

I went home to make myself presentable, and I had a message on my machine from Finger. Now, before you tell me to get out of the 1990s and get a real phone, I gave up carrying a cell phone after my last six got destroyed. Now, I wish I could say I wrecked them all doing something heroic — running into burning buildings, stopping bullets, fishing someone's car keys out of a sewer drain — but really, it's just easy to get careless when you're indestructible.

I can jump off a building just for kicks, and often do, but it's not until I hit the ground I remember there's a phone in my pocket. Or, more often, a pocketful of junk that used to be a phone. So I have my earpiece that picks up the police and fire scanners, for when I'm feeling heroic, and I have an answering machine. I have no problem being hard to reach. Especially when it's the police trying to reach me.

Cops and supers don't get along, as a general rule. The public thinks our lives are like the reality shows, all full of battling villains and superheroics. When in fact, it's really hard to actually fight crime. If you don't have a TV producer setting up a big fight with some phony supervillain (yes, spoiler alert, stuff on TV is fake), you really don't stumble onto any bank robberies or shootouts in your everyday life.

The real work of crimefighting is cleanup — finding out who did what after the fact, tracking down the who, proving the what, and all the kind of stuff that cops do every day. Most supers don't have the patience or the training for that, yet we get all the attention. So the cops resent that, and I kind of see their point.

But they don't like me in particular. The suburban cops just hate black people, no mystery there. Back when I drove, I tried to tell a cop I'm half white, so I should only get pulled over half as often. He wasn't amused.

The Buffalo cops don't like me because they've seen my record. When I went through my rebellious teen phase, I used to steal cars and crash them into things, or drive them off of things, just for the rush. Of course, I don't really remember the rush through the drunken haze I was in most of the time, but I assume it was a lot of good clean wholesome fun. I also knocked down a few abandoned buildings, tried to jump in the smelter at Bethlehem Steel (they had shut it down the year earlier and it was just a lump of solid metal, so that didn't pan out), and of course a lot of sidewalks got destroyed from me jumping off stuff. Mostly in the three blocks of downtown where there are tall buildings. It's not like New York, where there's a thousand skyscrapers and reinforced sidewalks.

Finger was the one who finally caught me at my shenanigans. Not because he was Sherlock Holmes or anything. I pulled down a building on top of myself and couldn't get out of it. I was trapped under a big concrete slab for a day and a half until someone finally bothered to dig me out. That was a fun day. This town's boring enough when you're not trapped under rubble.

Now, Finger would have been well within his rights to throw me in jail, and if some other cop had gotten the call I might still be locked up. And he was technically required by law to turn me over to the Secret Service. But he didn't do either of those things. My parents had done him a solid back before I was born, so he decided to look out for me. He made the charges against me go away, but he assigned me his own personal community service, which involved using my powers to help people occasionally, or at the very least not causing trouble. He stressed the importance of staying under the radar, if I didn't want to end up in the gulag, brainwashed, or getting blown up in Afghanistan.

Yeah, don't believe what you hear on cable news. The super-powered menace that's threatening your freedom? We've got a lot less freedom than you do.

Anyway, Finger. He looks out for me, I help him on a case when I can, and run into a burning building every now and again so he doesn't bitch that I'm squandering my gifts. Basically, he's my sole source of parental disapproval, and like any parent, he knows all the stupid stuff I did when I was young, and will never let me forget any of it.

I also have a private theory on why he keeps bringing me in for help. We're about the only two people in town who aren't in love with the Maestro. He's the "official" super, the city's protector, a job he took over from my parents when they left for New York. A job they probably thought I'd be doing someday. So I don't know whether I hate him for not doing the job as well as Mom and Dad did, or for doing it better than I would. And I don't know why Finger doesn't like him, but it's something we have to bond over.

His message was vague — he usually is — but he wanted me to come to the station, which is weird, because usually he's out on a case somewhere and needs me to go somewhere unsafe. Once, last year, he actually called me in to break up a standoff. Two drug dealers were holed up in an abandoned house, taking potshots at the cops through the windows. The cops were all behind barricades and cars, and I just walked right up the front walk. I thought maybe, an unarmed girl, clearly not a cop, they wouldn't shoot me. They shot me like fifty times. One dude was still shooting at me up until I walked up and took the gun out of his hand.

That was the one day I really felt like a superhero. Even the cops loved me that day. Firefighters get pissed if you rob them of their shot at glory, but cops are pretty happy if something you did means they don't have to take a bullet.

Even so, I'm never crazy about walking through the front door of police HQ, but Finger gets annoyed if he has to come up and unlock the roof. I find him at his desk, which looks just like every cop's desk in the movies. Stacks of paper everywhere with no rhyme or reason, multiple cups of cold coffee that could have been there since this morning or last year. Finger looks just like a cop out of the movies too — tall white guy, built like a linebacker, lantern jaw that has four o'clock shadow by the time he finishes breakfast. Lots of the other cops are overweight, or clumsy, or just don't seem serious enough to be cops. Finger's always serious.

"I need you to talk to this kid we brought in."

"Hey, nice to see you too. How was your weekend?"

He glared at me. Never any fun, this one.

"He almost burned down Sweet Home High School this morning. Teacher said he spontaneously combusted in the middle of class. Burned up his desk, his papers, his clothes, but he wasn't even singed. Not even his hair."

"So, he's super. You really needed me to work that out for you?"

"I was hoping you could talk to him. You and I know what his deal is, but he doesn't. He's scared shitless, and I was thinking it would be helpful if he could talk to someone who's..."

"Adorable?" No matter how much I bait Finger, he never responds. He's like one of those palace guards with the big fuzzy hats.

"You know what I mean."

"At...risk?" I say through gritted teeth. My least favorite phrase.

"Someone who's had to come to terms with their abilities. Right now he doesn't know how to turn it on and off. He's terrified he's going to go to bed tonight and wake up to find out he burned up his parents and is being shipped off to Gitmo. I thought maybe you could tell him he'll adjust to having these powers."

"I was born this way. I never had to adjust to shit."

"Damn it, I'm asking for your help, Marie. If you don't want to help, go fly off and get drunk again."

"Oh Finger, you know I can't say no to you." I bat my fake eyelashes. "Where have you got the little rugrat locked up?"

"You know where."

"The Rezsnyak Suite? Always nice to visit one of my old haunts."

"Just remember where you are, and why you're there. No screwing around. You're supposed to be helping this kid."

"Don't worry. I'll take him out, get him loaded, it'll be a good time."

Another glare. The glare continues as the phone rings and he picks up.

"Detective Finger. <pause> The explosion? They filled me

in. <pause> How is that possible?" He glanced up at me. "Sorry, stupid question. I'll be there in fifteen minutes."

He put down the phone and looked at me like he wasn't sure if he regretted asking me to come downtown. "I have to run down to the hospital. Please talk to the kid. Try and calm him down if you can."

Finger grabbed his coat and walked out. I guess he figured I had spent enough time in the station to find my own way around. I thought I'd take the opportunity to snoop around his desk, but there wasn't anything interesting, just cop paperwork I couldn't make heads or tails of — nobody I knew had their name on it, anyway. And the morning's paper. I don't see the word Rehab anywhere, which is always a relief. The big headline was the Maestro talking about retiring for, what, the eighth time? I think all the tributes and stuff the first time went right to his head. And you can pull off that heartfelt "my city still needs me" crap two, maybe three times, but after that give it a rest.

Of course, if he did retire for real, who would take over? Probably fucking Glimmer. As it is, I can barely stop myself from punching her every time I see her. The last thing she needs is an ego boost. There used to be a time when there was always someone waiting in the wings. When Vulcan retired, back before I was born, my parents were more than ready to jump in. And I'm sure the Maestro was beside himself when they got called up to the big leagues and moved to New York. But now there's really no good options. I guess I should keep rooting for the Maestro to stay on the job. Not that he needs my encouragement. He's like a little kid, grabbing onto the city's leg so they can't make him leave the playroom.

Then again, Dad never wanted to retire either. Damn stubborn old man. I keep thinking, if he had just listened to Mom. But then, Mom wouldn't have listened to anyone. All the time, I think, if only I could go back in time, and tell him not to go. But I never think about telling Mom — if there was trouble, she would have gone no matter what. Thought she was indestructible. Of course, she was, up until that day.

Of course, I think about this stuff and then kick myself for how selfish it is. If I could go back in time, my first thought isn't to stop the WTC attack from happening, it's just to tell Dad not to show up for work that day. Let everyone else die, just so long as my Daddy's safe. And that's why he's still a national hero, and I'm just his screwup daughter.

BURNS

The whole afternoon, waiting in the main office for the cops to show up, driving with the cops downtown, waiting in the cell they put me in, I was terrified that they would call home. But they never did. Which is even scarier. The worst thing I ever worried about was a lecture from a teacher or the principal, followed by a lecture from Dad. In-school suspension wasn't even on the radar. And now I'm in jail. Like, real jail.

I can tell right away this isn't the cell they put people in while they wait for their parents to show up. This cell is in the basement below the basement. There wasn't even a button in the elevator — the cop who took me down had this super-thin key that he slipped in the crack around the metal panel the buttons were on. You wouldn't even think to look for a place to put a key there. He didn't talk to me the whole way down. None of the cops did. I didn't even ride in a police car; they put me in the back of a van with no windows. I was afraid maybe they weren't even real cops.

Then they put me in this cell, which is not how you picture a jail cell. No bars, no windows, just stainless steel on every surface. Not even the little slot that opens for them to slip you a tray of food. There's just a little hole in the floor that I guess I'm supposed to poop into, but I'm really hoping it doesn't come to that.

This seems way worse than regular jail, and regular jail was way worse than anywhere I ever planned on ending up. You hear about the government taking people away who have dangerous powers. And I figured that must be what's happening, right? I mean, everything around me burned, and I didn't even feel warm. Is that my super power? Burning stuff? Can you even use that to help people? Crap, what if I'm a supervillain? I mean, The Maestro started off as a fireman — does this make me his enemy? Are they keeping me here until he can come and deal with me himself?

I always imagined meeting him one day. Just stupid, childish hero worship stuff. He'd come riding in on his motorcycle, maybe show off his powers, and I'd have a cool story to tell all my friends. I always wondered what I'd say to the guy if I ever met him. Now I'm pretty sure it'll be "please don't kill me."

I spend who knows how long down here, alone, working myself into a panic, when I hear the door start to move. I try to pull myself together, which is hard to do when all you're wearing is a pair of burned-up pants, which you nearly peed in from sheer terror. I feel self-conscious enough when we have to do shirts and skins in gym class. Bad enough the girls in my class see how scrawny I am next to the sophomores, I really don't need The Maestro deciding it'd be easier to snap me like a twig than it would be to talk to me.

But it's not The Maestro. And weirdly, it's not a cop. It's this black girl, not much older than me, wild curls everywhere, wearing a ripped-up t-shirt and a black leather jacket. She's about the least cop-like person I've ever seen. Still, whoever she is, maybe she can get me out of here. I have to play it cool. Act like I'm not crazy, or dangerous, or anything other than a well-behaved kid who didn't do anything on purpose. I just have to stay cool.

"Whoareyouyouhavetohelpmegetoutofhereididn'tdoany-thingididn'tknowwhatiwasdoingyouhavetohelpmeihavetoget-outofherewheresmydad?!?!?!"

Yep, cool like Paula Abdul. I always did know how to impress the girls. For a second, I'm convinced she's just going to walk right out again and close the door, but she laughs at me, which is maybe worse.

"So, enjoying your stay?"

"Y...uh....no?"

"Yeah, I spent a lot of time down here when I was your age. Fun times. So, what's your deal? You burned down your school?"

"N... uh... just a desk."

"Well, that's not so bad. You probably won't get the gas chamber for that."

I'm about 85% sure she's joking about the gas chamber, but it still hits me all over again how much trouble I'm in. I'm not proud to admit this, but I can feel tears welling up behind my eyes. Tears of panic. Is that a thing? It is if you're highly flammable, locked in a basement super-jail, talking about the gas chamber.

"Oh, relax, I'm kidding. I don't think you're in any real trouble. Okay, I don't actually know whether you're in trouble or not, but it doesn't seem like you did anything that bad. I bet they'll chalk it up to accidental. I mean, I'm not a lawyer or anything..."

"Yeah, who... who are you, exactly? Are you... with... the police?"

I don't even know what to ask her. She's pretty obviously not with the police, but then she's here in the police station, so... yeah. I have no idea what's going on.

"The police? No. I'm, well, let's say the cops and I are very dear frenemies. No, I'm like you. Check it out."

That didn't explain anything, and now she's pulling a gun out of her jacket. She points it at her head, and before I can even react, she smiles, and pulls the trigger. A deafening shot fills the room, and I instinctively take cover. Ten minutes ago, I was more scared than I had ever been in my life, but now I'm so scared I can feel pee running down my legs and soaking into my burnt-up jeans. This is far and away the worst day of my life. Tears stream down my nose, and I feel like I'm about to start sobbing, when I realize she's laughing.

The shock of it snaps me out of both crying and terror. She's still standing there, head cocked to one side, black powder marks around her ear, but other than that perfectly fine.

"You wanna try?" She uncocks the gun and tosses it to me. Even on my best day, I can't catch, and now, hands shaking, pissing myself in terror, I don't even reach for it, and it skitters away across the floor.

"Jesus, who are you?"

"You must not watch the local news."

Then it hits me. Who else would be able to shoot herself and laugh it off afterwards? And who else would be sick enough to actually do it?

"Oh shit. You're Rehab."

"That's not what my mama named me, but yeah."

"Why— why are you here?"

To torture me, is all I can think.

"Just to give ya a little pep talk. Buck up, little shaver, that kind of thing. Oh, and to explain why you've had such an interesting day. You see, when a boy reaches a certain age, his body starts to change. New and strange urges. A deeper voice. Hair, where there was no hair before. Flames, shooting from his hands. He starts to notice girls. The usual stuff."

My head is spinning. A minute ago, this girl shot herself right in front of me, and now she's cheerfully prattling on about God knows what? The cell door's still open. Maybe I can shove my way past her and get out of the cell. Although that would involve standing up, and I feel like that's way beyond me right now.

"I'm surprised your parents didn't give you this speech. You usually get some combination of their powers, so they must have seen the fire thing coming. Are both of your parents super, or just one? Because depending on what they can do, you might be able to do more than just burn."

"What? No! Neither... nobody... nobody's super."

I realize I'm not at my most articulate, but put yourself in my place. I'm still reeling from the gunshot thing. When I look at her more closely, I realize the rips in her shirt are bullet holes. Little circles of light brown peek out from the tears. It dawns on me that she isn't wearing a bra. One of the holes must be like an inch from her right nipple, and I find myself mesmerized for a second. Then I snap out of it. Damn it, brain, can you not think about boobs just this once? Focus!

I come back to reality and realize she's been talking about how powers are passed down genetically. Everybody knows this, at least everyone who knows how to use Wikipedia. Your genes don't actually give you the powers, but they make you receptive to the strings of energy, and the strings give you powers. At least, that's what Einstein said. I think about that for a minute, and realize something just as she says it:

"Your parents must be lying to you. Lying to their own kid about their powers, knowing full well he'll inherit them? That's pretty cold. But it's the only explanation. Oh. Wait."

Her eyes go wide.

"You need to talk to your mom."

Believe me, there is no one I would rather talk to right now than Mom. She died when I was a little kid. I want to think that if she were here, she'd be able to get me out of this, or make me feel better, or something, but who knows. And I really don't need to get into it with Rehab right now anyway.

"How do I... I mean, can I go home? And talk to my family? Will they be able to visit me? Are they going to let me out?"

"Kid, you're not going to jail. Not like jail, jail. They just want to hold onto you for a while to make sure you're not going to burn anything else down. You're going to get better at controlling your powers, but the first day? Not so much. Shit, that reminds me, that's why I'm here. I have to see if you're going to burn anything else down. So, let's start with this. Try and burn me."

"What?"

"Seriously. You can't hurt me. My clothes are fireproof. The only thing in the room that's flammable is your pants, and frankly, I think they're too wet to light at the moment."

I can feel myself blushing, which I didn't think was a real thing that happens in real life. I mean, obviously I know people blush, but feeling the blood rushing to your face, your cheeks getting tingly and hot? That must be a special thing that only happens when you're in jail, half-naked, soaked in your own urine, and being made fun of by a girl who just shot herself right in front of you.

She obviously notices, because her tone softens.

"Sorry, I know you've had a rough day. But I'm serious

about you burning something. If you can show them that you can control your power, they'll let you out sooner. Here, try this."

She reached into her jacket and handed me a pen. It was just a cheap Bic, the kind I had five of in the bottom of my backpack. "Melt it," she said.

I squeezed the pen in my right hand. Then my left. I opened my hand and stared at the pen, trying to focus on it as hard as I could. I closed my fist around the pen, and closed my eyes too. I tried to imagine the pen lighting on fire. I try to think of warmth, of the pen getting hotter and hotter. I try to imagine it melted, twisted, smelling like burnt plastic. But it's still cold and smooth in my hand.

"I can't do it."

She frowns. "How did you feel when you did it before?"

"Angry."

"Well, maybe that's it. Maybe you have to get emotional."

"How did it work for you?"

"I was born indestructible. When I was one minute old, they tried to prick my heel and the needle wouldn't go in, so they figured out pretty quickly what the deal was. Flying kinda started slow. I used to play basketball with a bunch of guys, and one day I dunked on them. They were all amazed. I mean, I'm tall now, but I was only 13. So I kept doing it to show off, and it got easier and easier, and I felt like I was just hanging in the air, until I realized that I actually was hanging in the air — I could go up and dunk and then just stay up there. After that, I told my Dad, and he took me up flying over the city with him every chance he got. He used to joke that it was my Driver's Ed.

"Anyway, let's try it again. Think about how you felt then.

Think about how pissed off you were."

I try. I think about Kevin, and what a jerk he is. I think about health class, and what a waste of time it is. I think about 9th grade, and how I can't wait for high school to just be done. They tell you a lot of crap about how high school is the best years of your life. I mean, no one expected it to be like in the movies, when high school kids all own cars and they spend all their time partying and drinking and having sex and are also 30 years old. But I expected at least the classes to be challenging, or interesting, or not complete bullshit. I wondered if they'd even let me back in, now that I had burned up a desk. I wondered if maybe there was some secret school for people with superpowers. Of course if there were, it wouldn't be secret, it'd have a reality show. The thought of that kind of depresses me.

"Anything?"

The sound of her voice reminded me I was supposed to be getting mad.

"Sorry, my mind keeps wandering."

"God, you're bad at this."

She walks over to me and slaps me. For a second, I worry she's going to take my head off with her super strength. Instead, she only hits me enough to knock me down. I'm still kneeling from when I ducked for cover after she fired the gun, so she easily knocks me off balance and sends me sprawling.

"Come on, fight back!"

The second I try and get my balance, she slaps me again and I go sprawling. In the back of my mind, I know what she's doing; she's trying to get me mad, so I'll use my power again. But I'm mostly just annoyed. Annoyed, and a little bit scared. Because what if it isn't an act? What if she is trying to fight me?

How do you fight back against someone who can't be hurt?

I get into a crouch and lunge at her legs, and this time I knock her down. Well done, sir. I know I'm not all that strong, but I'm fast. I was the best kid on the middle school track team, and yes, I know that's the most pathetic thing to brag about ever. I see daylight — the cell door's still open, and I climb over her and make a run for it.

I don't make it very far. Two feet from the door, she gets me in a bear hug, and spins me around so I'm facing back into the cell. She pushes me forward, and we both fall down, me going face-first towards the floor. Her whole weight lands on me, but she gets a hand in front of my mouth to stop me from cracking it on the ground. It's a strange feeling — her hands are soft, but in that moment of impact, when I should crush her fingers under my jaw, they're like solid rock.

"Come on! Burn me!" She has me on my stomach now, kneeling on my legs so I can't get up, grabbing me by the wrists.

"Stop hitting yourself! Why are you hitting yourself?"

You've got to be kidding me.

"What are you, eight years old?"

"Stop hitting yourself! Stop hitting yourself!"

Sad to say, I've been in this position before, and I find the only thing you can really do is hope it stops being fun for the other person. I stop fighting back, and let her slap me a few more times, until she relents.

"You're not even going to fight back?"

"What's the point? You're super strong and I can't hurt you."

She frowns.

"You're supposed to get mad! You're supposed to burn me! Shit, sorry, I thought that would work."

She gets off me, and I get to my feet, still wary that she might knock me down again.

"God, you're bad at this." I can at least throw that back in her face.

"Look, this isn't my job. They just asked me to help. You don't want my help, fine. I don't care if you stay in here or not."

"Help? How are you helping? Scaring the shit out of me then slapping the shit out of me? Hey, thanks for the help! I feel so much better now!"

"Fine, you can deal with the cops."

"Fine, I'd rather deal with the cops. The cops aren't completely crazy."

"Fine, good luck."

She turns to go, then stops in the doorway.

"Oh, before I go, your clothes." I look down at my smelly, burned-up jeans. I'm barely wearing clothes.

"There are a couple places online where you can buy fireproof clothes. You'll need them, if you ever do get your powers to work." She picks up the pen I didn't manage to melt and pulls a scrap of paper from her pocket. "Kevlar's always good. They can make it pretty thin and it's also bulletproof, which I hear is useful. Email me sometime, and I can show you where to go."

She hands me the piece of paper, and I can't think of anything else to say to her. Does she still think she's helping me? I'd always heard she was unstable, but I figured that was just the TV news, going after celebrities like they always do. Turns out they got it right for once.

She walks out and closes the door behind her. The stupid cops. They never even gave me my phone call, who knows what they've said to my dad, if they've even told him. I'm stuck in here without a way to even call the guard, and then they send this crazy girl to torment me. I feel more helpless now than I did a minute ago, when she had me pinned to the floor.

I look at the piece of paper in my hand. There's nothing left but ashes. Hey, it worked after all.

REHAB

So that went well. I don't know anything about that kid's powers, I'm sure he hates me after all that, and I'm doubly sure Finger's gonna be pissed. I really need to learn how to be more ah, shit, I forgot the gun.

I ask the officer on duty down here to let me back in, but he's not having it.

"I was instructed to give you one-time access to the prisoner. The detective was very clear."

"I just need to go back in for a second! I forgot something."

"Anything else you need to tell him can be relayed by one of the officers."

"No, I left something in there. I need to go back and get it."

"Left something? You weren't supposed to bring anything into the cell. What was it?"

"Um... nothing. Nothing important. I just want to go back in for a sec and get it."

Now his mood has shifted from bureaucratically annoyed to worried and mad at me. Isn't that the mood everyone ends up in, eventually?

"What. Did you bring. Into the cell."

"Just a... uh... gun."

"You gave the prisoner a gun?"

"It can't hurt me! It was just for a demonstration!"

You know who it can hurt? Everyone else in the world."

Wow, this guy is more of a smartass than I expected. I really hope he doesn't find out I just picked up the gun off of some cop's desk. I try my best to defuse the situation.

"That's why I'll go back in and get it. He can shoot me 'till he's out of bullets. Not a big deal."

"It's a very big deal."

"Just let me back in, I'll get the gun back, everything'll be cool."

He grabs me by the arm like an unruly child, and drags me to the cell and unlocks it.

"Hey, kid, I forgot the gun."

"I did it!"

I don't know what he did, but from his tone of voice, he did it to spite me.

"You did what?"

"I burned the paper you gave me!"

He holds up his hand, and his fingers are still a bit smudged with ash.

"Holy crap, you did it! See, that's why I was trying to piss you off."

"Yeah, you were a real help. But I felt it when it happened — I think I can do it again. Give me something else I can burn!"

"Totally. Lemme see what's out in the hallway."

I pick up the gun, and head for the door, but the second I get to the doorway, the cop cuffs me and drags me out of the room. I hear a shout from inside, and for a split second, I find myself hoping the kid sets the cop on fire. We can bust out of here and go on the lam together. It'll be fun. But the cop slams the door before the kid can take two steps towards us.

I seriously consider fighting the cop. Even cuffed, I could probably take him. He seems like he's in decent shape, he could be as strong as me, but I could wear him down. But that would raise a commotion, more cops, eventually one of them would pin me down, and then I'd just be in more trouble.

I consider it a sign of real maturity that I stopped to think about that and didn't just slug him.

Of course, the minute he throws me in a cell, I wish I had slugged him.

I've spent enough time in these cells to know the deal; there's no point trying to break out, the door's impossible to open from the inside, they're totally soundproof, so there's not much I can do until Finger shows up to yell at me. That's pretty much been the story every time I've been here — some cop locks me up, Finger yells at me, but he lets me out. So I just have to wait until that happens. I bet the kid would be happy to know I wound up as his next door neighbor. I wonder if they'll let me talk to him again after Finger lets me out. I wonder if they'll give him anything else to burn.

I wake up a few hours later to the sound of the door opening. I was out late and up early, so it isn't that hard to nap while I'm in here. I'm thankful for that. Being awake in these cells is the most boring thing imaginable.

Finger is as abrupt as ever.

"Come with me."

I put on my jacket and follow.

There's a different cop on guard duty, but he still grabs my arm and tries to tell Finger he's not allowed to walk out of here with me. Finger makes short work of him.

"Do you know who this girl's parents are? Do I have to drag you outside and show you the statue? This city would be a smoldering ruin if not for them."

Oh, God. The fucking statue. They redid the fountain in front of City Hall a few years ago with a shiny bronze statue of Mom and Dad striking a heroic pose. Brave protectors, symbol of unity in a racially divided city, blah, blah. They made Dad look like his power involved bludgeoning people with his chin, and they somehow managed to make Mom look Asian. I hate to even go near that block — I can just see the picture in the paper of the poor, screwed up girl mourning Mommy and Daddy after all these years.

What's worse is, the fountain they tore down to build it was put up to honor Vulcan. He was the city protector before my parents, and I always got the impression he was the guy Dad wanted to live up to. He was a big deal to Dad. But at this point, hardly anyone remembers him. I'm not sure anyone knew where the fountain came from when they tore it down. But Dad remembered. He would have been pissed if he'd known. I find myself thinking about the best way to leave the station so as to avoid Niagara Square, but I realize I'm going wherever Finger wants me to go.

"I don't have time to read you the riot act. I need your help, right now."

'Cause I did such a bang-up job the last time? I don't say anything, I just follow him up to the street and get in the car with him. He always makes me sit in the back, the seat where the criminals go, and usually I give him a hard time, call shot-gun, that sort of thing, but today I figure he's fed up with me enough already.

We drive a few blocks before he speaks up.

"A week ago there was an explosion at a warehouse downtown."

"Yeah? I didn't hear anything about it," I say, indicating my earpiece.

"We covered it up. Four people, that we know of, were caught in the blast. The explosion shattered windows a block away, burned every tree on the block to a cinder, and melted the street signs. But those four people were untouched. They're all comatose, but otherwise completely unharmed.

"Those four have been under observation at Millard Fillmore since the explosion. One patient glows in the dark; one is semi-transparent; one gives everyone who touches him electrical shocks. And then there's the blonde girl."

We drive a few blocks in silence before he elaborates. We pass by the big Greek Orthodox church. I used to love the view from on top of the steeple. You could look all the way down Delaware to Niagara Square. Of course, now the damned statue is there. Still, you can look down the cross street and just about see the river, so I still go up there sometimes.

I finally get tired of waiting and just ask: "So who's the blonde girl?"

Finger takes a deep breath.

"I said four people were untouched in the explosion. Actually, three were untouched. The fourth wasn't burned, or bruised, or harmed in any obvious way by the explosion itself. But she has a fresh scar across her face, and we don't know how she got it.

"The third night, a nurse heard a commotion in the girl's room. When she got there, everything in the room was broken. Furniture smashed, windows cracked, every light bulb broken, the TV wasn't working, and every light, screen, or readout on every machine she was hooked up to was smashed. And she was hooked up to a lot of machines."

"So, how did they subdue her?"

"They didn't have to. She never came out of the coma."

"Well, that's freaky."

"Yeah. After that, the hospital upped security, but two days later an orderly making the rounds got knocked unconscious when he stepped into the room. Now they're all afraid to go in there, and for good reason. And that's where you come in. We want to move her to a secure location, but we don't want to risk someone getting hurt."

"Okay, I'm game." This could be worth doing just to see her blow up the room in her sleep again.

He nodded his assent and we drove on in silence for another minute.

"You know, I did get the kid to use his powers."

"I'm sure there was a way of making that happen without breaking any laws."

"What, pissing off a teenager is against the law now?"

"How about bringing a gun into a jail cell and leaving it there? It's certainly frowned upon."

Is Finger making a joke? I hope that's a sign he isn't that mad about the whole thing. Maybe if I shift the conversation, he'll even forget all about it.

"There's another thing I wanted to talk to you about. The fire this morning?"

"Another arson case?"

"No. Well, maybe. But when I was in the building, I thought I saw something. I thought I saw a face in the flames."

"A face? Someone you didn't get to in time?"

"More like the fire was starting to take the shape of a person.

I think your arsonist is a super. You don't think it could be this kid, do you?"

"I have it on pretty good authority he was playing the oboe in band while your fire was going on."

"So two different people with fire powers we're just finding out about this week? That's odd. And there's another weird thing. He said neither of his parents are super."

"That he knows about."

"Yeah, that was my thought too. But what about this coma girl? And the other people in the explosion? That's a lot of new powers on the scene all at once. They can't all have super parents — that's a hell of a coincidence, unless the warehouse was hosting a family reunion."

"Sure. But how else would they get their powers? The thing's genetic, however it works."

"But the first generation, back in the 40s, they got their powers from somewhere."

"The atomic tests."

"Yeah. You don't think someone's..."

"Risking tearing apart the universe? I certainly hope not."

"Yeah, well, I think we need to figure out what's going on here. And hope there's some other explanation."

"I need to figure out what's going on here. You need to do what I ask you to do, and try and stay out of jail for once."

"Oh, I get it. You use me when it's dangerous but you don't pay me to think? You know, I'm pretty smart, I could help you."

"Go to college first, then we'll talk."

"Touché."

We pull up in front of Millard Fillmore. It's one of Buffalo's worst-kept secrets that this is the hospital with the supers wing. I'm sure that brings to mind someone flying around in a wheelchair, or bending crutches into a knot with their bare hands, but mostly it's a typical hospital, pale green paint, disinfectant smell, and TVs playing daytime talk shows.

They're expecting us at the nurses station. The nurse at the desk has a seen-it-all expression, and she probably has. She barely looks up from her book. "She's over in the O.R. You know the way."

It was nominally a question, but we do know the way. The supers "wing" isn't that big — if everything Finger said was true, the supers population of Buffalo probably increased by half this week. It's mostly for a few permanent residents, whose powers make them dangerous to the general population, but don't really deserve to be in jail, and the government doesn't really want for whatever reason. You've got to put people like that somewhere, so they may as well be someplace their families can visit.

And then there's Jodi. I'm not sure how she avoided government service, as I'm sure they could use her, but she somehow worked out a deal where the hospital gets her, and she keeps a low profile. I suspect half the reason for the supers wing is to keep her under wraps, but I don't know how she got them to agree to it. I'm also not sure whether she's an actual doctor or not, although I'm pretty sure she went to med school. For someone I think of as a friend, there's actually a lot I don't know about Jodi.

Still, I like her. She's not exactly a barrel of laughs, but I seem drawn to antisocial loners who hate everyone. Go figure.

The supers wing has its own operating room, and while the security guard on duty brings Finger up to date, I watch Jodi through the window. In front of her is a young boy on the table, five or six years old, black, tubes coming out of his arm, a breathing mask over his face, and a chest wound bleeding profusely. A man and a woman were in scrubs, with masks. Doctors? Nurses? They all looked the same to me. Jodi had green scrubs on, but no mask or gloves. She placed her hands over the wound and closed her eyes.

"Left superior pulmonary vein's definitely torn. Just keep the blood coming. Heart's okay, aorta's okay. Bullet went right through the lung and out the back."

Eyes still closed, Jodi started spreading out and closing her fingers, in some series of movements only she understood.

"Repaired the vein, keep an eye on heart rate. Arteries next, then the lung."

She worked in silence for a few minutes, her colleagues not doing much more than watching the heart monitor and cleaning up blood, although the flow had stemmed considerably. Finally, she flattened out the wound with her hands, and when she pulled them away, it was closed up entirely, a fresh pink scar standing out where there had been a gaping hole a minute before. She opened her eyes.

"The back's still open, flip him over, please."

She placed her hands over the exit wound, and a few minutes later, all that was left was a matching scar.

"Get the blood out of his lungs, keep checking his BP, but he should be fine."

"They always are, once you get your hands on 'em." The male doctor/nurse spoke for the first time. Could he be an orderly? All he did was flip the boy over.

"One inch to the left and the bullet would have taken out his aorta. One inch lower and it would have gone into his heart.

He wouldn't be fine then. Make sure he gets plenty to eat. Those new cells need nourishment."

Chastened, the man kept quiet as she washed her hands and stepped out into the hall.

"I'm just curious, why did it leave a scar? Couldn't you erase that too? I'm not criticizing, I'm just interested how it works."

"Too many questions. If there's a scar, we can tell his mother the bullet passed right through him and it was a lucky shot, and she'll be happy enough to have her boy back she won't think too hard about it. No scar, and it's not a lucky shot, it's a miracle. And once word gets out they're performing miracles down at the Mill, everyone will want one."

"I thought word had gotten out, as busy as you are."

"I'm busy because the city's overrun with poverty and crime, and people keep trying to burn it down. Shouldn't you be doing something about that?"

"Oh, so it's my fault people are poor? Or that it's easier to get a gun than a job interview? When I win the lottery, I promise I'll reopen the Trico plant, but until then, my flying around brawling isn't going to change much. You know that."

"You could at least try. I can't save everyone who comes through the front door, but I at least make a dent."

"I know you, Jodi. You probably do try to save everyone who comes through the front door. You need to take a break sometimes."

She looked over at the unconscious little boy in the next room.

"Sweetie, you wouldn't mind bleeding to death so I can have a break, do you?"

"Okay, point taken."

"Some of us have more important things to do than getting drunk all the time."

"Okay, okay, I get it. I just hate to see you killing yourself—"

"So that others might live? Yeah, where are my priorities?"

I give up. She's pretty much impossible to talk to when she gets her hackles up like this. Did I mention we're dear friends? Fortunately, Finger shows up and cuts through the awkwardness.

"Do you have the girl ready?"

"She's in 403. The elevator's set up to go nonstop to the loading dock, where the ambulance is waiting. The keys are in the ignition. Security has strict instructions not to let anyone near it, and not to interfere when you drive out."

"Man, you're taking this seriously."

"It is serious." She gestures into room 403. It's just what Finger described, but it somehow looks worse in person than I pictured. Every available surface is damaged somehow. Wind whistles through cracks in the windows. The bed tilts down where one of the legs is twisted unnaturally. Plaster scatters the floor where chunks of it have fallen out of the wall at various points. It takes me a second, but I realize that I can hear the wind because the usual hum of hospital machinery has stopped. Every piece of equipment is broken.

In the middle of the room, slumbering peacefully to all appearances, is the blonde girl. She must have been pretty at one point, in a high-school-cheerleader kind of way, but the scar changed that. A red gash ran from her forehead, across her eyelid, and down her cheek. It was still red and raw, so it must have been as recent as the explosion. But if the explosion itself didn't hurt her, how'd she get it?

"You didn't fix the scar?" I ask Jodi.

"I really don't want to mess with this one. Usually I can see someone's cell structure pretty clearly, but this girl's just a blur. I'd be working blind. And I really don't want to risk her blowing me up if I make a false move."

Jodi's explained to me how her powers work, or tried to. She can see, and then manipulate, someone's body on a cellular level. She looks at you and sees your internal organs, arteries, nerves, the whole deal. She can fix things, like she did with that kid's bullet wound, but if she wanted to, she could grow you a third arm. At least I assume she could. When I suggested it once, she looked at me like I was an idiot.

A nervous-looking orderly wheeled a gurney into the room, and Finger and I lifted the girl's body off the bed. She weighed like 90 pounds; I couldn't feel that scared of her. We rolled her to the elevator, and Jodi watched us as the doors closed. We rode down in silence, and I listened to the hum of the elevator, half expecting it to jolt to a stop at any moment. But it opened to daylight, where an ambulance was parked and waiting. So far, so good.

"So, where are we going? Back to the station?"

"Up north."

"You mean—"

"Our friend has taken an interest. Thinks maybe he can help her."

Our friend. Every time we talk about the Doctor, Finger turns into a mobster, all euphemism this, and if-you-get-my-drift that. To be fair, I didn't know his name for the longest time. As a little girl, my parents introduced me to him as Dr. Science, and that's still how I think of him. As much as I grew up around this stuff and shouldn't be fazed by it, I still get excited by the lab in Niagara Falls.

"Woohoo! Road trip with Fing-ah!"

That glare again.

"Come on, even you have to see how serious this is. You saw what she did to that room. Imagine if she got loose and were roaming the streets."

"Roaming the streets? She's in a coma!"

"For now. God help us both if she wakes up."

Okay, he was actually worried about this, even if I wasn't. I made the obvious gesture.

"Why don't I just drive her myself? Then you don't have to risk getting hurt if anything does go wrong."

"I want you in the back with her. I'm driving."

"Are you sure? You were just saying how dangerous she is."

"That's the job."

"So, you trust her not to blow you up more than you trust me to drive twenty miles without screwing it up?"

"That's about the size of it."

"Wow. Thanks."

I-190 goes across Grand Island and right into the heart of Niagara Falls, the New York side, the run-down depressing side, but Finger wants to take Niagara Falls Boulevard. The Boulevard's the way people used to go to the Falls, before they built the interstate. You can still see the remnants of what once must have been a sprawling thoroughfare. In between the suburban sprawl are still hot dog stands and tiny motels that once thrived on a tourists and travelers, and are now just holding on. I always imagine those motels are 10% weary travelers, and 90% cheating spouses. But there was a time when they must have been packed with vacationers, back when the Falls was the "honeymoon capital of the world." That was even before Dad's time, the Boulevard's heyday. Now there's barely any traffic, but the run-down buildings still crowd either side of the street. If there's one thing we're not short on around here, it's empty reminders of what used to be.

I look at the girl again. She's young, to have been blown up, scarred, and put into a coma. Not like there's an ideal age. I start trying to think like a detective. She was caught in an explosion, but she wasn't burned, or crushed, or even hurt, seemingly. But she's not indestructible, she can't heal like Mom could, or else she wouldn't have the scar. Could she have caused the explosion? Given the state of her room, and the way everyone's terrified of her, that seems likely. Maybe that's why she didn't get hurt? She was at the center of it?

I realize I'm spitballing, but the more I look at this girl, the more questions I have. Why was she at a warehouse, downtown, late at night? She looks like every skinny, blonde suburban white girl. Even if she was a college student, the explosion wasn't near any of the campuses. Was she buying drugs? Probably. Why else do white people go into the city, if there isn't a hockey game on?

I feel the ambulance lurch into a sharp left. I glance at the back window to see if I can get my bearings, and that's when I notice the cracks in the glass and realize we're in trouble.

The sides of the ambulance are rippling, like they're made of fabric and not steel. The back doors start to fold in on themselves, like a giant invisible hand is crumpling them up. All this only takes a few seconds to unfold, before the explosion. It happens so fast, my last thought before the ambulance flips over is, I wonder if anyone in the neighborhood saw anything before the warehouse went up. I wonder if they told Finger anything and he's holding out on me.

I don't really get to finish that thought, as there's an ear-splitting sound of metal grinding against metal, and then a second later I'm somehow lying on the pavement with half an ambulance on top of me. The other half is twenty feet away — the two broken halves lying open like a cracked eggshell, with bits of steel, broken glass, and EMT equipment strewn in between. The jagged edge of what was once the wall is pinned across my torso. I don't really feel pain, at least not the way other people have described it to me. But certain things are uncomfortable, and half a ton of twisted steel squashing one of my boobs is definitely one of them.

I try to wriggle free, and find I'm pretty well trapped, but as I twist around, I see daylight, an empty street, and about half a block away, a skinny blonde girl in a hospital gown, arms limp at her side, walking away. Even from here, I can see the glass cuts on her back through the gap in the back of the gown. I try and lift the wreck of the ambulance, hoping I can catch her before she goes out of sight, but it won't budge. I turn my body around, and then I see the other half of the ambulance, and Finger.

He's on his side facing me, still strapped into the passenger seat, his face covered in blood from a head wound somewhere behind his ear, and a metal rod sticking out of his chest. From here, I can't tell if he's alive or dead, but if he is alive, he won't be for long. Unless I get him help.

A beat-up Toyota Camry skids to a stop about 10 yards short of the wreck. A heavyset woman in sweatpants and a Bills sweatshirt opens the door and sticks her head out.

"Are you okay?"

"I need your help. Come here."

She walks over, gingerly, like she's scared the ambulance might re-explode. I eye the Camry and come up with a plan.

"Listen. I'm not hurt. But I'm stuck. I need you to get me out, or the officer will die."

I indicate Finger, and she gasps when she sees the shape he's in.

"I can't lift..."

"You don't have to. I want you to crash your car into it."

Her eyes go wide.

"You have to trust me. You can run right over me and I promise you I won't even get a bruise. But you have to do it fast. It'll hurt your car, but the cops will pay to have it fixed. If they don't, I'll buy you a new one myself. I'm good for it."

She starts to nod in agreement, screwing up her courage to do what I'm asking her to do. I talk a lot of shit about Buffalo, but one thing I have to give a lot of credit for, people help each other out. When you're done shoveling your driveway, you shovel your neighbor's driveway without being asked. That's just how it is. Maybe it's a shared sense of catastrophe, but people have each other's backs. In Manhattan, you ask someone for help and they're convinced it's a ploy to get their wallet.

"I... I don't think I can do this."

I try my best to twist around so I can look her in the eye.

"You can do this. You're going to do this. You're going to save this guy's life. You just have to be a little brave."

She nods again. I think I'm talking her into it.

"Back the car up so you get a running start. And just don't take your foot off the gas for anything. Just remember you can't hurt me, and your car will protect you. Does your car have an airbag?"

"Yeah. I think so."

"I'm pretty sure it does. Still, wear your seat belt too."

"Seat belt." She nods again, but otherwise stays motionless. For a minute, I worry she's too freaked out to go through with it. Maybe another car will stop in a minute. Odds are good it'll be an SUV, which I'm sure would make short work of the ambulance. And what would the odds be of three vehicles in a row going down this street with none of them being an SUV?

She starts walking to the car. Maybe she's going to come through after all. She gets behind the wheel, and just sits there for a minute. Is she screwing up her courage, or deciding whether she can get away with leaving? I squint to see her license plate, so I can figure out later who to either congratulate or condemn. But I can't see that far, and I'd never remember the number anyway.

She sits there long enough that I start to get worried. I crane my neck to see Finger again. Is he breathing? Has he been dead this whole time? Even though he insisted on driving, I still have the nagging feeling that this is somehow all my fault. I hear the car engine roar, and I turn back around to see the Camry speeding towards me from a block away. She's doing it. Now, let's just hope she doesn't chicken out before she hits me.

I've been in many car accidents from behind the wheel, but this'll be the first time I've been run over by one. Somewhere, my teenage self is kicking herself for not thinking of it. Crashing into something, there was always that thrill at the moment of impact, then that minute of disorientation afterwards, when you couldn't tell which way was up or how wrecked the car was. It was visceral and exciting, in a way not many things are if you can't be hurt. This is different. I find I'm not excited at the onrushing car; I'm barely even bracing for the impact. All I can think about is, will this work?

A few seconds later, I get that unmistakable sound of metal tearing through metal, and my body's flipped over before I have time to think. I'm under the Camry, which means I'm free of the ambulance. I roll onto my back, and do one of my favorite tricks, which is to fly just along the ground, and swoop up so I'm standing next to the car. The woman looks appropriately shocked.

Or maybe she's just rattled from the crash. Smoke is pouring from under the crumpled hood of the car, but the car's midsection seems undamaged, and the airbag deployed, so other than a scare, she seems fine.

"You did great," I tell her. "You saved his life. You saved me. I'll make sure everyone knows that."

"Y-you're okay?" she manages. It's a dumb question, but I don't blame her — what else is there to say?

"Everything rolls right off me. You may have to take me up on that new car, though. Call 911 first, and tell them what happened. The cops should take care of you. Now, I need to get him to a hospital."

I pull Finger out of the wreck. To my relief, he's still breathing, although there's blood everywhere. I look back at the woman, who's still trying to gather her wits.

"You were a hero today. Thanks." Seemed like a super-hero kind of thing to say. Plus, it's the truth. I take off, cradling Finger in my arms like a giant 6-foot-3 baby. I say a silent prayer as we hurtle through the sky, to the one person on Earth who can save him.

BURNS

So, being in jail sucked. But since I've been out, things aren't as bad as I feared. Dad was understandably freaked out, but I assumed it would be in an, "oh my God, you're a monster, please don't burn the house down," kind of way, when it turned out to be in a "you must have been so scared, I'm going to try and make everything okay" kind of way.

Dad's super practical all the time, which usually means he doesn't want us to do anything fun if it costs money, and we spend way too much time thinking about recycling and cutting down on household waste. But for this, he like, sprung into action. The most fireproof place in the house is the garage, so he moved the mattress from my bed down there and that's my room now, which is actually kinda great because I won't have to hear my sister's music when she's home from college and if I want to stay up late, no one can see light coming from under my door and tell me to go to sleep.

Dad went to Home Depot and bought like four fire extinguishers, placed strategically around the room. He also bought two big plastic barrels, put them up on wooden slats, and filled them up with water. So if the wood burns, it knocks over the barrels and douses everything. Pretty ingenious, although now my room looks like I live in the old *Donkey Kong* game. I also got fireproof clothes — it turns out, a lot of motorcyclists wear Kevlar to protect them if they hit the street, so I've got a few biker outfits now. They're basically just black shirts and jeans, but I still think it looks cool.

The one thing he couldn't help me with was explaining why I have these powers. I didn't get them from him. For a second, I thought maybe Mom had been super, and I just never knew because, well, I don't remember a whole lot about her in general. But he said she was just a regular person, and that my getting powers must just be some fluke thing. That we still don't really understand how this stuff works. Which I guess is true.

He also decided not to send me back to school, which is a relief on so many levels. The classes were a waste of time, and the handful of kids I actually liked I just talk to online anyway. A lot of kids were freaked out by what happened and were kind of scared I'd come back. So I told my friends to start telling everyone I'm going to come back and burn up anybody who picked on me.

Oh, and I came up with a superhero name: Mr. Burns. Like on *The Simpsons*? I've been practicing saying, "eeeeexcellent" while making little jets of flame shoot back and forth between my fingers. And, yeah, I can make little jets of flame shoot back and forth between my fingers. I've been practicing all week, and I'm actually getting a lot better. I have a corner of the garage I use for practice, or I go out on the back patio during the day when the neighbors are at work. I can burn stuff by touching it pretty much on cue now. I can make fire come out of my hands, and make it not come out the whole rest of my body. I tried to burn stuff just by thinking about it, but that didn't work, I have to be touching it, or shooting fire at it. But it's still pretty cool. I'm starting to get into this having-superpowers thing.

Even the cops were actually okay after that first day. They brought me clothes, finally, and when those burned up, they just brought me more. They finally gave me a Kevlar vest, too, which I couldn't burn up, although I had fun trying. I had to give it back before they let me go, but it still felt pretty badass in the meantime.

My dad visited every day and brought me stuff from home, the police station has wifi, they even ordered takeout for me. It really stops feeling like jail if you have your iPhone and a chicken finger sub. It took maybe three days before I could get a handle on not burning stuff by accident, and then once they were convinced, I could go home. I have to come back every week — they have a social worker who specializes in supers. Apparently she's Glimmer's big sister, which must be weird, but I guess it'll probably be weird for my sister too.

Anyway, I've gone to see her a few times, but this is the first time there's someone else in the waiting room. It's a girl maybe two-three years older than me, long black hair with blonde streaks, with bangs that hang past the tops of her glasses. If I had to guess, I'd say she's half white/half Asian, but I hate playing Guess the Ethnicity. There's no prize if you win, and you look like a jerk if you get it wrong.

The important thing is, she's cute, she's way cooler than any of the girls I go to school with, and as little success as I've had with girls, I have a chance to make a fresh start as a bad-ass superhero instead of a scrawny nerdling.

I realize as I'm thinking all this that I'm just staring at her. I don't want to weird her out, so I look down, but even then I'm just staring at her skinny jeans. Now I think I really am weirding her out. Maybe I should just say hi, so she sees I'm not some perv. Hi.

"So, what are you in for?"

Man, what do I tell her? I have super powers! I can make flames shoot out of my fingers! I'm not bragging or trying to impress you at all!

"Oh, you know. This and that."

"Hmm." She eyes me skeptically. She takes a sip of her Vitamin Water. Personally, I don't drink anything that has water in the name but isn't actually water, but that's just me. She takes another sip, and I notice frost creeping along the outside of the bottle. She drops it on the floor with a thunk — the water is frozen solid.

"So, nothing special? Just here for no reason?"

Okay, busted. Obviously if she's here it must be for the same reason. Might as well put my cards on the table.

"Um, well, I can do this..."

I tent my fingers like Mr. Burns. I gently pull them apart, and little arcs of flame jet between my fingers.

"Yeah, that's not bad." She tries her best to sound bored and unimpressed. She picks up the frozen water, and by the time it gets up to her lips, it's liquid again.

"So, you can make things cold. I can make things hot. We must be soul mates."

Was that trying too hard? I'm trying too hard.

"I think it means we're enemies."

Damn, I was trying too hard. Maybe dial it back down to small talk.

"So, how long you had, you know, powers?"

She looks at me like I'm the hundredth person in a row to ask her this question and she can't believe she has to answer it again.

"Around the time I hit puberty, it kept snowing in my bedroom. In the summertime. I used to see Dr. Walters pretty regularly, but now I just check in two-three times a year."

"What's she like? I only just started two weeks ago."

"She's nice. She actually helped me a lot. When the freezing stuff first started, I couldn't control it and was just freezing everything in sight. She helped me get a handle on that. And then after that, gave me some tips on just leading a normal life."

"So, you just lead a normal life? You don't want to be a superhero or anything?"

"I'm not really that interested. I just go to school, try and stay out of people's way. I have a part-time job making liquid nitrogen."

I start to laugh, but then realize she's not joking.

"So, Dr. Walters could help me get a job... burning stuff?"

I need to find a less lame way of saying that.

"I guess so. Although burning stuff isn't that hard for regular people. I don't know if there's a practical application. Maybe you can be the Maestro's assistant."

Assistant? Now that's cold. I'm used to just letting stuff like that roll off me. I got insulted all the time at school, and all I could really do was pretend it didn't bother me and try to keep my head down. I'm sick of doing that. Maybe being in jail toughened me up, but I decided to strike back.

I grabbed the Vitamin Water out of her hand. I try to focus on just applying a little heat, not enough to produce flame, just enough to make it hot. The water starts to bubble as the label burns off in my hand. Steam pours out of the lid as the water boils away. Then the plastic starts to melt. Water pours over my hand and turns to steam on impact, and when the smoke clears there's nothing left but a lump of plastic. I hand it back to her.

"Assistant?"

"Well, if I'm ever attacked by water bottles, I'll know just who to call."

I try to think of something to say back to that, when the

office door opens.

"Hello, Charles. Nice to see you again. Chloe, here's, um, this." She hands the girl a manila envelope, which she clearly doesn't want to talk about in front of me. From what I can tell so far, she takes the whole doctor-patient confidentiality thing super-seriously.

I won't bore you with the whole conversation. Oh right, I can't! It's confidential! No, I'm totally kidding, it's just boring. Typical teen-counselor stuff, her asking me if I'm okay, me saying yes, her not believing me, that kind of thing. Except that unlike the school guidance counselor, Dr. Walters can make the whole room go dark. It's a pretty cool power, but she's pretty quick to admit it doesn't have a lot of practical value. She said she had issues about that for a long time, which led to her wanting to help other supers through their issues.

I ask her about Chloe's job, and of course she says she can't talk about other patients, so I rephrase and ask whether there's anything in the growing field of setting-stuff-on-fire that I can look forward to, and she says she's sure there's a use for my abilities, but she doesn't sound like she knows any specifics. So nothing terribly useful, but it's nice to know I have someone I can talk to who isn't completely out of her depth. I mean, Dad is handling this remarkably well, but it's all new to him. Dr. Walters was able to hook me up with a place to get fireproof clothes and give me important safety tips — mostly that I still have to avoid getting overemotional and lighting up, at least until I've had more time to get a handle on things.

Of course, what I really want to ask her is, how do I get Chloe's number? Confident, older, hip, pretty, and not at all interested in me? That's like everything I'm looking for in a girl.

Plus the fire-and-ice thing is too perfect. Opposites attract! It just makes too much sense! And, of course, I'll never see her again. The doctor wouldn't give me her number, even if I asked, and she said she only comes in a few times a year. What are the chances I'd ever run into her again?

Forty-five minutes later, I run into her again.

When my session is done, I'm surprised to see Chloe still there, reading something on her phone, looking even more annoyed than before.

"D'you miss me?"

I think making "did you" into one word is a Buffalo thing. The old joke is, there are lots of Jews in Buffalo — Jew eat yet? Jew see the game? I'm sure she didn't give me a second thought while I was in there, but I figure, if she can give me a hard time, I can give her one.

"My dad's late."

"That sucks. Mine should be here in a minute, can we give you a ride?"

"No, he told me he's on his way." She holds up her phone.

In these situations, when I'm interested in a girl I just met, I usually think long and hard about asking for her number or something, and then I wuss out and feel stupid for the rest of the week. But this time is going to be different. We have this weird thing in common; I have a perfect excuse because I do really want to know about using your powers to get a job. Plus, I really have nothing to lose. It's not like I'll ever see her again. It's not like having a girl shoot you down at school and having to sit next to her in math for the rest of the year.

"Look, do you wanna hang out some time?"

She gives me the kind of blank look that would usually

have me frantically sounding the retreat, but for some reason I decide to press on. Just play it casual. Just hanging out.

"I just— I mean— it'd be nice to have somebody to talk to. Who has the same issues. I mean, Dr. Walters is nice, but you've actually been through what I'm going through. I don't know, I thought maybe you'd want to talk to somebody who's like you. You probably already have super-powered friends or whatever—"

"Yeah, that doesn't sound so bad. Give me your number."

Holy crap, it worked. She puts my number in her phone, although she doesn't offer hers. Still, my heart's beating fast enough that I start to worry about starting a fire. The door from outside opens and snaps me out of it. It's her dad, at long last. He's Asian, younger than my dad, with spiky black hair with flecks of gray, wire-rimmed glasses and a leather coat. He looks like he'd be a cool dad.

"See you around."

It's funny, now it's her turn to be shy and fumbling. She doesn't say anything back, just manages a tiny wave as she follows her dad out the door. I guess parents do that to everybody. There's an upper limit to how cool you can be when you're getting a ride home in a minivan.

After she goes, I send a text to summon my own ride and reflect that things are going really well. I got to drop out of school, I just gave a girl my number, and I won at Guess the Ethnicity. Too bad there's no prize.

REHAB

Finger was okay. Jodi did her thing, and he was good as new pretty much immediately. He didn't thank me for saving his life or anything, but he also wasn't mad at me for losing the girl, so I guess that evens out. I think his boss was pissed at him. After all, we screwed up a pretty delicate high-stakes operation. But at least it's given me some stuff to do the past couple weeks. Obviously I'm looking for the blonde girl, although I don't really have any idea of how to find her, unless she blows all the windows out of wherever she's hiding. And I'm pursuing my theory about the super-arsonist, mostly by running into every burning building I can find and trying to catch him in the act.

That's not exactly easy either. Arson is far and away the leading cause of fire in Buffalo and has been for years. The city's got a potent combination of entrenched poverty, high crime, and loads of abandoned buildings. In the past few years, the city has beefed up its arson unit while also tearing down empty buildings at a pretty good clip. So, arson has dropped dramatically, and there's still one a day, give or take. Mostly houses in bad neighborhoods that probably would have collapsed under their own weight given enough time.

My house included. When my parents lived here, they lived in one of the city's many restored Victorian mansions in the heart of one of the city's two nice neighborhoods. But the whole reason I moved here was to stay out of the spotlight and try and get my shit together. That seemed tough to do in a house that everyone knows belonged to the city's most famous heroes.

It's actually easier to hide in plain sight. My house is in the worst neighborhood in a town that's mostly bad neighborhoods. About two thirds of the houses on the block have either burned down or been torn down by the city, and the remaining third probably should be torn down. I'm not sure anyone on the street, myself included, has ever held a job. Which isn't that surprising, given how few jobs there are to be had.

People don't really look at you too closely in this neighborhood, which suits me just fine. If I have a hoodie pulled up, I may as well be invisible. If my half-whiteness makes me stand out, no one lets it show. There's nothing to see, really, just another girl from the East Side with nowhere to go. I can understand all that, but what really blows my mind is that even my being able to fly isn't that interesting to people.

Granted, I try not to call attention to it or anything. I usually go behind the abandoned furniture store around the corner, make a 2-story jump onto the roof, then take off from there, so it doesn't look like I'm coming from anywhere in particular. But the couple times I've just taken off from the street, people glanced up and went back to what they were doing. I'm sure anyone who wanted to put ten minutes of thought into it could figure out that the girl in the house at the end of the block is a super, but no one cares.

My parents owned this house too. It was a safe house, just in case anyone ever went after them at the mansion. I'm not sure they ever had to use it, but they made sure I knew it was here. The house next door got torn down a long time ago, and they took the opportunity to buy the property and build into that house's basement, so it's got a good-sized bunker underneath it. I keep the bunker well-furnished and the upstairs shitty.

When I go out, it certainly isn't in this neighborhood, so none of my friends even know where I live, apart from Jodi. I guess that tells you what good friends they are. "People I drink with" is probably more accurate. But the list of people who have actually been to my place is short enough that, when I hear a knock on the door, I know it's either the Jehovah's Witnesses, or it's Oakley.

As you may have picked up, I'm not shy about jumping into bed with a guy. But they don't stick around. Or I don't stick around. I haven't had an honest-to-goodness boyfriend since high school, although I've certainly kept busy. Maybe you think I don't want to involve some innocent boy in my dangerous lifestyle. Or maybe you think I'm just a slutty girl who can't commit. The truth is probably some combination of those. I like to think I'm like any other girl — I want to be loved, and I want to be left alone. Just a lot more of each than usual.

So, I haven't had anything close to a boyfriend, but I do have Oakley. What do I call him? On-again/off-again seems too romantic. Repeat offender is a bit closer to the mark. Frenemies with benefits? Is that a thing? It is for us. We hang out, casual-like, things are good, then we sleep together, and that's pretty good, and then either one of us meets someone else and blows the other one off, or I go off on a drunk and ignore him, and whatever happens, we hate each other and I forget about him for weeks or months.

And then he comes back.

"Oaktown."

"Hey, Ree, no one's seen you in a while."

"I've been working on a case."

"They sell vodka by the case now?"

"Asshole. What are you doing here anyway? I thought you were with that white girl."

That's our running joke. He always leaves me for a white girl, and by the time he comes back around to me, he's on the outs with a different white girl. I think he does well with them for the same reason he comes back to me; Oakley's a black nerd. White hipster girls love him, because he's black enough to piss off daddy, but nerdy enough that he drinks microbrew beer and can and will spend an hour talking about comic books, or the Coen Brothers, or Guided By Voices, or whatever other stuff nerds talk about.

And I think he and I keep coming back to each other partly because we're both black prep school kids. Not black enough for the black folks, not white enough for the white folks, all resentment and squandered potential. We understand each other. Which is probably why we can't stand each other.

"Nah, she was Asian this time. I'm broadening my horizons."

"And yet, here you are."

"Here I am."

I don't know whether there even was an Asian girl, or whether he's trying to wind me up. It doesn't really matter, we're both just skimming through the script until it gets to the good part.

"Do you want a drink or something?"

"Sure. You doing anything? You want to watch a movie or something?"

"Yeah, that's why you came over, the movies."

"Well, you want me to leave?"

"Yeah, and not come back. But you know I want you to stay too."

He kisses me. We both know why he's here, and we both know I'm not turning him away. The jumble of reasons why I shouldn't drifts away like it always does, and then he's got my shirt off and for a minute I think, one of these times I should make him work for it, or talk to him first, or something, but it's already too late for that.

And I have to admit, I like waking up next to Oak once in a while. It's nice to not be hung over and scrambling to remember someone's name. We do all the same stuff we did the night before, but it's somehow nicer in the morning. Last night it was urgent and rushed, like we both wanted to make sure we went through with it before the other one changed their mind. Now we take our time, just a lazy Sunday morning. Sunday? Wednesday? I can't remember but it doesn't matter. Oakley works odd hours, so it's all the same to him, I'm sure.

When we're finally up and out of bed, he makes these really good scrambled eggs with cheese and pepper and onions which I can never manage to get right myself, although, let's be honest, I'm too lazy to do anything with more than two ingredients, especially first thing in the morning. It hits me as I eat a forkful of eggs that the only reason I buy cheddar cheese is so he can make these eggs. If we don't hook up for a while, the cheese goes moldy and I throw it out, uneaten. I feel a stab of, what, guilt? Regret? Lust? Shame? Annoyance, I guess, that I'm just sitting here waiting for him, easy pickings, when I should be... shit, who knows what I should be.

This is a bad relationship, if it's even a relationship, and I shouldn't enjoy it as much as I do. But I actually feel good this morning, and my judgment is lax enough that I start talking about the arsonist, and the blonde girl, and before I know it I'm telling him how scared I was about Finger, and how I don't know what I would have done if he had died in that ambulance. I'm on the verge of tears, and I'm just waiting for Oakley to make some excuse to leave, but he doesn't.

"Look, I'm sorry, I know you didn't sign up for this. Being a shoulder to cry on or whatever."

"No, you're allowed. Besides, I've always been curious about your powers. What it's like, I mean. And whether you're a superhero who just slums it with someone like me sometimes or what."

I laugh a little as I brush away a tear. "I thought you were the one slumming, coming over to the East Side from Allentown! I don't work for the government, if that's what you mean. I just have one friend who's a cop. Friend of my parents, really. Sometimes he asks me to help him out."

"So this is the case you were talking about? Are you allowed to talk about it?"

"I guess so, not that there's a lot to talk about. Just this extremely dangerous girl on the loose, and I have no idea how to find her. And I feel like it's all my fault, although I don't know what I could have done differently. And hell, if the cops don't know how to find her, I don't know how I'm supposed to."

"So that's why you haven't been coming into the Pink lately? Flying around looking for this girl?"

"Actually, I have two cases I'm screwing up right now. I was in a burning building last week and I thought I saw a person made out of fire. I think there's a super arsonist on the loose. So I've been going on as many firefighting runs as I can, annoying the hell out of BFD, looking all over town for this guy. I assume it's a guy."

"Why look all over town? You don't got enough fires on this street to keep you busy?"

Something clicks when he says that. What if I assume the arsonist lives in the neighborhood? I saw him on Box Ave, not that far away. One thing I picked up from Finger is that small-time criminals don't travel. You're more likely to get mugged in a bad neighborhood because that's where the muggers live. If you're going to mug somebody, you don't get in the car and drive to East Amherst, even if people have more money there. You don't know the people, don't know the streets, and don't know the hiding places. That's why poor folks get robbed more than rich folks do.

I've also had the feeling all week, chasing this guy, that if I show up when BFD does, I'm already too late. Arsonists don't tend to stick around to get caught, so why should this guy be any different? It had to be a fluke that I caught him the other day. I need to get on the scene well before somebody calls 911. And that goes double in this neighborhood, where houses burn down all the time and nobody blinks an eye. So many of them are too decrepit to live in, so they're not worth anything besides an insurance settlement.

So I need to stick close to home and watch out for smoke. It still really comes down to me being in the right place at the right time, but I feel like my odds are better. I don't know — it's either a great idea or a terrible one, but I'm in a good mood, so it seems worth trying.

"Oak, I think you're onto something. Most of the garden-variety arson is in this part of town, so why wouldn't this guy be too? I just need to stick to this neighborhood."

"I'm just a genius crimefighter. No need to thank me."

"Do you have to be anywhere right now? Do you want to go for a walk?"

"A walk?"

"You know, you use your legs? To go from one place to another?"

Walking isn't that foreign a concept in Buffalo, but it's pretty close. This isn't New York, where you can hop on the subway no matter where you are. Not having a car is unheard of, and when the weather's bad, which is often, you drive to your next-door-neighbor's house. Hell, I had a car for a while, and I can fly.

"You can help me case the neighborhood. If I'm going to search the 'hood for this guy, I need to know my way around better."

"You mean you just want to walk around? In this neighborhood?"

"You'll come into the hood at night if it means you can get some, but you won't walk around in broad daylight? Aww... I'll keep you safe."

Attacking his manhood maybe isn't the best way to go, but after some grousing, he agrees to come with me and look around. The fact is, I don't really know my own neighborhood that well. There's not much to see, unless you like empty lots and weeds growing through the sidewalks, piles of garbage and broken furniture on the curbs, and piles of dirt that used to be piles of snow. If I leave the house, it's usually to fly off somewhere else.

We go up and down a few blocks, talking about this and that. I try to make note of which places are abandoned and likely to go up in smoke, although I remember that the first house had people living in it, so maybe that was no help. I have to admit to myself that I don't really have any idea what I'm doing. Part of this walking around was just an excuse to go somewhere with Oakley, and I realize I don't really have any idea what I'm doing there either.

We end up walking to Genesee Street. There's a long stretch in the middle of the block that's all empty lots, and it's a weirdly pastoral stretch of grass, a bird or two chirping over the hum of the highway that runs behind the line of trees at the back of the empty lots. On one side of the empty stretch is a house with paint peeling off clapboard, and the roof is in three mismatched shades of shingle, although on closer inspection, the darkest shade marks spots where the roof has caved in.

On the other side of the stretch is a large, ramshackle house that got converted into a bar. All of the windows are boarded up, and in a few spots the siding has fallen down and covered over with unvarnished plywood. Everything about the building screams out abandoned, but the awning is clean enough that I suspect the bar is open despite the state of the place. No one ever went broke selling booze in this town.

On the other side of the street is a red Victorian house that's actually pretty nice. Big upstairs porch, which a lot of houses in the city have, and both cars in the driveway are in good shape. The grass is neatly cut, and it just makes you feel like good people live there. But then you feel bad that those people have to live on a street like this one.

"Why do you live around here?"

It's a fair question.

"I had to get out of New York, and this is the only other place where I—"

"No, I mean the ghetto. I know who your parents were.

They must have left you some money. Even in Allentown, houses ain't that expensive. So why are you here?"

Oakley's never mentioned my parents before. We have this unspoken thing where he pretends I'm just some girl, and I pretend that's all I am. I look up and down the block. I guess I don't blame anyone for questioning the choices that led me to this place. Most people who live here don't have any other options.

"Partly, I wanted to hide out. I left New York because I was sick of being that trashy girl in the papers. As soon as the *Daily News* turned Ree into Rehab, I should have known to make a change, but I just kept right on. Drinking, getting into scrapes, eventually I couldn't get coffee in the morning without them putting my picture on page two with some made-up scandal for a headline. So I didn't just want to get out of New York, I wanted to go someplace where no one would notice me at all.

"Also, when I came back here, I wanted to see what this town is really like. My parents helped out everybody they could, but they were still in a bubble, living in a mansion and all. And they had a lot of spectacular rescues and stuff, but crime just got worse and worse. There's just no money in this town, and no jobs. I guess I want to remind myself that superpowers aren't going to fix any of that. My parents' way didn't work. And I want to find my own way, but who knows what I can actually do that'll matter to anyone."

Man, I'm really opening up to this guy today. I didn't mean for that to happen, like pretty much everything that happens between me and Oakley. To my surprise, he gets serious.

"Ree, it's not up to you to fix everything. And you don't have to keep punishing yourself because you can't."

He's actually a decent guy sometimes, this one. I kiss him. And not our usual, hey baby things are about to get freaky kind of kiss. Like a real kiss. A nice one. For a moment, I let myself believe that maybe this time, we won't screw it all up.

BURNS

And I never heard from that girl again.

That's what I assumed I'd be saying, anyway, as two weeks went by, and two more visits to Dr. Walters, and I never heard from her. But one night as I'm about to go to bed, I get a text from someone named iceqn.

iceqn: Hey have U burned down yr house yet? :p

At first I figure it's someone from school giving me a hard time. It takes me a minute to realize iceqn meant Ice Queen, and another minute to realize Ice Queen is her. Yeah, I'm dumb. But at this point I didn't think I was ever going to hear from her again. So I texted back,

charlesch: No, I'm coming over to burn down your house.
iceqn: oh, I'm totally scared.
charlesch: U should be. Ill melt all your frozen shit.
iceqn: who wd win if we had fight i wonder
charlesch: i totally would
iceqn: right youve been doing this like a week. I'd freeze yr feet in block of ice then have my way with U.

Have her way with me? Wow. What do I say back? Please, please have your way with me? Too desperate? I need to not seem overeager. Even the idea of fighting this girl is kind of exciting, maybe I'll stick to that.

charlesch: we should really have fight. might be good practice.
iceqn: ha i will beat you up
charlesch: i'm serious. see who wins, fire vs ice.
charlesch: get bucket of water, see if you can freeze it before I
boil it

The screen doesn't move for a long minute, before she finally replies.

iceqn: okay lets try it
iceqn: prolly cancel each other out
iceqn: room temp water

This is the most excited I've ever been about room temperature water. We make plans to meet at Glen Park, not too far from my house, and Sunday afternoon, I ride my bike down there and she's already waiting, sitting on a bench listening to her iPod, looking bored. It's a rare spring day that's actually warm and sunny, and I'm determined to enjoy it whether or not anything happens with this girl.

Ellicott creek runs through the whole park, and in the center is a 15-foot waterfall, which freezes into a giant sheet of ice in the wintertime.

"So. You think you could freeze the waterfall."

"Easily. What could you do, make the water warm?"

"Shut up. I bet I could boil the whole thing."

"It's a river. It's like a million gallons. There's no way."

I raise my arms towards the water. I'm actually starting to doubt myself. I mean, I know I can shoot fire out of my hands, but that probably wouldn't do much to a whole river. Maybe if I were in the water... I take a step towards the creek and she puts her hand on my shoulder.

"Maybe we shouldn't do this in front of all these people. I mean, we could get in trouble."

"Yeah, I guess if the whole creek turned to steam—"

"That's obviously not going to happen. But if I froze the whole thing, people might—"

"Oh, so you're so sure I can't do it but you can?"

"I can. I just don't think it's a good idea."

I want to do it, partly to show off to her, and partly to prove her wrong. But if I screw it up, I'd rather not do that in front of a crowd of people. And if I did pull it off... people at school freaked out a lot when they saw my powers in action. Who knows how people would react in the middle of a park.

"Come with me."

I take her by the hand, and drag her across the park, back to the street. One side of Glen Ave. has park benches and the waterfall and concrete pathways. We go across the street to the other side, which is just a dirt path that follows the stream, and is otherwise just woods.

We go by a guy fishing with his kids, and a few guys our age dragging skateboards behind, but after a few minutes, we don't see any people. I pull her further down the path, and now we have to step over the odd tree branch, or go around the big rocks I used to climb on as a kid. Finally, we get to the island. The river splits in two, then joins up again, making this little island in the middle. My friends and I always made that our kingdom, when we were kids, although there were always empty beer bottles, and once we found a used condom, so we knew it was mostly a place where older kids hung out.

Now I was the older kids. And I don't think they ever tried anything like this.

"Let's walk across to the island. You can step across those rocks. Just be careful, it's really easy to slip and fall in."

"Is that so?"

Chloe knelt down at the bank of the stream, and put just the palms of her hands in the water. The surface starts to turn white, as a sheet of ice spreads out across the water until it reaches the other side. She stands up and walks across the ice.

"Well, if you want to do it that way…"

"So, are we doing this thing or not? I'm impatient to beat you."

I kneel down in the same spot she had, and put my hands against the ice. Just as quickly as the ice spread across the creek, it vanishes, until the ice beneath her feet melts away and the water starts to soak into her pink Chuck Taylors. The water around my hands bubbles, and a second later, Chloe yelps and jumps out of the water. It's boiling hot.

It's funny, being fireproof. I can feel the heat, I know it's boiling hot, but it just doesn't affect me. Heat feels the same as it always did, but instead of being painful, it's like touching something rough or smooth or sticky. Just another sensation.

I don't have much time to think, as Chloe kicks the water, and I get splashed with shards of ice. They're cold and sharp and I vow to block them next time she does it. But in the time it takes me to think that, I nearly lose my balance, as I'm now standing on a sheet of ice.

I have to think about my next move carefully. I don't want to actually hurt her, and I could burn her pretty easily. I want to prove myself, but I don't want to put her in the hospital. I slip off my sneakers and step onto the ice. It feels cold on my feet, but then a minute later it's warm water and steam is rising all around me. It still feels weird burning things with my feet, but it's actually no harder than my hands. I could burn you with my elbows if I wanted to, it's pretty much all the same.

She paces the ground on the other side, figuring out how to get me. I'm keeping the water around me at a low boil, so she can't freeze it. She makes sheets of ice float downriver towards me, but they just melt before they get within three feet of me. Finally, the steam around me turns to snowflakes, which vaporize as soon as they get near me or the water. I'm not sure how that was supposed to get me, but I have to admit it was a cool trick.

"You can't touch me!", I cry out cheerfully. She looks annoyed. She looks around, probably trying to find some way she can get the better of me. Finally, she looks up. It takes me a minute to notice just one tree branch coated over with ice. Between the steam in the air and the sap in the tree, there's enough moisture to give it a pretty thick coating. I could cool down the water, and stop giving her steam to work with, but I'm curious to see where she's going with this.

The ice gets especially thick towards the back of the branch, and the ice turns solid white. It starts to give off steam — the cold kind. I later realize she's turning the air to liquid nitrogen, and the tree branch itself to who knows what. But I don't have time to think about that now, as the branch cracks, and falls towards my head.

I could step aside in time, but the whole point was to use our powers. I hold my hands up, and flame shoots out of both palms. By the time the branch gets to my head, it's a light shower of ash. I make a show of brushing it off my shoulder.

"That all you got?"

She doesn't say anything for a minute, and it's clear that she's out of ideas.

"Well... you can't get me either."

"I just don't want to put you in the burn ward. But I can still get you."

I run towards her, splashing. She screams, a little, and dashes for the trees. The island's only about 30 yards across, so she really doesn't have anywhere to run. I sprint towards her, skidding on a patch of leaves for a second, and it's only a minute before I'm right behind her. She goes left around a big tree, and I go right and catch her on the other side, pulling her down with me into the leaves. We wrestle back and forth until she's on top of me, hair in her face, leaves in her hair, laughing and out of breath and just achingly beautiful.

Now's the moment. Now's when I kiss her.

I grab the neck of her shirt, and I pull her down closer to me. She doesn't resist at all, in fact she leans in closer, until her face is just a few inches from mine. She parts her lips ever so slightly and says,

"Shit!"

She jumps up, and I frantically try and think of what I did wrong. I turn my head to follow her, and realize what I did wrong when I see the trail of burning leaves I left behind when I was chasing her. I forgot I was barefoot; I must have singed everything in my path. Now the dry leaves were actually burning, making a trail of fire across the island, which was spreading.

"Shit! What do we do?"

I can start fires, I don't know anything about putting them out. She runs to the water and freezes a stretch of the creek.

When water backs up and runs over the ice, she freezes that and starts building up a dam. But most of the water that trickles past only runs a few inches around either side. It's really just a tiny creek, where we need a raging river.

I'm frantically trying to stamp out piles of burning leaves, but it's barely doing anything. "It's not working!" I shout. The fire is spreading across the tiny island faster now. Chloe curses again, and starts to look scared. She flings her arms out in front of her, and just as fire shot from my hands a few minutes ago, a stream of solid ice shoots from hers. It coats the ground, and the fire's out instantly. She holds her hands out in front of her — I think she's as surprised as I am. She shoots out more ice, and quickly puts out the rest of the fire.

"Wow."

"Yeah. I've never done that before."

"I think you win."

She smiles, but I realize the moment we had a minute ago is gone, and I messed it up.

"Kid. We have to stop screwing around."

REHAB

As far as I know, no one has ever used the Old Pink's real name. Years ago, long before I started drinking, maybe before I was born, this bar was called the Pink Flamingo, and everyone drank here because it's cheap and dark and dirty and convenient to everything. Then the Pink moved to some out-of-the-way location, which is crazy, because the Pink has the best location in town, which is why everyone drinks here.

So someone new took over the Pink, and they gave it a new name, and no one ever used the name, they just called it the Old Pink. I couldn't even tell you what the bar's real name is — it isn't on the front of the building, it isn't even on the bar menus. It may be Buffalo's most closely-guarded secret.

It's a far cry from the places I used to drink in as a spoiled rich girl in New York. But it's basically the platonic ideal of dive bars. The bathrooms are disgusting, the lighting is almost non-existent, and most importantly, the drinks are cheap.

As Oakley pointed out, I haven't been coming in here too much lately, but after a solid week of patrolling my own neighborhood, looking for the super arsonist, I needed a break, so here I am, nice and drunk. People talk about booze killing brain cells, but it doesn't. I checked. Alcohol attaches to brain cells and stops them working for a while. Which is a good thing, because my brain is indestructible. If it killed brain cells, it wouldn't work on me. But it just knocks 'em out, so I'm good.

No one I know is here at the moment besides the bartenders, so I've been talking to these two college girls at the bar. They're acting all like they don't know who I am, but it's obvious they do. But I'm feeling indulgent, so I tell them my "secret," and they act surprised, and I tell them about some of the shit I've been through and now they'll have a cool story to tell their friends.

Another thing I like about the Pink is that, even when people do recognize me, I get left alone. I'm allowing tonight to be the exception. I guess, as much as I hate the attention that comes with being the horrible infamous celebrity spawn that I am, I like a little bit of attention sometimes.

Did that make any sense? Sorry, I'm a little drunk.

A guy comes up to the three of us with shots of that citrusy vodka, which I'm all too happy to accept. The drinks are for all three of us, but he's clearly got the eye on me. At least, I feel like he does. Plenty of nights, I'd let him buy me a few more, and I'd let him take me back to his place, and we'd be off to the races. But tonight's different.

"Thanks for the shot, but I have a boyfriend."

He plays it off like he doesn't care, like he wanted to talk to the other girls anyway, but I know he wanted me. But damn, I just told him I had a boyfriend. I guess I kinda do. Things have been good between us, anyway. We've upgraded our usual frequent-sex-with-occasional-conversations to frequent-sex-with-frequent-conversations. That's basically what a relationship is, right?

Whatever it is, a few more drinks and I'm fully embracing it, romanticizing it, when it strikes me that Oakley actually lives really close to the bar. And I have the brilliant idea that I will go to his house. Because I am his girlfriend, I just decided, and he will be delighted to see me. Unannounced. Drunk. At 1:30 in the morning. Who wouldn't want to see me?

I stagger out of the bar, fly up about ten feet and get snagged on some tree branches. I drift back down to the ground. I should walk. It's a nice night. I'll walk.

Oakley's place is a typical Allentown rental, a two-family house with an upstairs porch. Upstairs porches are my favorite thing in Buffalo — it's just like sitting on your front stoop in New York, except spacious, more comfortable and away from everybody. You can sit outside but still be in your own private kingdom. This one even has an overhanging roof, so it's out of the elements. Oakley's got an overstuffed couch that somehow almost never gets wet, and I've whiled away many a summer afternoon up there drinking beers, looking up the street and marveling at how, even on a perfect day, no one walks anywhere in this town.

By the time I get onto his block, I'm already drifting a foot or two off the ground, so it's the most natural thing in the world to just float on up to the porch. Why ring the buzzer and risk waking his roommate? Maybe I can just sneak into his room and surprise him, all sexy-like.

Sure enough, the door's unlocked, and I twist the handle as quietly as I can. I step out of my shoes and sneak across the living room in the dark. I think about taking off the rest of my clothes but decide, for once, I don't want to come across as too desperate. I stop in front of his bedroom door and think about my next move. I guess I'll try and crawl into bed with him without waking him up, and then wake him up.

I put my hand on the door handle, and pause just long enough to hear a noise from inside the room. Is he talking to himself? I gently turn the handle, still trying to be as quiet as I can. I hear a low moan from inside the room. What's he doing in... there... aw, crap.

I swing the door open and a glimpse of dirty blond hair is really all I need to see. I don't realize I've put my fist through the wall until I notice the plaster all over my hand. I'm just aware of myself shouting, and the girl freaking out, and Oakley shouting at us both to chill the fuck out like he's Sam Jack in *Pulp Fiction*. When I run out of curses to spit, I take a swing at him, but I'm drunk and angry and my reflexes are off, so he ducks out of the way and I put a crack in his headboard. He gets out of the bed, tries to cover the girl with the blanket, and gets between me and her. Sure, for her, he's a gentleman.

I pull him away from her, grabbing him by the shoulders, and throwing him against the bedroom door. He's slumped on the floor now, naked, covering his face with his arms. I scream at him some more, and kick him in the stomach. Should've left my shoes on. He groans loudly, and curls up into a ball. The girl's shrieking now, and I'm still yelling, and I'm about to kick him again when the voice cuts through everything.

"MARIE!"

I freeze. I actually wheel around to see who else is in the room before I realize the voice is in my ear.

"WAKE UP MARIE! Wake up, or sober up. We've got trouble."

It's Finger.

I only ever hear the police band in my earpiece, so it's disorienting to hear someone speaking directly to me. Has he been able to do this all along? Can he hear me back?

"It's the blonde girl. She just blew up a church in Clarence. I need you there. Now."

I look over to the bed, and there's a blonde girl in tears with a blanket wrapped around her. She blew up a church? Then I realize which blonde girl he's talking about. My blood runs cold and I feel a pang of guilt in my stomach. The one that got away. That sobers me up fast. She's been out there doing God-knows-what to God-knows-who because I let her get away.

"Our Lady of Peace. Main Street in Clarence. Come as fast as you can."

When most people say 'as fast as you can' it's a figure of speech. But Finger knows how fast I can. I fling myself through Oakley's bedroom window, knock a branch out of his neighbor's tree and I'm off like a shot, finding Main Street by instinct, then rocketing through the city, flying low, car alarms going off in my wake. I pass the UB city campus and city turns to suburbs, I pass the thruway and for a second I flash on Oakley's face, how scared he was, of me, and I feel a different pang of guilt, but I fight through it and keep flying and suddenly I've skipped past Amherst and I'm not sure how I'm going to find this church since I don't know Clarence real well but I see the flashing red lights in the distance and a second later I'm skidding to a stop in front of a fire truck.

"Where is she?"

A fireman points mutely to the church. It's pretty obvious where she is — the big, round stained glass window has been blown out, with chunks of glass scattered across the empty parking lot all the way to the street. The doors are hanging off the hinges. I walk across the parking lot, little bits of broken glass sticking to my feet — damn it, I forgot my shoes again. The flashing red lights from the fire trucks and ambulances lining the street cast an ever-moving array of shadows, but it's eerily quiet as I approach the doors.

Inside it's as still as, well, a church. Even with the pews in splinters, it just has that quiet, churchy feel, that churchy smell, and the skinny, weeping girl at the altar seems like she can't possibly be the cause of the turmoil outside.

"I did it!" she sobs, disturbing the silence.

"It's okay." My heart's still pounding from the flight and the fight before that, and I'm trying my best to sound soothing. "Tell me what happened."

"I smashed up the house. The TV. All the stuff on the shelves. I didn't mean to do it. I didn't want to. Why did He do this to me? I came in here to ask for help, I have a key from youth group."

"It's okay. I'm like you. I know people who can help you." I don't actually know if that's true, but I need her to stop babbling. As I get closer, I see her scar hasn't healed up any. If anything, it looks worse than it did in the ambulance, raw and red, a trench running through the skin like someone had tried to split her head open from the front with an axe. I realize that I'm not good at crisis negotiation or whatever the cops call this. I should have checked in with Finger before I just walked into the church. He's the one who called me, he must be outside somewhere. But after what happened last time, I don't blame him for keeping a safe distance.

"Tell me what happened. At your house." I try to use a soothing tone as I take a few steps closer. She sobs.

"They don't want me to ever come back! They hate me! I don't even know how I did it! I didn't mean to hurt him!"

I make a mental note to find out where this girl lives and send an ambulance there.

"It's okay. Sometimes, when you first get your powers..."

I feel like I'm giving the sex talk again, and I have to remind myself this is deadly serious and not a good time for jokes.

"...they're hard to control. It takes some time, and practice. But you get better. You'll be able to use your powers without hurting anybody."

Hurting anybody. Bad choice of words.

"Oh God! I didn't mean to do it! It just happened! I couldn't stop it!"

Tears are streaming down her face. I take her by the hands. She's not trembling, so much as her whole body is humming with energy. I'm a little nervous about that, but I press on. What else can I do?

"Listen. I have friends who can help you. I know a scientist who knows more about people like us than anyone in the world. I know a cop who deals with supers all the time, who can take you—"

"I don't want to go with the cops! I don't want to go to jail!"

"He can take you somewhere safe." I'm trying to stay soothing, but it's not working. Whatever I say just gets her more and more agitated.

"Don't let them take me away!"

She still looks tearful and scared, but then for a second, I see something else. Her eyes glare at me, the left one full of blood from where the scar cuts across it. For a second, I see a look of pure hatred flash across her face, and then something flings me across the room.

I don't know if this is what pain feels like; I have nothing to compare it to. But whatever it is that hits me, I really feel it. The only thing that's ever felt remotely like this is being struck by lightning. (Lightning's one of the chief hazards of being able to fly. People always seem surprised by that for some reason.) I don't think she even moved, but whatever she did, it hit me like an oncoming train. I smash through a support pillar and then through the wall behind it. I only have a second to get my bearings before I see the wall start to collapse, and the ceiling with it.

The only thing I can think to do is get on top of her and absorb the blow of the ceiling coming down. I forget sometimes, how quickly I can get across a room when I fly. I tackle her to the ground, trying to keep my body over hers, as the roof comes down on top of us.

To my surprise, that works. My indestructible body neatly covers hers and protects her from the brunt of the falling debris. The initial impact knocks the wind out of both of us, but she does start breathing again, so I did something right. But we're pinned under a big chunk of roof, and I'm not strong enough to just fly away with the roof on my back. So we're trapped for the moment.

"Are you okay."

"Ya... yeh...I don't know."

I'm pretty sure she's in shock; she can barely get words out. Her voice is high and trembling and she sounds like a little kid. She practically is, I guess.

"Does it hurt anywhere?"

"Yeah."

"How bad?"

"I don't know."

"Do you think anything's broken?"

"I don't know."

Wow, kid, you're really not giving me much to work with here.

"Let's try this. Can you move your arms and legs?"

I feel her trying to wriggle around, but there's nowhere for her to go. She's pinned under me, and I'm pinned under who knows how much wood, plaster and roofing tile.

"No, I'm stuck."

"But, they work, right? You're not in incredible pain when you try to move around or anything?"

"I guess not."

"In that case, I think you're okay. The bad news is, we're trapped under the rubble. The good news is, there are like eight hundred rescue workers lined up and down the street, so they're probably already digging us out. So, looks like we got time to get to know one another."

We were quiet for a while, lying together in the dark, both straining to hear sounds of the rescue we assumed was ongoing. Finally, she broke the silence.

"They hate me."

Her panic had subsided, and now her voice betrayed nothing apart from teenage bitterness.

"I smashed up the house, and now they hate me."

"Your family?"

I took her silence for a yes.

"You know they don't hate you. They're scared of what's happening to you. It's totally normal."

Actually, it wasn't normal at all. Usually, when someone's powers show up, they're ready for it, because their parents have powers, and can prepare them a bit, mentally. But hers didn't. Neither did that kid's from the jail. That's too weird to be a coincidence.

"So, stupid question, but are either of your parents super?"

She laughs bitterly.

"Super? My mom sells real estate, and my dad's a tax attorney. So not unless their power is being boring."

"Well, usually boring parents have boring kids. Not kids who blow stuff up with their minds. They had to be pretty shocked."

"I know you get powers from your parents. So where did mine come from? Am I adopted and they never told me? I look just like my mom did when she was my age."

"I don't think that's it. Tell me what you remember about the explosion."

"I... explosion?"

"You were downtown and a warehouse exploded. With you out on the sidewalk in front of it. That's how you ended up in the hospital. That's how you got the scar."

I feel her instinctively reach her arm to touch the scar, but of course her arm is trapped at her side. It must be very strange to have a scar, where there wasn't one before. Obviously I've never had one. It's a little hard to imagine.

"What happened before the explosion? Where in the city were you going?"

I wanted to say, what were you doing in the city at all? White teenage girls don't go into the city on their own. Hell, most white people in Clarence live their whole lives without going more than two blocks away from the light rail, if they go into the city at all. So why was she in front of a warehouse on the West Side?

"I... I don't remember any of that. I don't remember an explosion."

"Well, let's start with where you were going downtown.

Were you meeting anybody?"

"I don't know. I never go into the city."

"But you did that night."

"I don't think I did."

"You did. We found your body there."

"Could someone have taken me there... with their... powers... or something? I don't remember going, or planning to go, or wanting to go. Are you sure I was really there?"

"That's where the cops found you. You were in a coma for a couple of days, in the hospital. We tried to move you — one of the cops and I. That's when you woke up. Do you at least remember the ambulance?"

I can feel her nose brush against my face as she shakes her head.

"I don't remember any of this. The first thing I remember, I was in a cemetery."

"Like, dead?"

"Just walking around. It was all quiet and peaceful and stuff. I didn't know why I was there, though. I thought it wasn't real at first. I was naked, except for the hospital gown, so the whole thing felt like it was a dream. Behind the cemetery was a forest, and I wandered around the forest, barefoot, and that seemed even more like a dream. But then the forest emptied into somebody's backyard and that was it for the dream. I saw a girl's face in their car window, with this horrible scar. It took me a few minutes to realize it was me, and by that time, somebody heard me screaming and came out of the house. They gave me a ride home, and my parents told me I had been missing for days."

Jesus, somebody finds a teenage girl, wearing nothing but a hospital gown, wandering around disoriented, and they just give her a lift? Did it even cross their mind to call Missing Persons? I can just see Finger fuming about it.

"Obviously something had happened, but I couldn't remember, so there wasn't a lot anybody could do. My parents called all the hospitals to see where I had gotten the gown from, but none of them had a record of me."

"You were in the supers wing. They're pretty hush-hush. The rest of the hospital isn't allowed to acknowledge that they exist."

"We talked to the police, but they weren't any help and didn't even seem that interested. A few days of lost time, and a scar — I think they just figured I was drunk or on drugs or something. They didn't really care where I had been. I was fine now, they said. So eventually my parents started to say the same thing. I was fine now, I was home, everything was okay.

"Except nothing was okay. I mean, I was scarred for life. That was bad enough. But then on the fourth day home, stuff started happening."

"Stuff like windows breaking? Things getting smashed up without you touching them?"

"How'd you know."

She said it so flatly it was barely a question. I think she was getting fed up with me knowing more about what was happening to her than she did.

"I saw your hospital room. Even in a coma, you did a number on it."

"It couldn't have been worse than my bedroom. I woke up like I was having a bad dream, and everything was smashed. The windows, the TV, the clocks, soccer trophies, everything. My parents were freaked out; they thought someone broke into the house and tried to attack me or something. But deep down, I knew I had done it. My mom was really upset about all my stuff, too — that seemed to bother her more than the idea that someone had broken in, or that I could have been hurt. That I had this expensive TV, and now it didn't work. Or that I wouldn't be able to, like, show my trophies to my own kids or whatever. But seeing all that stuff destroyed? It made me realize I didn't really care about any of it.

"I tried to tell them that I had done it. Or I thought I did, anyway. But they didn't believe me — my dad was out front half the night looking for footprints from the "attacker". Two nights later, they actually saw it happen. Then they believed me."

"What happened that time?"

"We were in the kitchen. Fighting. I was insisting that I had done it somehow, and they didn't believe me. Then Mom started saying that if I had done it, I should pay for a new TV. How stupid is that? That's what she was worried about. The stupid TV. I started yelling that they didn't get it, that something was wrong with me, that why didn't they listen to me, when there was a smashing noise all around. Inside the cupboards, everything was broken. All the glasses, all the plates, all the nice china that's supposedly for special occasions but we never actually use? All of it was just shards of glass. It just came pouring out of every cupboard, so there were little piles of broken glass all along the counters and on the floor.

"She just freaked out. I mean, I'm sure she was freaked by what happened, who wouldn't be, but it was like she was way more concerned about the stupid dishes than she was with me."

"I'm sure she just couldn't deal. Hell, I'm freaked out about what you can do, and half the people I know have super powers."

"So, that's what this is? I have powers?"

"Looks that way."

"Wow, I have really crappy powers."

"You'd rather be super boring?"

"Yeah. Maybe. I don't know."

"Look, everybody takes a while to get a handle on their powers. This'll get better. You'll figure out what you're doing, and it'll be okay."

"It doesn't feel like it. I didn't even know I was doing it. Half the time it happened, I was asleep! How am I supposed to get a handle on that?"

I don't have an answer for her, so that question just hangs in the air for a minute.

"I killed my brother."

Now that hangs in the air, and it's way worse.

"I'm pretty sure. He flew against the wall, and I heard something snap, loud, and he just fell to the ground in a heap. My parents were screaming and I was horrified at what I'd done. I ran and ran until I was too tired to keep running, and by that time I was in the middle of town. So then I came here, to ask Jesus to help me.

"Nice one, Jesus!," she called out into the darkness. I couldn't help but laugh.

"Look, I don't know about Jesus, but I'm here. I'll help you. You don't know that your brother's dead. He's probably hurt pretty bad, but I can help him. I have a friend who can heal pretty much anyone. That's her power. She was taking care of you when you were in the hospital. Whatever happened to your brother, he'll be good as new tomorrow, I promise."

I realize as soon as I say it that it's a promise I can't keep,

91

if he really is dead.

"If she can heal anything, why do I have the scar?"

I wait a minute, not sure what to say. But I realize there's nothing I can say that'll make her feel better, so I stick with the truth.

"She can heal anything but you. I don't know why. She doesn't know why. You're a mystery."

More silence. I don't know if she's waiting for me to elaborate or what, but I don't really know anything else, so I just leave it at that.

"Wow, lucky me."

I feel her sigh, like her whole body deflates a little bit under mine.

"You don't really know if you can help me or not, do you?"

"Look, I'll admit you're a little more complicated than the typical super-strength, see-through-walls kinda gal. You're a special case. But really? We're all special cases. And no matter how good your powers end up being, it's always difficult at the beginning. You know Glimmer?"

"Of course."

"Girl barely has any powers at all, and she still managed to wreak havoc when she started. Her mom actually went blind for a few weeks! Of course, it saved her a month of seeing that girl's tits hanging out all over the place, so she was probably grateful."

She laughs, and for the first time it's a real laugh and not just a bitter, grim chuckle. We're not exactly having a slumber party down here, under the wreckage of the church, but I'm hoping she feels a tiny bit better about things.

"I'm Amberly, by the way."

Amberly. Of course you are. What is it with these suburban parents? One trendy name isn't enough, they have to smush two together.

"Marie. But most people call me-"

"Rehab? I know who you are."

"I was going to say Ree, but yeah, I get that one a lot."

"So why did they start calling you that?"

"Well, I went through a phase where I was drinking pretty heavily. Thankfully, that's all behind me and now I'm only drinking moderately. Moderately-to-heavily. I'm much better now. But the papers started calling me Rehab back when I was in New York and now I'm stuck with it. I got into some mischief now and again, and eventually the same gossip rags that loved me when I was a little kid realized it was way more entertaining to make fun of me.

"It mostly started with one reporter. He had always been cool to my parents, wrote heroic-sounding stuff about them, made sure a flattering photo ran, and then one day I was on the cover of the *Post* chugging a bottle of Jack under the headline 'Pour Little Rich Girl.' P-O-U-R. After that, it was open season."

We continue the superhero gossip for a while, me hoping I can keep her in a good mood, and her asking, with depressing predictability, if I really know the Maestro. You'd think people would put it together for themselves that the guy took over my parents' job, does it half as well, with twice the ego, has insulted me publicly, more than once, so maybe I'm not all that keen to talk about the guy. But no, I get more questions about him than his publicist.

Still, I give Amberly a pass, in the interest of keeping her spirits up. Partly because she's had a shitty day already, and partly because I don't really want anything else to get blown up.

It's only when we start to hear the sounds of someone clearing rubble away that she tenses up.

"Don't let them take me away." She almost whispers it, but I can still hear her voice tremble as she says it.

"Look, whatever happened with your brother was an accident. I'm sure they'll be—"

"Not because of him. Because of my power. I know it's not safe for me to go home. But I don't want them locking me up somewhere."

I honestly don't know what they would do with her. But it's hard to convince myself locking her up is a bad idea. Having seen how much damage she can do, I can't bring myself to tell her she has no business being locked up, because she does. But at the same time, I can sympathize with the colossal unfairness of what she had gone through, and what she was facing next.

I feel a section of wall being lifted off of us, and am momentarily blinded by klieg lights the rescuers had set up. I guess I shouldn't be surprised that, once my eyes adjust, there's a circle of cops around us, pointing their guns.

"Circle of guns? Come on, guys, such a cliché."

They really commit to the cliché, all cocking their guns within a span of a few seconds.

"Are you gonna shoot me? 'Cause you know how much good that'll do. Or are you going to shoot an unarmed 16-year-old girl?"

"Step away from her. She's dangerous." The lead cop barks that out, but I can hear the fear behind it. He's out of his depth. The Buffalo cops, Finger's people, they deal with this kind of stuff. Not all the time, but once in a while. Enough to stay cool about it. Out here in the sticks? There's no real crime, in sharp contrast to the city, so they don't have much to do besides speeding tickets and racial profiling. A girl who can blow up a building with her mind has to be more than a little scary for these guys.

I try and defuse the situation. With humor.

"Now, now, boys, shooting a kid in church makes baby Jesus cry."

The cops look at me stone-faced and their guns remain pointed at Amberly. Why do I ever think jokes will work on these guys?

"Okay, let's just talk about this for a minute, before anyone does anything rash."

Aren't the cops supposed to say that, not hear it from an unemployed drunk?

"There's nothing to talk about. We're taking the girl into custody, please step aside."

From behind me, I hear Amberly's trembling voice.

"What are you going to do with me?"

"You're extremely dangerous to yourself and others. We're going to take you someplace safe."

"Like jail? I don't want to go to jail! I didn't do anything on purpose!"

She's starting to get hysterical, and I worry she's going to blow something up again.

"Kid. Look around you. Look at what you did to the church. You did this. Who's going to fix all the damage?"

Is he trying to guilt-trip her? I knew this guy was an amateur.

"I hear prayer works."

And then we're gone. I grab Amberly and it only takes a few seconds to get up about 20 feet in the air but by that time the idiots start shooting. I try to keep my back to the cops and shield the girl as best I can. I feel a bullet get me in the small of the back and silently hope she doesn't get grazed, but the further up we go, the quieter the shots get, and I figure we're safe.

I figure wrong.

The enormity of the situation — half a mile in the air, with cops shooting at us — must hit Amberly all at once, because suddenly I'm thrown across the sky and she's plummeting like a stone.

I have the same moment of disorientation I have when she threw me into the wall, so she's nearly halfway to the ground when I catch sight of her again. At least she's wearing white — she shows up like a comet, streaking across the sky. I just try and streak faster.

I don't really have any idea what my top speed is, but I hear the wind tearing past my ears, I feel the wig fly off of my head, and I know I'm pretty close to it. I get within about 20 yards of the girl, and I feel the air crackling with electricity. Whatever it is that she does, she's still doing it. At a standstill, I might get knocked back, but at top speed, I just plow through whatever the energy is that surrounds her. I feel a lot of resistance, and it's slowing me down, but I'm still going.

I see a cloud of blonde hair, I see the ground rushing up towards us, and then our bodies collide and I've got her. I hold her as tight as I can, but nothing's pushing me away any more. I swoop back up, over the ruined church, over the town, and I hang there, in the sky, trying to work out my next move. Amberly's out cold — I wonder whether she was even awake for any of it.

I look over at the tiny skyline, trying to think of where I can take her. I could take her back to my place — if she blew it up it'd fit right in with the rest of the neighborhood. But of course somebody would think to look for me there. A different house in the ghetto? A blonde girl from Clarence wouldn't exactly blend in. Lucky for me, if there's one natural resource Buffalo has in abundance, it's empty buildings. And I know just the one.

BURNS

Over the next few weeks, I hung out with Chloe a few more times, but I never got to make a move. Usually because we always ended up someplace where there were tons of other people around and I wanted to spare myself the embarrassment if it blew up in my face. We had a good time together, though. She even invited me over for dinner, so I got to meet her family. Well, her dad and her little sister anyway. Her mom owns some hipster shoe store downtown, and usually works evenings. Chloe's dad says they sometimes call her "Ghost Mom" — she's home when they're at school or working, and she's at work when they're home and awake, so Chloe doesn't see her for days on end, but the kitchen will magically restock itself with groceries, and notes will appear on the dining room table reminding her to study or who'll be picking her up after work.

I laugh at "Ghost Mom," but Chloe looks mortified. It's funny, her parents seem super-cool — I mean, I don't really know what "hipster shoe store" even means, except they must sell shoes, but it sounds way cooler than the optician's office where my dad works. But she's constantly embarrassed by everything her dad says. And he's like the least embarrassing dad ever.

He doesn't ask if I'm her boyfriend or press us with awkward questions or anything. He doesn't even want to talk about my powers that much. I mean it comes up, but we mostly talk about normal stuff — how I like homeschooling, whether the Bills could beat Miami, just like we were old friends and it wasn't a big deal at all that I was there.

Chloe had described her sister Abby as a pain in the ass, but I thought she was adorable. She's seven, and clearly got all her genes from her Dad, because she looked a smaller version of him, if he had somehow been turned into a pigtailed little girl. She was obsessed with Harry Potter, but was only on book three, so most of our conversations are her begging me for spoilers, then begging me not to give anything away.

"Is Snape really evil?"

"Well, he's never nice to Harry, and he does some bad things, but he also—"

"Ohnodon'ttellme! Don't tell me! I want it to be a surprise!"

"Yeah, it gives away a lot if you talk about—"

"Does Hagrid die? Ohmygod is Ginny Harry's girlfriend?"

That goes on for a while. Chloe acts like she had already been through this conversation a hundred times, and she probably has, but I was entertained.

We have mochi for dessert, which are these Korean dumplings that are basically pierogies but made of ice cream. In other words, the greatest thing ever. Chloe seems super-impatient to get away from her family, but I'm having a great time.

"One day, someone should open a restaurant where everything's just a shell with stuff inside."

"Totally," her dad says, his mouth full of ice cream.

"Tortellini, samosas, pierogies, mochi,"

"Tiny buns," he offers.

"Tiny buns? Like rolls?"

"They're Chinese dumplings, with fried pork inside. This place in Chinatown made them — I'm not sure anyone else even calls them tiny buns, but I had them for every meal when I was in high school."

"Wow, so you grew up in New York."

"Sure. Back in the bad old days of graffiti and supervillains. Before Titan and Hydra cleaned the place up and Giuliani took all the credit."

I want to mention that I met their daughter, but I don't really know how to get into that. Yeah, we hung out, she shot herself, I peed in my pants, and then they put her in jail. Cool story, bro. Maybe best not to derail the conversation.

"So, why'd you move here? You're supposed to move to New York, like Titan and Hydra did."

"Went to grad school at UB. And then fell in loooove." He pretends to swoon, and Chloe looks like she wants to crawl under the table. "She wanted to stay near her family, so I stayed too. I got one of the few remaining jobs in Buffalo, and we scraped enough money for her to open the store. "

"How did you get the money for that?" Chloe finally joins the conversation. Everybody loves to hear about that murky time when their parents were together but they hadn't been born.

"Robbed a bank," he says with a grin. Chloe rolls her eyes. I try to envision him holding somebody at gunpoint and threatening to blow their head off, it just doesn't work. He's too laid-back and nice. Instead I pictured him putting his arm around the bank teller chummily — "don't you just love this bank vault? Isn't it great?"

Trying to picture Chloe's dad as a bank robber makes me think of something.

"Mr. Pang?"

He looks amused that I was addressing him like one of my teachers, but I feel weird calling grownups by their first name, and besides, I can't remember his.

"Do you have any, you know, powers?"

"Just my good looks."

He smiles warmly, but his eyes dart over at Chloe for just a second, and I see what he's thinking, like he knows the question in my head. How did she get her powers? I guess it could still be her mom. But if Mom has powers, why does she run a shoe store? I guess she'd have to have cold powers — you get some variation on what your parents have. Maybe there's just no demand in Buffalo for making things even colder.

I think about coldness for a minute as I hold a mouthful of mochi on my tongue. Just to see if I can do it, I fill my mouth with fire, and a warm stream of liquid ice cream runs down my throat. It's simultaneously tasty and kind of gross. Still, cool trick. I wonder if I can breathe fire. I'll have to practice that some time.

Before I can finish the rest, Chloe takes me by the arm and pulls me into the other room. Her Dad's busy washing the dishes, and she's been eager to get away from Family Time for a while. But it turns out, she also wants to talk.

"Hey, I got a weird problem. It involves a naked guy at work."

Damn it! I hadn't even gotten to first base, and some guy she works with is getting naked with her? How much had they done? My stomach churned. Of course there's some other guy. As pretty as she is? As cool as she is? Of course there's some other guy. There's probably like ten other guys. Why would she waste her time with a scrawny nerd who's younger than her and doesn't know how to drive?

"Apparently, someone broke into Delspan, bare-assed naked, rummaged through some files and vanished."

Wow. So totally not what I was expecting. And I probably shouldn't think, "Yay, it's a criminal sneaking around her office" but, yay, it's a criminal. I try to hide my relief.

"Naked? Was he some kind of perv? Was he looking at pictures of all the girls who worked there or something?"

"It's a defense contractor. I'm like the only girl. Under age 50, anyway. And I think he was looking at some pretty technical stuff. I mean, they don't tell me anything, but that's the rumor."

"Wow. So how did he get in? And why was he naked?"

"Well, those are the two big mysteries. And I was hoping, maybe, you could help me figure it out."

My pulse quickened. She wants my help. She could have gone to the police, or her parents, but she wants me. Okay, it's not, "I'm madly in love with you," but it's something. We'll hang out more, sneak around, get into trouble, eventually an opening will present itself and I'll make my move. But I can't seem over-eager. Play it cool. Skeptical, even.

"I thought you weren't into using your powers for good."

"This is different. This is where I work. It's like somebody breaking into your house."

"You've got to defend your turf."

"Exactly."

"Okay, so let's go. What do we do?"

Her shoulders slump and her face goes slack. "I have no idea."

REHAB

A hundred years ago, Buffalo was one of the most thriving cities in America. We were the first city to get electric streetlights. We had more millionaires than anywhere else in the country. And the city was the second-biggest rail junction behind Chicago. Between the Erie Canal, the Great Lakes, and the railroads, everything that moved through the North came through Buffalo.

Then shipping went away and the railroads did too. But like so many things from our glorious past, the city's big central train station stayed behind gathering dust.

Somebody bought the station after it shut down, and did the quintessential Buffalo thing: talked about restoring a useless eyesore to its former glory, and then ran out of money. But he liked the place so much, he built an apartment for himself in the old manager's office. There's no running water any more, but otherwise it's in pretty good shape. I've known about the place for a while — you can find a lot of interesting stuff if you're unemployed, curious, and unfazed by run-ins with the law.

I always had the vague idea that it might make a good safehouse if anything happened to the safehouse I actually live in, and it turns out I was actually planning ahead for something. It's not the suburban comfort Amberly's used to, but no one will look for her here, and if she blows the place up, it's abandoned and empty and no one will miss it. It's conveniently located in an isolated stretch of urban blight next to the worst neighborhood in town. Which is handy, since I live in that neighborhood.

Jodi and I have been taking turns checking up on Amberly. It's rare that anyone manages to drag her away from the hospital, but she seems fascinated by the girl. Maybe it's that she can't fix her — that has to be a first, or close to it. I keep catching Jodi staring at Amberly, and I can see the wheels turning in her head, trying to solve the puzzle.

"I can't figure this girl out. I can't see inside her, I can't fix her scar, I can't change anything about her. She just has this... energy. It's like..."

"That charge in the air when you get close? Yeah, I feel it too. I kept almost dropping her when we were flying here because I kept expecting her to go off."

"I don't think either of us can do anything for her. We have to call Finger."

I hadn't spoken to Finger since I pulled the girl out of the church. I guess I was probably a wanted fugitive again, so I couldn't exactly fly down to the police station and say what's up.

"Finger can't help her either. I think we need to stick to the original plan — we have to get her to Dr. Science. He knows more about us than anyone. If anyone can figure out her deal, it's him. As disastrous as the ambulance ride was, I think I just have to fly her up there and hope for the best."

Seeing Jodi look worried was a new experience. She was always calm and detached with her patients, because she knew she'd fix them and then never see them again. But the girl was clearly affecting her.

"There's something else I have to talk to you about."

"You like a boy in your class and you want me to tell him for you?"

"This is serious. I overheard Finger talking about something when he came around looking for you. Someone broke into a defense contractor in town, without setting off any alarms or any guards noticing, but a security camera picked him up, using a computer in the security-clearance area, stark naked."

"Naked? Is he some kind of pervert?"

"He's my brother."

"Your brother's a pervert?" Sorry, couldn't resist. Jodi sighs and continues.

"My brother can walk through walls. He can pass through anything, in fact. But no one's invented clothes that can. So when he walks through walls—"

"His boxers stay behind to hold down the fort. Are you sure it was him?"

"No. Maybe someone else has the same power? I don't know. But I'm scared it's him."

"Is he the kind of person who would break into a defense contractor?"

There's a long pause as she tries to find a way to put a positive spin on her eventual answer.

"Yeah. He mostly uses his power to steal things. Usually simple things, though — cars, small piles of cash, glimpses of girls' locker rooms — he's a real class act. But this seems too big and sophisticated for him."

"So, you think he's met someone with some ambition?"

"And that scares me a lot. We're powerful, he and I. He could really do a lot of damage with the wrong person doing the thinking for him."

"So this is why you're the martyr all the time? To make up for the bad shit he's done?"

"Not exactly. But I do still want to keep him out of trouble if I can. Which is why I need your help."

I know asking for my help is a big deal. Jodi's made two things clear on several occasions. She considers me extremely flaky and unreliable. And she likes me anyway, because I'm the one person on Earth who will never, ever need anything from her. So I'm sure needing something from me is no fun for her.

"I'm afraid of what'll happen if the cops get ahold of him. This seems like a bigger deal than any of the stuff he's pulled in the past."

"How would the cops even get ahold of him? And if they put him in jail, couldn't he walk right out?"

"Well, that's my worry. If jail's off the table, they either put up with him or kill him. I lie awake at night worrying about when they'll decide to deal with him once and for all."

"But how would they even kill him? Won't bullets go right through him?"

"If he's paying attention, they will. But you can sneak up on him. He has to eat, you could poison him. If you could get him deep enough underwater, he'd still drown — he can't breathe while he's out of phase, so he has to come up for air sometime. Ree, he's my brother. I've thought long and hard about all the ways I could kill him."

"So, how can I help stop your adolescent fantasies from coming true?"

Jodi's shoulders slumped.

"I don't know. I don't know how we find him, or talk to him, or stop him, or anything. I was hoping maybe you had an idea."

Several thoughts race through my brain — I already have an arsonist I can't find. I lost the girl, and only found her again because of the cops. Who are now looking for her and me. My only real resource is Finger, who I can't really go to given that I'm probably wanted for kidnapping a dangerous criminal... how do I find Jodi's brother? That's not even that high on the list of stuff I have no idea how to do.

"I'll do whatever I can."

Did that sound reassuring? Boy, I hope so.

"So, back to the girl. Do you want me to go with you? Up to the Falls?"

"No. I appreciate all your help, but no. Finger went halfway up with me and almost didn't come back. I have to take her on my own, and just hope she doesn't blow up the Doc when we get there."

We say our goodbyes, and she goes home, by which I mean work. I knock on the door to the bedroom, where Amberly's going through the clothes Jodi brought her. She raided the hospital Lost and Found for anything that might fit the girl, who was now sorting everything according to how likely it was she'd be caught dead in public wearing it. Lucky for her, this is Buffalo and not Milan, so the standards are pretty lax. Our biggest fashion rule is, if it keeps ya warm, who cares what it looks like?

She's sitting on the bed, with a New York Rangers jersey spread out across her lap, picking away at the thread that holds the lettering onto the back. I'm sure no one was in a rush to claim it from lost and found here in Sabres country. Who knows what she's doing with the letters. Player she doesn't like? It takes her a minute to realize I'm watching her.

"Everything okay?"

She starts to gather up the shirt, like she's self-conscious about what she's doing. "Yeah, fine. Just going through clothes."

"You called your parents?"

She rolled her eyes. "Yeah. They were all like, 'you have to come back, you can trust the police, blah blah blah.' I ended up hanging up. Tyler's doing okay, though." Her brother had cracked a vertebrae when he got flung against the wall, but Jodi fixed him up easily enough. She said he would have been paralyzed otherwise, though. It's very easy to see why the public's always had a distrust-hate relationship with us. A 14-year-old kid's minding his own business, one super comes along, he's paralyzed, another comes along, he's fine — they must feel like the ancient Greeks did, just living at the whim of the Gods. Zeus decides to turn you into a swan and sex you up? All you could do was cancel whatever plans you had for that day and just go with it. I suppose it's pretty much the same thing if your church gets blown up by that girl from the youth group.

I guess it's no different for her, though. A week ago, all she was was the girl from the youth group, and now she's a wanted fugitive living in an abandoned building, which she'll probably end up blowing up at some point.

"Are you ready to go?"

No point hanging around here waiting for the explosion. If the Doc can really help her, then the sooner the better. She pulled the jersey over her head and stood up.

"This guy can't really help me, can he?" She sounded like she had already convinced herself of the answer.

"I think he's your best bet. You should at least give him a shot. Wear a coat. It gets cold up in the air."

She picks up a coat from a pile on the floor without really looking at it, and we're off. I pull out a couple belts and two sets of handcuffs, and she assumes the position.

Okay, that sounded wrong. But I spent a lot of time thinking

108

about how to fly her all the way to Niagara Falls. I could just pick her up and carry her, *Officer and a Gentleman* style — it's how I got her here — but I'm worried that, like last time, I'd drop her at the first sign of trouble. Better to tie her down so she can't go flying off on her own.

I bought two oversized belts, designed for fat guys but more than big enough for strapping two average-sized girls together. One went around our waists, one under our arms, and I handcuffed each of her wrists to mine. That way, even if she zapped me so hard I blacked out momentarily, I couldn't drop her. Of course, I'd have to come to before I hit the ground, for her sake at least, but all I could really do was hope that didn't happen.

The nice bonus is, she gets to fly the way I do. Arms outstretched, wind whipping past her, gazing down as the sagging rooftops of the East Side give way to the trees and green lawns of the Northtowns. It only takes her about a minute and a half to go from terror to giddy excitement. I decide to show off, flying in circles, doing a barrel roll, diving down towards the ground, then swooping back up to the clouds at the last minute. All the cliché moves, but they're still fun. Hell, they're fun for me, and I do this stuff all the time. For Amberly, this has to be the most exciting thing she's ever done that didn't involve blowing anything up. She lets out a whoop as we go soaring just over the treetops. The girl's been through enough; let her have her fun.

Once we get well north of the city, I cut over to the river and fly low over the waves. Sometimes if it's a warm day, I just dive in and cruise underwater. For a second, I think that might be fun for the girl, before I remember that she'd drown pretty much instantly. Maybe not so fun.

But I can still show her a good time. We follow the river as it curves around Grand Island, and then widens once we're past the island. Over the wind whipping past our ears, you can hear the low roar of the falls. And then you can see the mist rising up from downriver. And then the roar gets deafening as we fly in low over the rapids, and then the water drops away and we drop with it over the falls.

Amberly screams, in delight or terror I can't tell, and we get soaked to the skin as we plunge into a cloud of mist towards the base of the Falls, pulling up just before we hit the water, skimming past the ferry that takes tourists past the waterfall, and speeding over the waves. I have to admit, that's a hell of a lot of fun. Maybe not as good as buzzing the Statue of Liberty, but it's certainly my favorite flyby anywhere near Buffalo.

Whether the girl tied to me saw her life flash in front of her eyes or not, her screams were now definitely teenage girl enthusiasm, as we looped around the big casino on the Canadian side, cut across the Horseshoe Falls, and finally landed on the island.

For the uninitiated, the Canadians have the cooler of the two waterfalls — the horseshoe-shaped one — and the better view, the nicer hotels, and all in all the better tourist experience. But the New York side, with its slum of a town and bus-depot-looking casino, also has a great state park on Goat Island, wedged in between the two waterfalls. The park's just woods, paths, a few roads, and spectacular views on every side. In its quiet way, it says, yes, this town is a big tourist trap, but at the end of the day, it's still Mother Nature's show.

Except, of course, for one very unnatural thing on the island.

We fly over the center of Goat Island, and I abruptly drop us down in the woods. Abruptly, so that once we drop below the treeline, no one will be able to mark quite where we landed. Not that it matters too much — security's pretty damn good.

I undo the handcuffs and the belt, and we stroll through the woods as casually as possible. Whatever Amberly wants to tell me about her experience flying with me, I shush with a finger over my lips. We really don't want to be noticed when we get to the spot.

I couldn't show you on a map where the spot is, but I can still see, in my head, my parents bringing me there as a kid to meet a man they called Dr. Science. The trees must be taller, but in my mind, once I find the spot, it perfectly matches up with my memories of the place from my childhood.

I take Amberly's hand, as we walk through the trees. I stop her, and say, "This certainly is a lovely afternoon for a walk in the woods." I guess he hasn't taken me out of the voice recognition database, as I haven't finished the sentence yet when we start sinking into the dirt.

"Ohmygod, quicksand!" Amberly's eyes go wide. "We're sinking!"

"On purpose," I tell her firmly. I can tell she's nervous, but she goes with it. It hadn't occurred to me that she might freak out and blow everything up here. Who knows what kind of trouble that would cause, but she keeps it together and pretty soon we're chest-deep.

"Close your eyes and your mouth," I tell her calmly. I hold my breath for a minute, and then, with my eyes still closed, the light hits me. I open my eyes in a grey room, with cement floors and walls, and an unmarked metal door. Amberly's staring in disbelief at the dirt ceiling. "How does it work?"

"Science!"

I have no idea how it works. But it's apparently really good at keeping the riffraff out.

The metal door has no handle. I put my palm against the center of the door, and after a second, it clicks and swings open. We enter what looks like any corporate reception area, totally devoid of distinguishing features or personality. Frosted onto a glass wall is a logo of the Earth with electrons flying around it that reads World Academy of Art and Science, and under it the inscription J. Robert Oppenheimer Laboratory.

Even from underground, you can hear the muffled roar of the Falls, but once we get past the deserted reception area, it combines with the thrum of machinery and a radio playing the Led Zeppelin/Pink Floyd station, two bands that never really went away for Buffalo. The big room looks like someone filled a warehouse with every kind of weird scientific equipment in existence, but ran out of boxes after the second one. Odd-shaped chunks of titanium, glass and semi-transparent plastic were stacked precariously around the room, on the floor, on big metal work tables, leaning against the walls, and in a few spots, hanging from the ceiling. I'd be worried about getting electrocuted just walking through the place except that doesn't work on me.

It takes me a few seconds of scanning through the piles of junk before I see the doc. In my head, I always pictured him clean-shaven and in a lab coat, but I'm not sure I had ever seen either of those things in real life. Most of the time I see him, the smartest man I've ever met looks like a pretty typical middle-aged Buffalo guy — heavyset, moon-faced, beard shot through with grey — but less kempt, if that's a word. His hair is messy, his pants have a sizeable hole in the knee, and he seems not to notice that his shoelace is untied. A cloud of tiny robot helicopters buzz around his head, but he seems not to notice them either.

"Marie!" He waves at me and shouts across the room, nearly tripping over cables as he heads in my direction, faking out the helicopters so they speed on ahead. "I'm so glad you're here! I want to shoot a laser at you!"

"Wow, you're totally getting a second date!"

"I may have finally created something that can actually penetrate your body."

"You wouldn't be the first guy."

The doc doesn't listen to half of what anyone says to him, so I can bounce all the off-color jokes I want to at him and most of them sail right by. Probably for the best.

"You have exactly the right properties I need to test—"

He stops abruptly when he noticed I had brought someone with me. He shoos away some of the helicopters with a wave of his hand, but they simply regroup a moment later.

"Now I remember why you're here! This girl sounds quite extraordinary!"

I take the girl by the hand and pull her closer to the Doc.

"Doc, this is Amberly, Amberly, this is Dr. Science, not his real name."

"So, what is your real—oh. Sorry."

It only just occurs to her that someone who lives in a secret base under Niagara Falls might value his privacy. In fairness, I didn't get that the first time either, but then again I was six. My parents told me we weren't supposed to know his real name, although I gathered that they did. But I've never asked or tried to find out. The story I tell myself is that he works for some branch of the government so secret most of the government doesn't know about it. Or he's working to bring down the government. One of those. Either way, someone gives him a hell of a lot of money and resources to pursue whatever futuristic technology interests him at the moment. Apparently, his latest one was a laser.

"So, you're the little girl who blows things up."

Amberly looks like she just got caught farting in church. "I guess so."

"No, don't feel bad. It's remarkable. Marie says you hurt her! That's amazing!"

Yes, it's wonderful. I wonder if his lab assistants ever quit because they're sick of him being enthusiastic about every damn thing under the sun.

"I wasn't hurt, I don't think. I definitely felt it."

"Well, that's something, at least." He doesn't look at me when he says it. He's focused completely on the girl.

"I'm going to start by measuring you."

She gives me a nervous look, but I try to nod reassuringly.

He leads us across the lab. Around the edges of the room, we see glimpses of white-coated lab assistants scurrying around to one project or another. I walk past a table with no legs, floating three feet off the ground. On the table is some unidentified organ floating in a fish tank full of blue liquid. It looks too big to be human, and doesn't resemble any body part I've ever seen. I shudder and try my best not to look at the other stuff in the lab.

We go through a door on the far side of the lab into a cramped vault of a room, with unadorned concrete walls. It's like visiting the inside of a cinderblock. Most of the room is taken up by what looks like an MRI machine that's at the center of an orgy with several other types of machine. The familiar white tunnel the person lies in is at the center of it, but other hunks of metal with flashing lights are either welded on at odd angles or connected by pipes and wires that tangle around each other like the whole contraption was just coughed up onto a beach covered in seaweed.

"So, if you'll just lie down in here..."

Amberly looks at me wide-eyed, shaking her head 'no' ever so slightly. I want to reassure her and can't think of anything to say. I'm pretty nervous about whatever the hell this thing is too.

"Doc, what does this thing do exactly?"

"It measures several types of energy. We can't observe the strings directly, but we can infer their existence from how they affect surrounding matter."

He turns to Amberly and goes into lecturing professor mode. "I don't know how much you know about physics, but Einstein postulated that the universe is made up of strings of energy. When mankind split the atom, the resulting explosion made some of the strings come unmoored. Certain people with the right genetic predisposition could channel the strings' energy, and those are what you call supers."

Amberly's looking wide-eyed, glancing back and forth between the Doc and the machine she's supposed to go into. I'm not sure whether she already knows this stuff, or if she's even taking in what he's saying. But I am.

"I've been wanting to ask you about that. The, uh, predisposition or whatever, it gets passed down from your parents."

"You know that firsthand."

"But Amberly doesn't. Her parents aren't super."

"Well. That's something else we have to investigate."

"Everyone else caught in the explosion has powers. So did this kid who caught on fire in school one morning. His parents aren't super either."

He looks annoyed, maybe because I'm interrupting his train of thought, or maybe because I brought up one of those rare things that he doesn't know the answer to.

"I was hoping you'd have a theory or something."

"Hmm. I do have some suspicions. I hope I'm wrong. Let's not jump ahead. I want to take some readings."

He indicates the MRI bed again to Amberly.

"Jodi said your powers manifested while you were comatose, so there's no point in sedating you. Let's just cross our fingers and hope for the best, then."

He knows Jodi? I guess I'd be more surprised if he didn't.

"Um... I'm not sure I really want to do this."

He looks annoyed again.

"All you have to do is lie still for a few minutes."

I squeeze her hand and nod reassuringly. She lies down on the bed and it slides into the cavern at the machine's center. Even from here it looks claustrophobic. Dr. Science walks into the adjacent room, like doctors do when they take an x-ray. The bed clicks into place once she's all the way in, and the machine starts to hum.

"Just pretend you're trapped under some rubble!" I shout into the opening.

"You're not helping," she shouts back.

The machine hums loudly and the interior glows with a deep blue light. A clanking noise emerges from one of the smaller machines attached to the main one. The clanking gets

116

louder and louder, until it sounds like someone was hammering on the thing with a wrench. A dull echo comes from the cement walls, until the room is completely filled up with noise. I worry about Amberly, whether she's freaking out inside that thing, and find myself bracing for impact.

But the impact never comes. Eventually the noise dies down and the light changes to white, and she slides out of the machine. Dr. Science comes back into the room looking disappointed.

"Hmm. I expected your powers to manifest. Now I'm not sure what to do, to be honest."

"That was what this whole thing was about? You wanted to set her off in here? She'd blow up all your science junk, and probably bring the roof down on top of us."

"I don't think you're giving the roof enough credit. This place was designed to withstand a nuclear blast. In fact, if World War III starts, the Vice President may show up here and I'll have some explaining to do. Anyway, I needed her to blow up. I can't measure what isn't happening."

"You asshole! You couldn't at least tell one of us that in advance?"

"I had reason to believe her power was activated by periods of stress. It's not very stressful to say 'I'm going to put you under stress in a few minutes'. Surely you know that much about elementary psychology."

My anger eases into annoyance, but I stay annoyed. "So, what are we supposed to do now? Go home and try not to blow anything up ever again?"

Instead of answering me, he seems to finally notice the cloud of helicopter robots around his head. He stares at them with a puzzled expression, like he'd never seen them before and had no idea where they came from. Just as I'm about to give up on the conversation and walk away, he glances over at me, startled, like he just noticed I came in.

"What? Well, no. I think there are a few more tests we can do. MAL!"

He shouts across the room to one of the lab coats scurrying around. A lanky, frizzy-haired scientist rushes over. He gives me a nod in what I assume is an attempt at Halfrican solidarity, or maybe he recognizes me from the newspaper, but I don't respond. I'm too worried about what happens to Amberly next to try and make friends. If the Doc can't figure her out, I honestly don't know what to do next.

"Malcolm. Would you mind taking this young lady across the way and get a blood sample? I'd like to run a DNA test, check for elevated mitochondrial activity, and a few other things."

Mal gives him a quick look that says, "is this really why I got my PhD?" but obligingly leads Amberly back into the main room. Once they're out of earshot, Dr. Science focuses his attention on me.

"I did get a reading, of course. I didn't want to tell her the truth, because what I found is terrifying. Her energy is an order of magnitude higher than yours. However she got them, she doesn't have what you'd call ordinary superpowers. She's bursting with energy, on a level I've never seen before."

"Look, I've always known there are more powerful supers than me. People with all four grandparents—"

"Oh, you have no idea. But that's not what this is. Even with the most powerful supers, your energy is like a faucet, it comes out slow and steady. You use a little more when your powers are active, a little less otherwise, but all within a normal range, if anything about you can be said to be normal. This girl, however, is streaming energy like a fire hose. One too strong for us to pick up and aim. One we don't know how to turn off. This isn't a matter of her learning to control her powers. This power is uncontrollable and incredibly dangerous to her and everyone around her."

"Marie." He spoke quietly for the first time since we arrived. "You know there's a chance we won't be able to fix this. And if that's the case, we can't just have her running around creating havoc." He's ultra-serious now, and for the first time since I've known him he looks less like an overgrown kid, and like what he was, a man smart enough to grasp every single one of the world's problems and too responsible to ignore them. "I don't want that to be the case, but sometimes we have to make tough decisions to keep people safe."

He never said the words, but we both knew what he was talking about. If it came down to it, we'd have to kill the girl, before her powers killed someone else. And let's face it, the me part of we would be doing the heavy lifting. I look at her across the room and it hits me all over again how young she is, and how unfair it all is. What's worse, she knows how unfair it is, and just has to live with it. Her back is to me, and for the first time I can see the back of the Rangers jersey. She had pulled off the R and the S. Now it reads ANGER.

BURNS

So, it turns out, I'm a really lousy detective. It's not like TV, where you ask a bartender about some guy who ordered a drink three months before and he remembers his eye color, shoe size, and Social Security number. Plus, there was really nobody to ask, except the other people at Delspan, who didn't want to tell anything to a couple of kids.

Chloe brought me into work with her, introducing me as one of her "superhero friends." Our plan was, if she told them I was "working on the investigation," they'd be so impressed by my powers they'd spill all their secrets. Lighting my hand on fire impressed the receptionist enough that she let me into the office, and Chloe's immediate boss was just a young guy who clearly had no authority except over the interns. (Chloe was considered an intern because she was young, never mind the other interns were making photocopies and she was making liquid nitrogen.)

After some stammering, "I don't know..." and "I don't think we can," he finally took us to meet his boss, who stonewalled us with a lot of, "the police are already working on it," and "ongoing investigation blah blah." I tried to sound as serious as I could, saying that whoever broke in was super-powered and very dangerous. I shot a jet of flame from one hand to the other, which I thought was my best trick that didn't involve actually destroying anything. But he immediately sized me up for what I was — a scrawny, overeager 15-year-old who really had no idea what he was doing.

So that was that. I lamely said goodbye to Chloe, and she went to work and I had a long walk home. Our master plan didn't take into account that she was my ride.

So, now I'm where anyone in Buffalo goes when they want consolation — a hockey game. Now, usually the Sabres console us about how bad the Bills are, mostly just by being less bad. But in my case, it's just nice to hang out with my Dad and not think about superpower stuff, or girls, or solving mysteries. Nothing takes your mind off stuff like watching a bunch of insane Scandinavians beating each other with sticks. And, you know, occasionally trying to score a goal.

A lot of my conversations with Dad lately have had to do with either taking homeschool tests, or not burning the house down, so it's nice to just hear him grousing about the quality of the goaltending, or how expensive the concessions are, not that that stopped him from loading us down with snacks.

I want to thank him for how cool he was after my powers showed up, and just for being a good dad in general. But it sounds weird to say that out loud. Neither of us are the kind of guy to say I love you to another guy, even each other. So I tell him how good the giant pretzel I'm eating is, and pretend to be more interested in hockey than I am, and assume he knows what I mean.

Dad's in the middle of his usual rant about the refs stealing the '99 Stanley Cup against Dallas, most hated of all cities, (we still have a "No Goal!" bumper sticker on our car), when the crowd roars. We crane our necks to see who scored, but no one did. The players are still skating. It takes me a second to realize no one in the crowd is looking at the ice. They're all looking at us.

Past us, it turns out. Even over the crowd noise, we can hear the fight that had broken out a dozen rows behind us. Usually when that happens, it's no different than a fight in the schoolyard. Two guys shout and threaten, but it's all posturing. Both of them want to look tough but neither of them wants to throw the first punch.

This is different. A man is slumped across his seat at an unnatural angle, his head caked in blood. People in the rows between us are streaming for the exits. Standing over the bleeding man is another, much bigger man, who looks like a bodybuilder who's gone to seed. He has muscles, all right, but he's unshaven, with long greasy hair, and he's swaying unsteadily. I've seen drunk people, mostly in this hockey arena, and it seems like this guy was pretty drunk.

A guy two seats away is talking to him, maybe trying to reason with him. "Mind your own business!" the drunk shouts, loud enough for us to hear over the crowd noise. The other guy tries to grab his arm, and gets swatted away like a fly. The drunk barely does more than brush him away, but the guy flies backwards along the row of seats and lands on his butt in the aisle.

"Mind your own goddamn business!!!" the drunk shouts, and he rips the seat in front of him out of the ground and throws it at the guy. Lucky his aim is lousy. But those seats are bolted into the ground. The way he pulled the seat up like it was nothing; the way he tossed that guy into the aisle — this isn't just some drunk who likes to work out. This guy is a super.

You hear about supers going on a rampage sometimes. Not people using their powers to steal money or whatever, but just good old-fashioned senseless violence. But you usually don't hear about it until after the Maestro had fried the guy and he was in jail. I don't know what happens before the Maestro shows up.

Looks like I'm about to find out. Three security guards show up, standing over the guy who got thrown into the aisle. The lead guy is black, maybe about 6'5", and looked like very few people have ever messed with him in his life, and the ones who did regretted it almost immediately. "Sir," his voice booms out, "I'm going to have to ask you to come with me."

He responds by making the jerking-off motion with one hand. "I'm watchin' the game." He takes an empty seat next to the one he tore out.

"Sir." The security guard raises his voice even louder. "You're creating a disturbance. I'm going to have to ask you to come with me."

This time the drunk responds by ripping out another seat. He throws it well to the left of the main security guard — one of the two guys behind him easily sidesteps it. But by the time he does, the drunk is running towards them down the aisle. The main guard pulls handcuffs out in one smooth motion, ready to slap them on the drunk when he gets too close.

But he never gets the chance. The drunk charges, the guard takes a step out of his way and then grabs him from behind by both arms. I've watched enough episodes of *Cops* to learn two things. One, cops have a lot of experience dealing with drunks. And two, if a strong guy is holding you from behind by both arms, you're pretty much already in jail.

But not this guy. He tears his right arm free, whirls around and grabs the guard, who's still holding on to his left arm. I brace myself for a punch to fly, but he picks up the guard, and throws him. This is not a small man we're talking about, but he picks him up and throws him like he's playing catch. His body sails over our heads, and he disappears over the side of the upper deck.

I can hear the crowd below, crying out as the guard lands wherever he lands. There's bedlam from the opposite side of the arena, who all must have seen him fall. But I'm already looking back at the drunk. He's definitely super — no regular person is that strong. There's no way the other two guards stand a chance against him. They don't have guns or anything. Dad's grabbing my arm, trying to pull me away, but all of the noise of the arena is fading to the background, as a thought enters my head.

It's up to me.

I shrug off my Dad's grip, and shout as loud as I can.

"Hey!" I know it doesn't sound at all tough, but I hold out my palm, and shoot a jet of fire three feet into the air, and shout it again. Now I have his attention.

What do I say to him? Stop doing that, please? Let these nice men take you to jail? There really isn't anything to say. So when he turns to look at me, I throw both arms out in front of me, and send a pillar of fire straight at the seat in front of him. It only takes a few seconds to melt down to nothing, and I'm hoping that scares him. I'm not ready to just start roasting the guy alive, whoever else he's hurt. I'm hoping once he sees he's not the only one with powers, he'll back down.

No such luck. He rips out another seat and throws it in my direction. It skitters across the tops of a few rows of seats and ends up somewhere behind me. I'm no longer aware of where the rest of the crowd is, even whether Dad's still standing next to me.

I shoot fire straight at him this time. His aim may be lousy, but mine isn't. I hit him square in the chest, and he roars as his shirt catches on fire. For a second, I worry I've gone too far, that I just burned him to death or something. But a second later he's ripping off the shirt like Hulk Hogan and vaulting over the rows of seats towards me. His chest is red, but he doesn't seem that burned — he must be super-tough as well as super-strong.

I barely have time to think about it, as he jumps another row and lands two rows away. I shoot more fire at his chest, he screams and rips out another seat. The seat is rushing towards my head, and in the half second I have to react I try to duck, I try to run, I try to burn him, I try to look for my Dad, but all I see is a wall of flame and then everything goes black.

REHAB

Have you ever woken up underwater? Okay, stupid question, of course you haven't. But I have. My body isn't just tough, it's impenetrable. Every cell is as solid as a diamond. So apparently not even oxygen or food gets in. Who knows what the hell keeps me alive. I mostly eat because I enjoy it, and I breathe out of habit. I don't really need to do either.

It feels weird to wake up underwater, naked, in my bathtub, not knowing how I got there, but I still deal with it better than you would. It's happened a few times, if we're being honest. I assume my favorite unindicted co-conspirator, alcohol, was involved. As I hunch over the side of the bathtub, vomiting up water out of my lungs, I start to think that I really need to make some changes. But I've had those thoughts plenty of times before, and they always pass.

I stumble into the bedroom, and see a bit more than the usual disarray. My latest wooden chair was a pile of sticks, there was a hole in the plaster above the headboard roughly the shape and size of my fist. All the blankets had been thrown off the bed, and there was a condom, used, nestled in the middle of the sheet. Conscientious motherfucker, whoever he was. I must have been too far gone to explain I'm impervious to disease and my eggs are just as bulletproof as the rest of me.

Shit, I wonder if he saw me without my hair. I try and think back and sort through what I can actually remember about last night.

After we got back from the Falls, I needed a break. I

couldn't take any more of the routine — trying to keep the girl safe, trying to find the Arsonist, trying to figure out what to do about Jodi's brother, failing at all of it. And as much as I didn't want to admit that what the Doc said was true, there was no getting around that he was right. I was probably going to have to kill Amberly before too long. That's a tough thing to face. So I went back to my old routine, hitting the town with the distinguished gentlemen from Kentucky, Senator Beam and Congressman Daniels.

Honestly, I don't remember too much more than that. I remember those two bottles, all right. And I remember just not wanting to think about all the shit that's going on right now. Looks like I got my wish there. It's funny, I haven't seen Finger in two weeks and I can hear him in my head, bawling me out.

I don't really get hungover, like other people do, but I still feel awful. It's mostly that feeling that I did something shitty to somebody last night, which I'm sure I must have at some point. From the looks of things, the house is hungover enough for the both of us. The place is hardly immaculate at the best of times, but I try not to let things pile up. But there's clothes and half-eaten food on the kitchen counters, the couch, and spilling off the coffee table, which no longer has the correct number of legs. Looking at the accumulated debris, I start to wonder if I blacked out more than one night.

I have to get out of here. I can't face cleaning up this mess. I can't face this wreck of a house. I can't face, well, most things. That's what the booze is for.

I pull on some clothes and walk outside, hoping to clear my head, maybe think of somewhere to fly away to. I have certain haunts I go to when I get bored and I want to go somewhere other than a bar. The top of the Marine Midland building — the one moderately tall building in town. I play this game sometimes where I dive into Lake Erie, and see if I can touch the bottom before I freak myself out and fly back up again. I don't need to breathe, as I mentioned, but it still feels freaky not to. Plus it gets cold and dark under all that polluted water.

I can't really take the thought of that today, so I start to walk around my cheerful neighborhood. Sometimes it's weird to walk places. And not just because this is Buffalo and everyone drives everywhere. It's just, why would I, when I can fly? I can feel the pull of it, sometimes. The open sky beckoning me. It's just so much faster, for starters. But there's still a thrill of doing it. Being indestructible doesn't feel like anything, because I've always been that and I have nothing to compare it to. I have no idea what it feels like to feel pain, or bleed, or bruise, or anything like that. But I spent my whole childhood stuck on the ground, so I still get that feeling of, oh my God I can actually do this.

But today I don't have anywhere to fly to. I stare up at the grey clouds, thinking about where I could go or what I could do, and I only realize how long I've spaced out for when I hear a girl's voice.

"Naw, I don't watch the news, I just heard about it."

It was my neighbor walking by, talking on the phone. She's not technically the girl next door, as she lives about six houses down. But five of those six houses have been torn down and the last one's abandoned. I look at her as she listens to whoever's on the other end. She's around sixteen, blacker than me, like just about everyone in the neighborhood, skinny, athletic, and beautiful in a way that even I, with flawless skin and perpetual youth, am jealous of.

For all the good that'll do her. I sometimes wonder how anyone in this neighborhood makes it out of the neighborhood. But I don't wonder that hard or for that long. And I sometimes feel a pang of guilt about not caring more, and then I forget all about it. No wonder the public loves me.

The neighbor girl gets close enough that I can hear what she's saying, and it's impossible not to listen in.

"Maestro got his ass beat." Pause. "Yeah, he old as shit." Pause. "They probably just get somebody to replace him. You comin' over tonight?"

The Maestro? Got his ass beat? I definitely missed something while I was out. Is that really what happened? I know the guy's not getting any younger, but I still wouldn't want to fight him. If somebody actually beat him in a fight, it'd have to be a super. But who? I mentally flip through my personal most wanted list. The arsonist? Shit, it's the Maestro — he'd play a guy made of fire like a violin. Jodi's brother? I'm sure he could escape the Maestro easy, but how would he actually hurt him? Then my heart stops when I get to the next name on the list. Amberly.

Damn it. That girl could fuck him up. I very nearly fly away on the spot to check on her, but I want to get more information first, and my neighbor just put down her phone.

"Hey." I feel painfully aware that I have no idea what this girl's name is, and I can feel her baleful look. Is she wondering why the light-skinned girl never bothered to talk to her, or anyone else in the neighborhood, before now? Or is that just guilt, and she's just annoyed the way anyone would be when a stranger comes up to them? I press on.

"What happened to the Maestro?"

"Got his ass beat by someone. At the hockey game."

"Like, right in the middle of the game?"

"I guess so. It was on TV, but I didn't see it."

"Do you know anything about the guy who did it?"

"Naw. I only just heard about it."

"Thanks. I'm Marie, by the way."

"I know who you are."

She just looks at me, and I feel the blood rush to my head. So maybe hiding in plain sight doesn't work as well as I thought. She's still just looking at me, seeing if I have a response. I don't.

"Okay, then. Thanks. Bye."

Damn, that wasn't awkward at all. I fly away. If she knows who I am anyway, no sense in hiding it. If it was a guy, at least it wasn't Amberly. Unless she didn't know and just assumed it was a guy. It probably wasn't her. But I find myself flying to the train station just in case.

When I get to the train station apartment, my first thought is that somebody else broke in. I barely recognized the girl sprawled out on the bare mattress in the room we set up as a bedroom. Amberly cut all her hair off. It's shaved down to almost nothing on the sides, and spiky on top. Her plain white tank top does nothing to hide how skinny she is. I had only seen her in conservative clothes that covered up a lot, which I guess made her look not so tiny. But looking like this, I barely recognize her. She's a frail little thing, to be so dangerous.

"I always wanted to do something drastic with my hair. I knew my parents would hate it, so I never did. But now, I figured... what the hell."

She stumbles over "hell," like someone who isn't used to saying even mild curse words. It's pretty fucking adorable.

"My whole life I just wanted to keep them happy. Stay out of trouble. Now they're terrified of me and I'm wanted by the police and could explode and kill you at any moment."

"Pretty sure you can't kill me, but let's not test that theory if we can help it."

She doesn't really hear me. Most of this is addressed to the grimy train station window, more like she's working through all this in her head then telling it to me as an afterthought.

"I always just kept my head down and did what they wanted. Go to school. Go to church. Meet a nice boy and settle down." She runs her across her scalp, ruffling her hair. "I don't care about any of those things. I hate school. I hate boys." She looks stricken for a moment. "I do feel bad about the church, though."

"It's just a building." I try my best to sound reassuring. "They'll put up another one. Nobody was in it but you. Nobody got hurt." She doesn't look reassured.

I'm surprised to find a TV playing in the background. The train station hasn't had electricity in decades, so my first thought is that she has a power I didn't know about. But then I hear the hum of a generator.

"Jodi brought me some stuff. She's been coming over at least."

I feel a pang of guilt. I hadn't asked Jodi for help, figuring she wouldn't want to leave the hospital for any stretch. But now she's stuck taking care of my mess. I hate when I'm the kid and she's the grownup, even though, let's face it, I'm the kid and she's the grownup.

I start to worry she had been doing more than feeding Amberly. She told me she was afraid to try and fix this girl, but maybe she got over it. Which is a good thing, in theory. But in practice, if something goes wrong with this girl, I feel like it's going to go very, very wrong.

Still, the apartment is in one piece, so she hasn't exploded in a few days. I think that's a record. This may be the first time I've come up with a plan and it actually worked.

"What else did she bring ya?"

"Minifridge. Some food." I kick myself as I realize I haven't been feeding the girl. No wonder she's so skinny. "She didn't give me any extra gas for the generator, though. I guess she's worried I'd blow it up."

"Yeah, I think that's a smart move."

"So, where have you been?"

I guess I should have expected this question, but I honestly thought I'd just swoop in and she wouldn't notice I'd been out of it for—I'm actually not sure how many days. I try to think up a convincing cover story. Something that sounds important, mysterious, and totally worth blowing her off for a few days.

"I was drunk."

There's that air of mystery I was going for.

"I just needed a night off from all this shit. I went out and had a few drinks. And then a few more. And a few more. You know how it goes."

She looks at me blankly. She doesn't know how it goes.

"You told me not to leave the train station! You know how much fun it is hanging out all alone in an empty train station with no electricity or water? I'm amazed I didn't blow up again just to have something to do."

"Look, you can joke about it if you want, but you're incredibly dangerous. You know that. You blowing up anything at all could be catastrophic."

Shit, I'm starting to sound like Finger now, all scoldy and serious.

"Well then give me something to do! Or find a way to fix me! Or — God — don't just go away for days at a time like I don't even exist!"

I felt an even bigger stab of guilt. Of course, she was right. I went on a drunk so I wouldn't have to think about her. But even this morning, I wouldn't have remembered she was even here if my neighbor hadn't mentioned the Maestro.

"Shit. I'm sorry. I got caught up in other stuff, I've been working on another—" Another what? Another case? The arsonist guy hadn't crossed my mind in days. I was just making excuses. Which I do a lot, but this poor, doomed girl deserved better.

"Sorry, I wasn't working on anything. I just needed like, half a day off, and it got away from me. I just couldn't deal."

She glares at me, and I swear the scar gets a little redder. I feel her eye burning into me, the one with the bloody, jagged red line through it. I brace for her to explode and throw me through a wall. I can't really say I don't deserve it.

"You can't deal? How do you think I feel? Just sitting here for days, hoping I don't bring the ceiling down on top of myself? I can't go home, I can't talk to my friends. My phone was like the first thing that blew up — I can't even text anybody. What am I supposed to do while you and your scientist friends figure out whatever you're supposed to be figuring out?"

"I don't know — watch TV. Take naps. Stay out of trouble. I promise I'll do everything I can to keep you safe, but sometimes being safe is boring. You can't be around people. You do get that, right? That next time you go off you could kill somebody?"

"Yeah... I know... but..."

"But nothing. I really hope there's a way to help you, but until that happens, you're one of the most dangerous people on Earth. So you can either lay low here, quietly, bored, or I can let Homeland Security take you away and you can be bored in a cell someplace."

"How is this place not a cell? I can't leave. I can't do anything."

Man, that shitty feeling I had when I woke up is starting to come back with a vengeance. I promise myself to cut down on the booze. But then I have a better idea and promise myself never to help anyone ever again.

"It's temporary."

"Until when?"

"I have no idea. Until someone works out how to help you."

"But what are you actually going to do to help me?"

"I don't know, okay. I don't know."

I don't know.

BURNS

"...out eight to twelve weeks with the injury, prompting another round of speculation that the city's protector might finally retire for good. Police are not releasing the name of the young man who was injured fighting the suspect, but witnesses report he exhibited powers, fire-based in nature. Could the city have another superhero on its hands? Time will tell. Up next is April with the weather; looks like we might finally get some sun!"

The TV rattles on for a few minutes before I realize they were talking about me. It takes me a few more minutes to realize I'm in the hospital. My head's pounding, my left arm hurts, and I feel groggy, like I can't completely wake up. I look back up at the TV, and there's a goat driving an SUV. A man is in the back seat, and he starts taking his clothes off while the goat talks to him. A commercial for something, I guess, but who knows what for. Everything that comes up on the screen is incomprehensible.

It takes a few more minutes before I notice that someone else is in the room.

He's standing in the corner, the one that isn't close to the bed or the door. I guess he was looking out the window, but now he's looking at me. He's maybe a few years older than me, with a dirty t-shirt and the kind of scraggly mustache guys try and grow when they can't grow a mustache. Kind of white trashy. Probably not a doctor.

"Do you..." It's hard making words come out. "You don't work here. Sorry. Do you? Who are you?"

"You're that kid. From the hockey game."

I'm a little wary about saying yes, but he already knows I am so I nod my head.

"Lemme show you something."

He starts to pull his shirt over his head. Just like the guy in the commercial. With the goat. Am I dreaming this whole thing? It all has an unreal quality. He unbuttons his jeans, and as he pulls them off I'm not even freaked out, because it can't be real, right? He starts to take off his underpants. I don't know why he's doing that. I don't need to see his dick. I don't usually have that kind of dream.

I try to sit up, but my arm hurts like crazy, and I get a stabbing pain in my head. It's the scar on my forehead, I think for a minute. Voldemort must be getting angry. But then I realize that's somebody else who has that scar. I'm lying back down on the bed, but the white trashy guy sees me try and get up.

"No, don't worry. Sorry. I'm just running out of underwear. I just wanna show you. This is what I can do."

And then he's on fire. I feel the heat from across the room. The air starts to get thick, to match the fog in my head. Everything gets even more dreamlike as he just stands there, burning. Wait. That's what I do. That guy is me. I'm Harry Potter, and that guy is me, showing me his magic trick. It's starting to make sense now.

But I keep looking at him, looking at the swirling flames, and I realize it's not quite like me. I can burn things. My clothes might burn. But I don't burn. His whole body is burning. It's almost like he's made of fire. I try and fight through the fog in my head and make sense of this. He's not me. He's like me. He can do what I do, kind of. He has a power.

"You're like me." I manage to get some words out that make sense to both of us.

"Yeah. I'm like you." He's back to normal, naked and sweaty, but not on fire. His hair isn't even singed. He looks embarrassed and pulls his underwear back on.

"I saw you on TV. They showed you on the news. Fighting that dude. It was pretty awesome. I just wanted to meet you. I don't know anybody else with powers."

The dreamlike quality is starting to fade, but my head is still swimming and I'm not sure what to say to this guy. He doesn't seem like someone I can just recommend my therapist to.

"We both have fire powers." I offer lamely.

"Yeah. We should hang out."

Isn't that what I said to Chloe? Is he flirting with me? No, that doesn't make sense. He wants to hang out. Burn stuff together.

"Does it feel weird? When you turn into fire?" I don't know why that's my first question, but I can't really think of good questions.

"Yeah. It's like my whole body disappears. It's pretty trippy. But isn't it the same for you?"

"I don't turn into fire. I just burn stuff." I start to reach around for something to burn, but when I try and move my left arm it hurts like crazy, and when I move my right arm, I realize there's a tube coming out of it that's attaching me to the bed. I look at where the tube connects to my arm, and I start to feel woozy. My arm hurts, and my head hurts, and I get dizzy for a minute and my eyes unfocus.

I turn to look at the guy, and his hair suddenly got long. And he doesn't have a mustache. Also, he's my sister.

"You can turn into my sister? And fire?"

Laura looks confused, and more than a little worried. "It's okay. You're okay. You broke your arm, and you have a concussion. You might be a little confused for the next few days. But the doctors are taking good care of you. I've been here since last night. Dad went home to get some sleep. You're going to be fine."

"But you're not... there was a guy here. He could turn into fire."

"You're just confused from the concussion. It was probably a nurse."

Nurse. Right. I know male nurses are supposed to be gay, but this guy was flaming. God, shut up, brain, that was homophobic and not even funny. Why can't I think straight? Oh, right. Concussion. So did I dream up that guy? I don't even know. I feel like there was definitely a guy here. But was there? Why do I have a concussion? And why did I break my arm? Oh, right. The drunk guy.

"What happened with that guy? Is Dad okay?"

"Dad's fine. He's just worried about you. He said you were very brave, and he heavily implied you were crazy for picking a fight with a super."

I assume Laura decided that second part all by herself.

"What about the guy? The angry guy?"

"The doctors said not to worry you with that kind of stuff."

"Worry me? I was there. I fought with the guy. What happened to him? Did the cops get him?"

"The Maestro showed up. It was very exciting, I guess. They had a big fight."

"So the Maestro got him?" I felt my pulse quicken despite myself. A real superhero fight! That I was kind of a part of.

"No. The Maestro's hurt. The other dude ran away. The

police are looking for him. You shouldn't worry about him. The police will take care of him. You just need to get better, and not get involved with those kind of people."

Those kind of people? People who get into fights? Drunks? Hockey fans? She means supers. People like me.

"I am people like me."

That came out wrong.

"Dude. You've been through a lot. You should try and sleep."

Sleep. I thought if you fell asleep with a concussion you'd die or something. Still, I don't want to talk to her, so I start to roll over onto my pillow. I get the sharp pain in my arm again. Oh, right. Broken. I keep forgetting. I reach for a glass of water, and I see a scrap of paper on the table. I can make out part of a phone number and a name. James. That guy from my dream. He was a real guy. He was people like me.

REHAB

In the mind of the public, that cops spend most of their time catching crooks. Drug dealers, murderers, the occasional hit man. But the truth is a lot more boring. As far as I can tell, most cops spend the bulk of their time either waiting for something to happen, or trying to corral people who need to calm the fuck down. People who are too drunk, too high, or just can't control their temper. The whole job is just one decades-long middle school lunch period.

Being a super's kind of like that. At least, if you decide to "use your powers for good," like they say on TV. Lots of us just use our powers to do regular jobs (I'd make a hell of a window-washer), or just to impress people in bars or whatever. But because there were so many high-profile "super-heroes" in the fifties, there's this idea that, if you have powers, you should use them to better society, and the way to do that, supposedly, is to run around fighting people like my parents do. Did.

But just like your garden variety criminals, supers aren't generally scheming masterminds. They're just like the regular people — either greedy or desperate enough to rob somebody, or drunk or high or short-tempered enough to cause trouble without really planning to. And the cops aren't Sherlock Holmes, piecing together some trail of clues to solve the mystery. It's usually a lot simpler than that. For example, this guy who fought the Maestro? Somebody recognized him on TV, so the cops went to his house, and surprise, surprise, he was home sitting on the couch. There's your criminal mastermind.

I pieced that together from the police band. I had originally planned on spending the afternoon easing the pain of being a drunk screwup by drinking some more. But now I have a new plan: I'm flying in to save the day. If I can just do this thing right — succeed where the Maestro failed, even — it's going to make up for a lot of crap that I've done. I don't care about being the hero or anything, I just want to show them all I'm not a complete fuckup.

Of course, I don't know how to find the guy's house, so I'm not off to a great start. I need to get a new phone. One that has Google Maps. And can get reception 2000 feet in the air. Okay, maybe I need to think that through more.

Turns out, I don't have to worry, because his block is wall-to-wall sirens. So's the block behind. When I get over the house, I can just make out a cop yelling through a bullhorn at the house. My guess is, they've got him pinned down inside, but nobody wants to actually try and slap the cuffs on a guy who could beat up the Maestro.

I hover over the house for a minute, trying to figure out my move. I don't know what this guy's powers are, I don't know what he looks like, and all these cops lined up outside probably want to arrest me almost as badly as him. So I'm off to a great start, as usual.

I don't know anything about him, maybe the best move is to catch him off-guard. Even the score a bit. The house is a dingy one-story, and you can guess the layout from the roof. The bedrooms are probably in the back, the living room's on the side with the fireplace, so the kitchen must be on the other side. He's probably in the living room, maybe looking at the cops out the windows, maybe trying not to do that.

I fly up. Up and up until the house is a tiny speck. Then I do a flip, and start flying down, arms outstretched, aiming for the living room. I try my best to hit top speed, hurtling down nearly out of control, and then just before I get to the roof, I curl up into a ball so I can cannonball through. Just as I do that, I hear the cop shouting through the bullhorn. Is he shouting at me? I guess he'll have to tell me later.

There's a crash, and a cloud of plaster dust and shingle fragments, and I'm surprised to land on something soft. I jump up and shout "surprise!" but there's no bad guy. I'm standing on a bed, debris from the ceiling strewn all over, and a scared girl about my age is crouched in the corner, cradling a small child to her. The bedroom. Was my aim off? Who the hell has their bedroom in the front of the house?

"JESUS! What the hell did they do?"

A voice comes booming from the next room, and a second later the door flies off the hinges and he bursts into the room. This must be our guy. White trashy, shirtless, haggard. Maybe 30 but he's already done some hard living. He also has burn marks across his chest and a recent gash in his forehead. The Maestro may as well have left his autograph on the guy. He looks to his girlfriend and kid first.

"You're okay?"

But then he sees the ceiling, and me in the middle of the wreckage. I expect him to ask me what I'm doing here, to scream at me, to say something. But I have to give him credit, he knows the first rule of fighting. Don't stand around bullshitting, just hit the person you're gonna hit.

Half a second later, I'm embedded in the wall — his punch knocked me clear across the room. As I pry myself out of the plaster, the woman scurries out of the room, carrying the kid with her. I fly at him. It's usually a good move, as I can fly with a lot more force than I can move on the ground, but it's like running into a wall. He grabs me with both hands, and then slams my spine into his knee like he's breaking a baseball bat.

I'm sure if I were a regular person, that would have messed me up. Since I'm not, I spring to my feet with a smile on my face. I hold the pose for just a second, just long enough to see that I'm not hurt at all. Then I start swinging.

I keep thinking I should take karate lessons or boxing or something, but honestly I don't get into that many fights and being indestructible is usually enough of an advantage. But when I clock this guy in the jaw a couple times he doesn't even flinch. It's like hitting a brick wall. He can't have what I have, since he's got the gash on his head. But he's pretty damn tough.

I'm tougher. All I have to do is wear him down. I hit him a few more times, aiming for the gash. He swats me away with one arm and again I'm halfway through the wall. He's going to bring the house down on top of him if he's not careful. In fact, that's probably the best way to get this guy, except that little kid would probably get crushed to death.

I extricate myself from the wall, thinking about my plan of attack. I have to keep going for the head — he's already hurt there. I'm barely on my feet when he grabs me by the throat. He can't choke me, or, he can but it won't bother me much. But he has other plans. He grabs my pants by the waist, and for a second I think he's going to tear them off and try and rape me with his girlfriend and kid in the next room. He gives me the heave-ho instead. I crash through the window and land in the side yard in a shower of broken glass.

Good, I think, as I hit the ground. There's a million cops out here, and no ceiling to pen me in. I roll from where I'm sprawled on the grass into a crouch, and take off.

A second later, I'm jerked back down. The guy's got me by the ankle. He either followed me through the window, or busted through the wall like Kool-Aid Man. Either way, he's pulling me back down towards him. I kick at his face with my free leg, but he just grabs that foot too. I hear a cop shouting through a bullhorn as he tries to drag me down.

"PUT HER DOWN, RIGHT NOW!" shouts the voice through the bullhorn. I struggle to get away, to kick at him some more, but he's so much stronger, I can't get free of him.

"DROP HER RIGHT NOW, OR WE'LL—"

And then I'm careening through the air. The guy just swings me around like a wiffle ball bat, and throws me at the cops. They're all in a crowd, and I knock into several guys all at once and we end up in a heap on the ground. I scramble to get up, to free myself from the tangle of arms and legs I'm in the middle of. A bullet hits me in the confusion. Good, I think. Somebody's smart enough to know I'm bulletproof, the cops are armored, and they have nothing to lose by taking a shot at this guy. Or they see that I'm black and unarmed and are just doing what comes naturally.

But they don't get a clean shot. The second I disentangle myself, I glance in his direction and just see flashing lights. He's lifting up a police car and using it as a shield. I see a few sparks as bullets ricochet off the transmission. I only get to watch for a second before I realize he's not shielding himself with the car, he's throwing it at me.

I don't know if my reflexes are off because I'm still hung

over, or whether I'm just not as fast as I think I am, but no sooner do I try to dodge out of the way than the side door hits me square in the head. I have a second of midair disorientation, and then I'm on the ground, my stomach pinned beneath the roof of the car, part of the siren poking at my leg uncomfortably.

I'm not hurt, obviously, but I can't get away. I took that guy for a dumb brute, but it only took him about a minute to figure out how to handle me. I get into fights now and again, some heroic, some not, but I never go in thinking I might lose. Now, lying pinned under the car, it dawns on me that I've never really fought anyone on my level. It's always regular people, who I have every advantage over. Sure, there was that one dude who could give people electrical shocks, but he found out pretty quick that his trick didn't work on me, and half an hour later he was in jail. Finger was nice to me for like a week after that one.

But I'm sure I'm going to catch hell this time. I hear more shouting from the cops, more shots fired, but this one is clearly not going our way. The brute steps back through the hole where the bedroom window had been and the noise drops a few notches while the cops figure out their next move.

It's weirdly boring, being stuck here. The cops make no move to help me — they know I'm not hurt, they know they can't get the car off me until later, and I'm sure they don't care what happens to me anyway. The guy stays in the house, the sirens flash, and not much happens.

Then *he* shows up.

BURNS

After a few days in the hospital, I stop getting headaches and start getting visitors. Laura went back to campus, but she still calls to check up on me. I hadn't talked to her much since she went away to school. We had the typical annoy-the-crap-out-of-each-other sibling relationship, so I think we've both been pretty happy to have a break from that. I don't really even know what she thinks about the whole superpower thing, apart from her lecture in the hospital.

It's nice having people here besides the nurses, but honestly it's also good that Dad leaves to go to work during the day. He flips back and forth between fussing over me and scolding me about how dangerous picking a fight was and all that. Neither extreme is especially fun. At least Chloe comes to see me.

A few days ago, her mom dropped me off, so I finally got to see her. It's funny, if anything Chloe's mom is more punk rock than she is — Elvis Costello glasses, sleeve of tattoos down one arm, about six different piercings in each ear. I guess if you sell shoes to hipsters, you have to look the part. Today, though Chloe comes on her own.

"So, how's your vacation? People cooking your meals, nurses giving you sponge baths — remind me to get my ass handed to me some time."

"Hey, nice to see you too. Glad you're still so concerned."

For the record, there hadn't been any sponge baths.

"Sorry, but some of us still have school to go to."

"Oh, please, you have like a week left."

146

"Oh, yeah. I don't know if I told you, but I'm not going away for school. Buffalo! The cheap option!" She gives me a fake smile and thumbs up. Her smile immediately fades. "For rich kids who can't get into a good school, and smart kids who can't afford a good school. Guess which one I am!"

"Well, sorry you don't get to go anywhere, but I'm... like... glad you're not going anywhere."

"Yeah, I bet you are. You'll still be able to come around and bother me. At least, if you don't get yourself killed before then."

"I wasn't going to get killed!"

"Oh, right, that guy who beat you over the head with a chair wanted you to live a long, healthy life."

"Yeah, but that guy was... hey, that's him!"

Out of the corner of my eye, I saw his face flash on the TV. Then it cut to him in the hockey arena. A jet of flame shoots out of the stands and hits him square in the chest.

"Holy shit, that's me! I'm on the news!"

I stab at the remote attached to the side of my bed. It takes about twenty stabs before the volume gets loud enough, and then of course it's too loud.

"—cornered inside a house in South Buffalo, which we have reason to believe is the suspect's home. Despite his injuries at the hands of the suspect, the Maestro has been called in to bring his assailant to justice. We go now live to—"

I stab the volume back down. The Maestro's going to finish this guy off. It might be my only chance to confront him.

"Chloe, how did you get here."

"I drove! My parents actually let me take the car into—"

"Great. Great. We need to go. We need to go there." I point at the TV with my good arm.

"Kid, you can't fight this guy again. You're lucky he didn't kill you as it is. No offense, but what are you even going to do? The Maestro will be there."

"I know. That's why we have to go. I'll explain on the way."

"I don't understand. Why—"

"I know you don't understand, that's what 'I'll explain on the way' means. Are you going to help me, or do I have to take the bus?" I get out of the bed and pull the tube out of my arm. It hurts, and I get woozy for a second, and I start to think this is a bad idea, but then I see the look on Chloe's face. I think she's starting to take me seriously.

I look around the room for clothes, but I don't seem to have any. Of course, Dad took the stuff I was wearing home to wash. I was really hoping I could have this confrontation in my Kevlar jacket, or at least something that looked cool. Or failing that, not a hospital gown that left my butt on display. But there wasn't time to think of anything. We needed to go, now.

We rush past the nurse's station, but it's empty. I was worried someone would try to stop us from going, but no one even notices us. A few minutes later we're in the car, and I'm doing anything but explaining on the way. I use the GPS to find my best guess as to where the house is, based on what they said on the news. Then I text the number that guy James left me, and tell him to meet me there.

We drive in silence for a bit, both nervous about what will happen when we get there. What if the Maestro can't beat this guy? Do we fight him? Would he kill us? I don't really want to think about what's going to happen, so I think about the other thing I don't want to think about.

"Chloe?"

I rarely call anybody by name, so when I say hers it sounds weird. Like I'm building up the question I'm going to ask, when I don't really want to do that. It's an awkward enough question as it is, and maybe I shouldn't say anything.

"If both your parents are Korean, how come you're half white?"

She doesn't say anything, but her shoulders slump as she's driving. We coast in silence for a minute.

"I mean... you are... aren't you?"

She slows to a stop for a red light and lets out a sigh.

"Yeah. I am."

She doesn't say anything else for a minute. Maybe I shouldn't have asked. Who knows how she feels about whatever the story is. But there's something I have to know.

"He's not my biological father. My dad. Not that it matters. I mean, I don't remember a time when he wasn't my dad. I've never even met the other guy. All I got from him is my stupid — is this really what you want to talk about right now?"

"No. No. I'm sorry if it's weird to talk about. I mean, I don't care at all — I didn't even want to bring it up. But there's something I have to — holy shit."

I lose my train of thought, as I hear a roar in the distance, and see thick black smoke billowing on the horizon. Chloe still looks irritated, but the engine roars and we speed towards whatever just happened. We drive on in silence until we get to a police car blocking the road. Just past it I see a dude with a wispy mustache standing on the sidewalk.

"That's the guy I told you about. From the hospital. James Flames."

We get out of the car, and he runs over to us.

"Bro, it's all over. I think the Maestro blew his ass up or something."

"Let's go see."

I start running towards the commotion, hoping they're both following me. My arm gives me a little jolt of pain every time I step with my right foot, but I don't slow down. I see fire trucks lined up along the street, police sirens flashing, even a police car that got flipped upside-down somehow. There must be cops around, everywhere, but they all seem to have bigger things to worry about than a couple of kids trying to get a glimpse of the action. The smoke's starting to dissipate, and through it I see the source — a house, one half burned up, the roof and half of the front wall caved in. The other half is pristine. There's practically a straight line down the middle. That looks like his doing, all right.

In front of the house, EMTs are loading a man onto an ambulance. He's a big guy, burnt very badly, his clothes nothing but charred rags hanging off of him. That must be the guy from the arena.

I keep looking, until I see a glint of red up the block. The motorcycle. Even from a distance, it's unmistakable, every surface bright red, except the golden flames painted on the side, practically glowing in the sunlight. He can't be far away.

The other two catch up to me, but I ignore them for a minute and keep looking.

"Well, they got him. Looks like we didn't need to rush over here after all."

I look at the crowd of cops. I look up the street in the other direction. I look back at the house.

"They just put the guy into an ambulance. It's all done.

What are you looking for?"

"Him."

He steps around from behind the ruined side of the house. He's walking with a crutch, and the side of his head is bandaged up, but even beat up he looks bigger than life. It's always weird seeing someone in person you only know from pictures and TV. But I've seen a few of the Bills around town, and it's always a shock to see that they're just regular guys, not these monsters in shoulder pads. They always look smaller in person. But with the Maestro, he actually seems bigger and more impressive than he does on TV. He's the furthest thing from regular guy, it's like even when he isn't using his powers, they just magnify him somehow.

He hobbles along, dragging his crutch through the ashes, talking to one of the cops who's walking with him. He laughs at something the cop says, and I take a deep breath, hoping my voice comes out in an impressive yell and not a squeak.

"MAESTRO!"

He looks up, and squints at me, trying to work out who I am and why I'm yelling at him. He looks a bit bemused. Again, I try to make my voice as deep and serious as I can.

"We have to talk."

He snorts out a laugh and limps a few steps closer. He looks the three of us up and down.

"What are you supposed to be, my fan club?"

I hold my good arm out and send a jet of flame in the air. Behind me, I feel heat from my left as James Flames lights up, and cold from my right as Chloe sends a cloud of snowflakes past my peripheral vision. I take another deep breath, and look him in the eye.

"We're your kids."

SELFDESTRUCTIBLE

THREE
MONTHS
LATER

BURNS

"All right, kid." He always calls me kid. "If you want to do this for real, you have to learn to deal with somebody dangerous. Because sooner or later — usually sooner — somebody like that comes along."

"Like the guy at the hockey game."

He snorts. "That guy wasn't dangerous."

"Um... he did kill a couple of people."

"Yeah. Dangerous to them. Not to us."

"He also broke my arm, and, uh..."

He looks annoyed, like he usually does when I disagree with him. I'm not sure he's used to being disagreed with. "You were dumb. You could have handled him, but you didn't know what to do. You panicked."

He cuts a piece of steak and uses it to scoop up some eggs. While he shovels it into his mouth, I stay quiet. It's not a great feeling, being scolded for having my arm broken by a super-strong guy half the cops in town combined couldn't take on.

He always picks the place, and he usually picks this place. They're only open for breakfast. The guy who owns the restaurant will always multiply your check by some random power of ten, so $8.49 becomes "eight hundred and forty-nine thousand dollars, please!" And, yeah, you can get a huge breakfast for $8.49, so I understand why we keep coming back here. I mean, he's rich and all, but a good cheap breakfast is a good cheap breakfast.

"Wait a minute! He beat you up! After me! Isn't that how your leg got messed up?"

156

Now he's really annoyed, but it's because I'm right. He's just being a jerk, giving me a hard time about losing a fight to a guy he lost a fight to.

"Is that what you heard? He did this to me?" His crutch is leaning against the table, and he tips it up for emphasis. "That fuckin' white trash dirtbag never touched me. Shit, he turned and ran as soon as he saw who he was up against."

"So, what happened?"

He stabs at his eggs for a second and lets out a deep breath.

"Kid, I'm an old man."

He lets that hang in the air, like it explains everything.

"When I chased him. I tried to take a whole flight of stairs at once. I landed badly and tore a knee ligament. I could do that shit when I was younger. Not any more. Too fucking old."

"So... why not retire?"

As soon as that's out of my mouth, I realize it's probably a touchy subject, as that's all they talk about in the news and have for years.

"Yeah, that's all anybody wants to know. When am I gonna drag my saggy ass out the door. Kid, if I quit, who takes over? Glimmer, the Human fucking Christmas Ornament? Rehab? The liquor stores would stay in business; I don't know about the rest of the city. Somebody from out of town? Nobody wants to get stuck here, managing Buffalo's decline. Not for what they're paying.

"Maybe, maybe, if you pay attention and keep your head on straight, I can teach you and those other kids enough that one of you can step up in a few years."

Wow. So that's why he keeps meeting with me? He wants me to take over? That... that sounds great, actually. A real superhero, not just some nerdy kid with powers? I wonder if he'll give me his motorcycle.

"Seriously? You'd want me to take over?"

"My son? Who else would I rather have replace me?"

I feel a flush of pride for a minute, but only for a minute before I realize he doesn't have any better options. His other kids aren't so happy to be part of the family. Chloe won't talk to him — heck, she barely talks to me these days. James Flames was all gung ho at the beginning, but every time he turned to fire, Frank couldn't resist flinging him all over the place. (Yeah, the Maestro's real name is Frank. Not very maestro-ey, but it fits him better, blue-collar lug that he is under it all.) We get it, you can control fire. Do you have to be a dick about it? To your own kid? Eventually James got fed up and I haven't heard from him since.

I'm not sure whether I'm actually enjoying these meetings either, but I do enjoy the fact that I'm sitting here at 10:30AM on a Tuesday. They wouldn't let me back to school for the new year, for insurance reasons, which I guess makes sense. I mean, I wouldn't burn the school down intentionally, at least probably not, but who knows what would happen. So I'm still doing homeschool, which is great because there's no one actually home to school me. Dad's at work during the day, so I spend maybe two hours doing schoolwork, I try and spend an hour looking up interesting stuff on Wikipedia, and that leaves me with a lot of free time. So I may as well spend some of it getting to know the guy I got my powers from.

Chloe knew all along, by the way. Not about me, but about the Maestro being her real dad. Biological father, sorry. She gets pissed if I say that wrong, as the guy who raised her is her real dad, in her mind. Which is fair enough. I feel the same way about my dad. But, jeez, it would have been helpful at some point to say, oh, by the way, this is where I got my powers from and boy isn't that suspiciously similar to your situation?

Of course, it is and it isn't. Her mom wasn't already married. They didn't even meet until after Chloe was born. Or they met, but they didn't get together until later, or something. The point is, she was single, so of course she slept with a famous, good-looking guy who had just saved her life. I'm sure he got tons of girls that way. Probably still does.

But my mom was married. She had a kid. And she cheated on my dad with, well, the famous, good-looking guy who had just saved her life. Still, how could she do that? I mean, I guess I have to be glad she did, because I wouldn't be here otherwise. But still.

And then Dad not telling me! When I was a kid, sure, why get into that stuff. But once I started lighting stuff on fire? That was really the time.

I almost burned the house down when I came home that day, after I talked to Frank for the first time. That was my plan, anyway, burning down the house. Or never coming home at all. I talked to Frank a long time that day, long after Chloe and James had gone home. He gave me a ride home on his motorcycle and I just stood there at the edge of the driveway, heart pounding, hands and arms burning, as he sputtered away.

I stood there, staring at the house, wanting to burn it. Wanting to burn him. Wanting to just burn everything and run away and start a new life. Then I wanted to kick the door in and scream at him. How could he lie to me my whole life? How could my Mom? How could he see my powers show up, and still not tell me anything? Let me go through everything alone, with no explanation?

I started having the fight with him in my head. He just wanted to keep me safe. He didn't want me to get any ideas, running off with the Maestro fighting criminals, getting hurt. He just wanted to protect me. As always. Because I'm a useless kid who can't do anything for himself.

I could see how this fight ended, and it ended with me storming out. Maybe after burning the house down, maybe not. But I couldn't say everything I had to say and then just go to bed like everything was okay. I'd have to leave.

I went over the fight again and again in my head. I thought about where I'd go next, or what I'd do on my own. And the imaginary fight just wore me down to the point where I couldn't face the real thing. So I did just what he did. I didn't talk about it. I came home like nothing had happened, and Dad didn't even say that much about me leaving the hospital on my own, and it's been like that ever since. Doing schoolwork, sneaking out to see my other dad, acting like I'm not mad about anything.

Not that things are going that much better with my biological family. Frank doesn't really talk about much either. I mean, the guy doesn't shut up, but he doesn't talk about how it feels to find out he has kids, or even any decent advice about using powers. He mostly just talks about people he doesn't like or people who don't like him, or things he's annoyed about. I guess if I want any actually useful information, I have to drag it out of him.

"Say, another thing about your leg. Isn't there, like, super... doctors or something? Like, supers with healing powers? Somebody's got that power, right?"

"Yeah. That bitch won't help me, though." He swigs his coffee and squints off into the distance. How is it that everything I've said to him this morning seems to strike a nerve?

"So, there's one...uh... bitch... in particular?"

"Doesn't know how to take a compliment." He takes another drink and thinks about that for a second. "I guess the ol' charm doesn't work on everybody. Anyway, she won't help. I've gotta go to an HMO just like everybody else.'

For a guy whose main gig is saving lives, he really seems to upset... everyone he meets? Maybe just most of the people he meets? It's funny, everyone who doesn't know him loves the guy. You'd hear about other cities' heroes getting into drugs, or picking fights, or electrocuting their girlfriends or whatever. But The Maestro seemed like the real deal — a superhero who was actually heroic. I guess he is, when it comes down to it. If a warehouse is on fire, you certainly want him conducting the flames. Who can even count how many people's lives he's saved. I guess it doesn't matter what he's like in person. Still, it's a bit of a letdown.

REHAB

So, jail's fun. You don't wanna know what a girl has to do to get a drink around here. Actually, it's not really all that awful, it's mostly just boring. Nobody really fucks with me, at least not since they learned I'm the strongest girl in the room and I can't be hurt. My parents have been gone too long to have put anybody in here personally, so there aren't really those kinds of grudges. So it's just boring, the food sucks, there's a lot of gossip, bitchiness and the occasional fight. In other words, it's basically middle school except nobody learns anything. So, it's basically middle school.

Just when I'm getting used to the idea that this is going to be my routine for the foreseeable future, the guard comes by and tells me I have a visitor. Who on earth would visit me? The only person I could think of who might is Jodi, but after the first few weeks, I gave up hope that anyone was going to bother.

I make my first trip to the visitors' room — a row of seats behind thick bank-teller plexiglass, just like in the movies. It actually takes me a minute to recognize my visitor. I'm not sure I've ever seen him not wearing a suit or a uniform.

"I think it goes without saying that you're in a lot of trouble this time. Too much for me to just wave away. They're trying to decide whether it was kidnapping, or aiding an escaped fugitive."

"Fugitive? She was a scared kid." Finger never was much for small talk.

"I'm just telling you what I hear. Personally, I think you did the right thing. She is just a kid, and locking her up or dissecting her isn't going to help anyone." I hope he's kidding about dissection. Does Finger ever kid? I try and remember if it's happened before.

"I didn't do it for her sake; I did it for yours. I saw her powers firsthand. If those dudes tried to take her away, she could have killed any of you without even knowing she was doing it. After the ambulance, I didn't want to risk your life again."

I almost see a flicker of a smile cross Finger's face. At the very least, he looks less annoyed than I've seen him in a long time.

"You risked a lot of lives by letting her run around loose. Who knows what's going to set her off next — so far we've been lucky there haven't been a ton of people around when she's exploded. What if she goes off on a crowded street?"

"It's Buffalo. There aren't any crowded streets."

Okay, there's that annoyed look I've missed so much.

"Marie, three months ago we had two people killed in the middle of a hockey game. Can you imagine if it had been your girl in that situation? The whole arena might have collapsed. What if she's got season tickets for the Bills? Or decides to go to a concert? Or even a busy restaurant?"

It dawns on me that he's worried about this stuff because it could actually happen. They don't know where she is. When they hauled me in, I told the cops where she was hiding. I figured the jig was up, and without me bringing her food, it was only a matter of time before she started wandering around on her own. Police custody wasn't my first choice, but it still seemed safer than just setting her loose, and better the cops than the Department of Intelligence. But if the cops didn't have her, either DOI sent her to Guantanamo, or she's still out there somewhere.

"She got away, didn't she?"

"It took a week for us to sort through the rubble of the train station. There was no trace of a body, so either she got away or she incinerated herself. My money's on got away."

"Shit."

"So, when are you busting me out of here so we can find her?"

"Nobody's busting you out. I don't have the authority, and even if I did, I probably wouldn't. You've caused enough trouble for the moment."

"So what happens?"

"Nothing happens. You stay here. That's what happens when you're in jail."

"I didn't have a trial! You can't just keep me here!"

"You're a special case. That's why I've been able to keep you out of jail in the past, and that's why they can keep you in now."

"So, I don't have any rights."

"Not since the World Trade Center, you don't. You're too potentially useful to the government, and too potentially dangerous. I keep waiting for you to realize how powerful you are, and how important you could be if you dried out and got your act together. You must have had some idea the government had an interest in you. Not everyone gets a dedicated handler."

"Handler. I thought you were... like... a friend of my Dad..."

Even as I say it, I realize how stupid that is and how I should have seen through it. I never heard my parents mention Finger. I just assumed they knew a lot of cops, and I certainly didn't keep track. Of course he hasn't been putting up with me out of the goodness of his heart.

"I had a great deal of respect for your parents. Never met them, but at one time I had high hopes you'd live up to their example."

"So all this time you've been... what? Waiting for me to be less of a fuckup so I could go kill people for Uncle Sam? Isn't that what boot camp is for?"

Finger sighs, like after revealing that it's his job to put up with me, he can finally admit what a shitty job it actually is. "We've been waiting for a situation where your abilities would be useful. Useful enough to outweigh how unreliable you are. Your latest adventures have convinced them it's not worth the wait."

"Them?"

Finger stands up. "Goodbye, Marie. I do sincerely hope you straighten yourself out. But we're done waiting around for that to happen."

I watch him walking away until the door closes behind me and a guard oh-so-gently reminds me it's time for me to go too. Shit. I guess that's that. Looks like I'm going to be here for a while.

I know that's supposed to be awful, but in a way, I'm okay with it. I feel weirdly at home in institutional settings, probably because I was raised by one. After my parents died, there was nowhere for me to go; Mom's parents died long before I was born, and she never talked about any other family. My grandparents on Dad's side were around when I was a kid, but neither of them outlived him. She was the World's Strongest Woman, at least, that's what they called her when she was young. But she wasn't stronger than cancer. Grandpa's the one I get my flying powers from, and he wouldn't stop flying even when the doctors told him it wasn't safe anymore. About a year after Grandma went, he had a heart-attack in mid-air, and the fall killed him.

So, that's the family. All gone. I didn't have any uncles or aunts — I guess both sets of parents decided one super-baby was enough. I was certainly enough for my folks. So when they were gone, there was nobody to raise me. Shockingly, it was tough to find foster parents who wanted to take in an indestructible 14-year-old budding alcoholic who liked stealing cars and destroying things. So they put me in juvie until I was old enough to legally inherit the home I had lived in my whole life.

I hated it back then, of course, but there's something weirdly comforting about being back in the old routine, lights out at a certain time, eating shitty food and sitting around trying to kill time with other head cases. And just like juvie, I'm one of the head cases, but at the same time, I'm not one of them. Most of these girls grew up poor, single parent if even that many, shitty lives from start to finish. They all have pretty good reasons to be screwed up and to have done something that got them here. Me? Rich girl who went to expensive schools and had every advantage, not to mention powers? I'm just in here because I'm an asshole.

And I was twice as much of an asshole as a kid. When my parents were alive, I was a spoiled rich kid who thought she could get away with anything. And after they died, I felt like the world owed me, like I deserved to get away with anything. Except the whole world seemed designed to teach me I neither could nor deserved to get away with much. I'd sneak out, get into mischief, they'd drag me back, until I aged out of the system.

Of course, by the time I was old enough to move back home, there was no home, just a pile of money where an apartment had been. You can't just sit on prime New York real estate waiting for some brat to grow up and then trash the place. The lawyers at least kept the Buffalo properties in my name. We could afford to just pay the taxes and let the dust accumulate.

But now I'm back in my real home, with my real parents — the Proper Authorities. Like so many parents of twentysomethings, Dr. and Mrs. Authority had high hopes I'd move out of the house and make something of myself, but they always have my old room waiting for me when I fuck up.

BURNS

When the snowball hits my window, I don't immediately put together that there isn't any snow on the ground, and that it must be Chloe. She's been avoiding me lately — we hung out a few times after confronting the Maestro, but things were weird after that. When I brought her to meet him, I really didn't realize how much she hated the guy. Maybe she didn't until that day either. She knew he was her biological dad, but he must have been like, an abstract concept she could mostly ignore, but now he was a real guy.

She was mad at me for even talking to him. But how is it up to her whether I talk to him or not? I got my powers from him. He's technically my father. I think I have every right to be at least curious. Anyway, we got into a fight about all this stuff, and I haven't heard from her since.

But the snowball gets my attention. I go over to the window, and of course see green grass, but nobody standing in the backyard under the window. Instead, there's a slide. She made a slide, out of ice, going from my window down to the lawn. It's like four inches thick. I'm not sure it'll support me, but I open the window and stick my head out. I still don't see her, but come on, it has to be her, right?

I swing my legs out and test the weight of the slide. It actually seems pretty solid. I push off and realize that it's not slippery. My butt's sticking to the ice. I have to push myself along the slide, awkwardly inching forward. I get about two feet from the window, and the ice starts to melt. Am I doing that? I'm not lit up, I don't think I'm any hotter than normal. Before I have time to figure it out, I land on my back on the lawn, chunks of ice all around me.

"Jeez! What the hell?!?"

The Ice Queen is leaning up against the back of the house, smirk on her face.

"I need to talk to you."

I'm still rubbing my bruised tailbone. "You couldn't have rung the doorbell?"

"This way was more fun. You remember the naked guy?"

"At Delspan? That was months ago."

"I saw him. I fought him, actually."

"Oh my God. You had, like, a real fight? With powers and everything?"

"I'll get to that. There's something I never told you. That day. When you left the hospital. I saw something."

When I left the hospital? It takes me a second to realize she's talking about when we confronted the Maestro. Does she not even want to mention the guy by name?

"You were talking to that guy."

That guy? You mean your father? I stop myself from saying it out loud, because I know it'll make her mad. But come on.

"I couldn't even look at him. I really didn't want to know him before, I didn't then, and I don't now. So I looked away, at anything else but him. And I saw some strange things.

"That girl, Rehab? She was there, trapped under a police car. I don't know why she didn't just flip it over and fly away. She was just lying there, like she was already bored with the whole super-fight that had just happened. There were cops milling around, talking into radios, people from the TV news with cameras set up. And then there was this guy. I just saw him out of the corner of my eye, up against the wall of the neighboring house. He was there. I swear he was there. But then, a second later, he wasn't there.

"I have this image burned into my brain. It's an empty suit of clothes, just collapsing in mid-air and falling to the ground. The guy was wearing those clothes, and then he vanished into thin air. I only saw it out of the corner of my eye. But I know I saw it. And I'm pretty sure she saw it. Rehab. After the clothes fell to the ground, our eyes met. She had the same what-the-fuck-was-that expression I must have had. She must have seen the guy vanish too, but I never got to ask her about it. I couldn't really just walk away from you, and by the time he had said his peace, the cops had taken her away."

"And you never told me any of this? Like you never told me about the Maestro? What am I supposed to-"

Before I got the sentence out, my hands were encased in a block of ice, frozen together. Is that her way of telling me to shut up? It only takes me a second to melt the ice and ignite my hands. The flames illuminate her face. She's not even really looking at me.

"Eventually, the cops came for me. Well, not the cops. Just one cop. He knew you and I had been asking questions about Vaporware. He wanted me to use my powers to help catch the guy."

"Vapor-"

"That's just my stupid name for the guy. I have to call him something."

"So did you? Help catch him?"

She looks away again, like she's just talking to herself and letting me listen in.

"I really didn't want to use my powers. I just wanted to be a normal college freshman. Drink. Have sex. Occasionally study. That's all."

Shit, has she had sex? The fact that she's my sister now makes me feel like I shouldn't want to know.

"I told the guy no at first. I didn't want to get involved with any of this shit. But I had to know. I'd come across this guy twice now. Even if neither time had anything to do with me, I couldn't leave it alone. I wanted to find out what he was after. So I went with the cop.

"They put me in this police jacket that was like three sizes too big. I look like I'm twelve as it is, so I'm sure anybody walking by thought I was there for Take Your Daughter To Work Day. But they did at least take me seriously, like I was part of the team. It was the cop, and this scientist guy, and me. The scientist had that thing Spock carries around, and he was talking about radiation levels, so I may or may not have cancer now."

She gives me a fake smile and a thumbs up at the mention of cancer, which I'm pretty sure she doesn't have.

"We went to this warehouse where the guy was. The plan was, I was just going to freeze him, and they'd take him to jail or something. But things went wrong. We burst in, and the guy had all this machinery. This big, humming thing that looked like a giant bell. As soon as he saw us, he disappeared. Just like before — clothes crumpled to the ground, no sign of him. I should have started freezing the whole room right away, but I didn't do anything. I froze up. Bad choice of words. But I didn't know what to do.

"Suddenly, the cop started choking. Like really rough coughs. And then a second later there was a guy standing there

— the naked guy — with his arm all the way down the cop's throat. Not just his hand. Like, his entire arm. Blood was leaking out from the cop's lips — the arm must have just been tearing apart his lungs, or his insides, or something.

"Finally, I snapped out of it and shot ice at the naked guy. He vanished again, but this time I was ready. I brought down the temperature in the room as fast as I could. The scientist had the sense to run out the door. I kept making it colder. Too cold for anything to survive. At first I thought naked guy went out the door too, but then I saw this on the floor."

She reaches into her coat pocket, and brings out a lump of something frozen. It looks like bone and gristle, like someone cut a chunk out of a frozen side of beef. I feel a wave of nausea as I realize what it must be.

"It's a piece of Vaporware. I got him."

REHAB

I hear the name "Rex Nyack" a few times before I realize the guard's calling for me. Come on, people, how hard is Rezsnyak? Spelled like it sounds! Anyway, any time one of the grownups calls you over, it usually means you get a break from being in a small, windowless room and get to go sit in a small, windowless room for a bit. I try and think of what I did this time, just so I can brace myself for whatever I'm going to be lectured about. But it's never the thing you think it's going to be.

And whatever the thing is, no one ever wants to talk to me to say something good. No one sober, anyway. So it's a great shock when I get to one of the Deputy Wardens' offices and he tells me they're letting me go. He doesn't say anything about my sentence being up, since I was never sentenced. It can't be good behavior. I'll spare you all the drama, but suffice it to say I've gotten into a few scrapes in here. He just says I've been released and refuses to give any details.

"That's it? I'm free? I can just fly outta here?"

He mulls this over for a minute.

"I suppose you can."

It's hard to tell whether he's pissed that he has to let me go, or if he's pissed I got dumped in his lap in the first place, or whether he doesn't care about me one way or the other and just looks pissy all the time.

An hour later, I'm walking out the front door. It feels like forever since I've been outside — they didn't let me use the yard, since I'm a pretty obvious flight risk. The leaves have changed color, and the air has that fall smell, and right now it's the most beautiful thing I've ever seen. All I want to do is fly as high and as fast as I can. And just as I lift off the ground, I notice her.

There's a woman standing in the middle of the road, black suit, white shirt, standing stiffly upright like a Marine, staring at me. She's not out here for the fresh air. As quickly as I launch myself into the air, I pull myself back down and clumsily land in front of her. She's white, with reddish-brown hair cut super-short, almost a crew cut. Maybe she is a Marine. She's got freckles, which seem out of place, given how super-serious the rest of her appearance is. I almost smile at the thought of calling her adorable just to see her reaction, but I hold back. I feel like I shouldn't kill the mood. I'm about to ask if she's waiting for me, as stupid a question as that is, but she speaks first.

"William Finger is dead."

That knocks the wind out of me. I guess you shouldn't be shocked when a cop dies, it's part of the job. But he just seemed like he'd always be there. Like... well, shit. Like my parents. Who were always there, until they weren't.

"Jesus, what happened? Who killed him?"

There was no question that someone killed him. A hardass like Finger doesn't just get hit by a bus and die. Shit, if he had a heart attack, he'd probably just glare at his heart until it apologized and started beating again. No, it had to have happened on the job. I'm just not sure why they had to spring me from jail to tell me about it.

"We'll catch you up on everything that's happened. But not here. We'd like to keep this as quiet as possible."

"Is that the royal 'we'?"

"My organization. I believe you're familiar with our

research arm."

She hands me a tiny plastic cylinder, with a tangle of wires inside. It looks like a bug trapped in a jar, but the robot version. My earpiece. It's what lets me hear the police and fire radios. It's possible she got the prison to turn it over after they confiscated it from me. But she might have gotten it from the guy who gave it to me — Dr. Science. So he and Finger... I guess that makes some sense.

"I thought you guys were done with me."

"We were never interested in you in the first place. Rehabilitating you was William's pet project."

William? Oh, right. I always assumed even his grandma called him either 'Finger' or 'Lieutenant'.

"So... you never wanted me, but now you do. Why the change of heart?"

"We have a situation. I'd rather not talk about it here."

I look around at the empty field we're standing in and the prison gates behind us.

"You think somebody's bugging this field?" I look around extra shifty-eyed, but she either doesn't get the joke or won't dignify it with a response.

"No, I'm cold. But you'd be surprised at how well the right person can eavesdrop."

"So, are we waiting for your ride to show up, or what?"

"You're my ride." She looks at me expectantly, like I'm supposed to just, what, bend over and give her a piggyback?

"I'm not your damn chauffeur. You think you can just ride me around like a pony?"

"You've carried people before. I assume you can again."

"You assumed I'd be your pack animal?"

"Would you rather go back to jail?"

"Yes." Maybe.

She gives me a look like the stick up her ass just went a few inches deeper. She must be used to people following her orders, no questions asked, so I must be a fun change of pace. I float just a few inches off the ground, just enough that I can look down on her for a moment.

"Call a taxi."

Most people look up when I fly away, it's probably involuntary. But she doesn't flinch. She stands stock-still, looking at where I used to be, like if she waits long enough, I'll turn around and come back to her.

I don't.

BURNS

House of Breakfast seems to have become our regular meeting spot, so I decided to order everything on the menu at least once. I had never tried corned beef hash, and it's better than it looks or sounds. No corn in it anywhere, for starters. I have to get excited about breakfast, because the real exciting thing, Frank showing me the ropes, hasn't really happened. I mean, he said he was going to, and I was very eager to learn. But we mostly get together so I can listen to him complain about stuff. Right now he's talking about motorcycles and how the Japanese ones don't have any power. He keeps calling them "rice burners," which seems kinda racist, but I'm not sure what to say about it, so I just try and enjoy the free breakfast and keep my mouth shut.

He's still going on about motorcycles — probably how much better his one is than some other one, but to be honest, I haven't really been paying attention — when he stops in mid-sentence. He pulls his phone out of his pocket and curses under his breath.

"Kid, I gotta go." He takes a gulp of coffee, stands up from the table, and throws down two twenties for the meal. "We can do this some other time." He turns around and walks halfway to the door, off the crutches but still limping a little. He pushes the door open, and then stops and looks back at me for a long minute.

"Shit. You wanna come with me?"

"Um... where? What's going on?"

"Some kids in the ghetto taking shots at each other. No biggie. Come on, you can help."

Holy crap. He wants me to help him. I'm a superhero. Assistant superhero. Superhero intern? Superhero-in-training. That works. I try to be less terrified than usual as the motorcycle roars away from House of Breakfast. I can barely hear Frank as he shouts over his shoulder.

"You got your bulletproof shit on?"

"Always. It's fireproof too."

We zoom past houses that get progressively less nice, and Frank doesn't even slow down when we see police sirens ahead. He cruises past the police car blocking the street and skids to a stop a hundred feet from a black guy, maybe in his twenties, big jeans pulled way down and no shirt, pointing a gun at some other guys on the sidewalk. He was yelling something I couldn't hear over the motorcycle at those guys, and I got the feeling this standoff had been going on for a while. Frank doesn't waste any time with conversation.

"Light me up, kid."

It takes a second to realize what he wants. Everyone knows he carries a golden lighter; looks like I'm his lighter now. I guess I have to start at the bottom and work my way up.

I send a pillar of flame up from my outstretched hand, and for the first time, I see the Maestro in action. True to form, he waves his arms like a conductor, as the column of fire goes higher, splits into two, and then with a flick of his wrist encircles the gunman at a distance of a few feet. We can't see him through the circle of flame, and I expect him to start shooting, but he tosses the gun through the fire. Looks like he knows when he's beaten.

I look over to the sidewalk, and the guys he had been pointing the gun at are already running down the block. They almost knock over a kid with dreadlocks who had been watching the whole thing from a distance. "Hey!" I start to chase after them. They're witnesses, and I at least know from TV they shouldn't flee the scene of a crime. But I hear the Maestro's voice behind me.

"I got it, kid."

He points, and flame shoots off the circle in the middle of the street, flies down the block, and blocks their way. I can see him making small circles with his right hand, keeping the gunman trapped, while his left draws the wall of flame into a larger circle around the others. The kid with dreads look terrified — he can't be much older than twelve — but I can see the Maestro screwing up his face in concentration, and a tendril of flame reaches out and makes a circle around the kid too. I can hear his voice break as he shouts through the flames, "I didn't do nothin'! I didn't do nothin'!"

I wave my arms at the Maestro. "Wait, wait. He's right. That kid didn't do anything."

"Don't worry about it, kid. The cops will sort it out."

"There's nothing to sort out. He's an innocent bystander."

"No one's innocent in this neighborhood."

"He didn't do anything. Let him go."

"He was right in the middle of this shit. I'm sure he did something. Don't worry about it."

"You're sure? Why, because he's black? So he must be a criminal?"

"Fuck you, kid. I'm out here every goddamn day dealing with these people..."

"These people? He's a kid! He was just walking down the street and those guys ran into him. He wasn't shooting anybody; he wasn't part of this at all."

Now he's pissed. For a few minute, he was the Maestro, commanding and fearsome. Now he's back to scowling, irritable Frank. "You wanna tell me how to do my job, kid?"

"Your job's to stop criminals. Not any random dude who walks down the street."

"You know what, kid? You can't handle this shit. Time to go home."

"No wonder everyone wants you to retire. You're a dick." Was bringing up retirement too mean? So what, he deserves it. "I don't wanna work with you, if this is how you work."

"Then don't work with me. You think I asked for any of this bullshit?"

"This bullshit? I'm your son."

"Look. I'm sorry I fucked your mom. Okay? In fact I'm really starting to regret it."

"Asshole."

I shoot flames right at his face. He deflects them with a wave of his hand, like I knew he would, but it breaks his concentration, and the rest of the fires dissipate. Everyone runs, and Frank's torn between going after me and going after the gunman, who at least left his gun lying in the street when he took off.

"You little shit!" He glares at me, but he limps the other way as fast as he can, fumbling in his jacket pocket for his lighter.

I run the other way and get back on the motorcycle. I've never ridden anything but a ten-speed, but I'm pissed off enough that I don't stop to think about how dangerous it probably is. I just do what I saw him do — kick the pedal to start it, turn the handle to rev the engine, and I take off down the street.

"Goddamnit! Get off my bike!"

If there's one thing I've learned from talking to people online, when someone's being a troll, you don't hang around trying to get the last word in, you just walk away. I rev the engine some more and try not to ignite with anger as his curses fade into the background.

REHAB

"What the fuck?"

When I got to the Falls, I really wished I was my dad, and could just bust right through the ceiling in a rage and land on top of everybody in a cloud of dust. Could he bust into a concrete bunker this thick? Probably. Maybe. But me, I had to sink slowly through the ground like usual, fists clenched, wanting to punch somebody. I settled for punching the glass wall in the entryway, but it was really super-tough and I couldn't break it. That just pissed me off more.

"Marie, nice to see you."

If Dr. Science was surprised to see me barging into his lab, he didn't show it. He didn't even seem to register that I was mad, which just annoyed me even more.

"Finger's dead. He was lying to me all this time. And your super spy friends or whatever have been playing me for years. So I repeat, what the fuck?"

Not at my most eloquent when I'm mad.

"Yes. Well. It's a terrible shame about William. Terrible." He sounded regretful, but like food in the refrigerator had spoiled, not like someone he knew had been murdered. "The man who did this — well, I don't think any of us understood how dangerous he is. He's something I've never seen before."

"So he was killed by a super?"

"Well, yes, but there's more to it than that."

"What do you mean? Are his powers, like, worse than other people's or something?" That sounded stupid, but as soon as I said it, I thought of Amberly. If supers were getting stronger powers, she certainly qualified.

"No, it's just that, as far as I know, this time last year, he didn't have powers. It's fascinating."

He got his powers out of the clear blue sky? I would have said that was impossible, if not for Amberly. And the kid from jail. And those people from...

"The explosion. There was an explosion at a warehouse last spring. And people started showing up with new powers afterwards. This guy was one of them."

"Well, Detective Finger would know more about that..." he started to say, absent-mindedly, before catching himself. It hits me in the gut for the tenth time today. We can't ask Finger.

"Sorry," he said quietly.

I drift off for a second, thinking about Finger, imagining him dead. But that brings me back to wanting to solve this. Avenge him, or whatever. Make things right.

"So, who was this guy, and how did he get his powers? That's supposed to be impossible. Unless... did someone build another atom bomb? Einstein destroyed all the plans for it. He said it could destroy the universe if we ever made another one."

I've been coming to see Dr. Science since I was a kid, and in all that time, his mood has never changed. Absent-minded, rambling, chipper, but distracted, like he's only half-paying attention to you as a courtesy while his brain races through more important things. So it's a shock to see the wheels over his head stop. His brow furrows, and maybe for the first time since I've known him, he looks me square in the eyes.

"I can't talk about this."

"What? What can't you talk about? What do you know about this guy?"

"I... I can't. I shouldn't."

"Finger's dead! I'm going to find out who murdered him, and I'm going to take him down! I need to know who he is! I need to know what the fuck's going on! Who was this guy who killed him? Where did he get his powers?"

Without even realizing I'm doing it, I'm shouting at the doc, grabbing him by the shirt and pushing him against the wall. I see fear in his eyes — that's a first too. For some reason I flash on Oakley, in bed with that girl, terrified of me. Is that how people see me? Fine. When I find Finger's killer, he'd better be goddamn terrified. I give the doc my best Samuel L. Jackson glower — if I'm scaring him, I may as well go the full nine. I let my voice drop from a shout to a low growl. "What aren't you telling me?"

I see his expression turn from fear to resignation to maybe even sadness, like he was mourning the secret he had been keeping. His voice was a whisper, barely audible over the hum of machinery and the muffled roar of the falls.

"I can't. It's a shame about Finger but... what his killer did... it's not for you to know about. Someone else will handle him. Someone they trust."

"They?"

He nods sagely. "They." I already know who they are, but that doesn't make things less frustrating. I take a step back, let the Doc away from the wall, let go of his shirt. This is stupid. What am I gonna do, beat it out of him?

It's a glum flight back home. Finger's gone. I have no idea who killed him, or how, or why. The Doc won't give me any answers. That DOI agent, or whatever she was, probably had loads of answers but I blew her off. I need a drink. Which reminds me of the silver lining about all this: I'm not in jail! I can do whatever I want! And you'll never guess what I want!

I head for the liquor cabinet the moment I get home. "The liquor cabinet" is my nickname for the kitchen counter, which is where I keep most of the booze in the house. But I'm only halfway across the room when I hear a voice from behind me.

"Einstein lied."

It's Mal. The lab assistant. He's reclining in my one unbroken kitchen chair, drink on the table in front of him.

"Shit! How did you get in here? How the hell did you get here before me?"

"Science."

I wait for the punchline, or some further explanation, but that's all I'm getting. Even if I asked again, he either wouldn't tell me or I wouldn't end up caring that much. I pour myself a drink and let him get to the point.

"So what did Einstein lie about?"

"Powers. When he and Oppenheimer saw the destructive power of the atom bomb, they were terrified at what they had created. They knew that once it was used as a weapon of war, it was only a matter of time before it was used again, and again.

"In the first World War, 100,000 men died just on the first day of the Battle of the Somme. One day! That many people could be killed every time one of these bombs was used. And if we could build one of them, we could build a hundred. Millions could die on a single person's command. He and Oppenheimer were livid at the thought that their research could be used for mass murder on that scale.

"And when superpowers started showing up, they had

cause for concern too. If someone could give people these powers, everyone would want them. Can you imagine a whole world where everyone can shoot lightning bolts and bust through walls? Every bar fight, every schoolyard brawl, every bit of domestic violence would be potentially devastating. We'd have a World Trade Center-level disaster every couple of years. Maybe every couple of months.

"They saw these two great dangers to humanity, and when Roosevelt charged Einstein with explaining the superpowers, he saw an opportunity. He invented string theory, which may very well be correct — strings of energy, binding the universe together, loose threads giving you your powers, that's as good an explanation as anyone's come up with. But he completely invented the link between atomic testing and superpowers, surmising that no one would question Einstein on matters that very few people in the world even understood. He said the powers came from a tear in the fabric of the universe, and another tear could be devastating, even world-ending. But that doesn't seem to have any basis in reality. Einstein and Oppenheimer simply wanted to scare the world into never detonating another A-bomb, and they did. And they also tricked the world out of ever giving anyone more powers."

I guess I'm supposed to be shocked by these shocking revelations, but it makes a lot of sense. Given how close we and the Soviets came to obliterating each other with supers during the Cold War, I can't imagine how it would have played out if we had atomic bombs, too. That lie probably saved humanity. So the part that shocks me isn't the lying.

"Wait... giving anyone more powers? Someone gave these out on purpose? If it wasn't the A-bomb, then what happened?"

Mal looks around nervously, like the boss is going to show up and chew him out if he answers this one. He shakes his head and takes a deep breath.

"Hitler."

He stops for a minute, like that explains it all, then realizes he has to elaborate.

"The atomic bomb wasn't the only weapon being developed during World War II. Hitler knew he was losing the war long before it was over. He realized pretty quickly that invading the USSR was a huge mistake. He was losing tons of men, tons of tanks and planes, but he couldn't back down. What could he do, send Stalin an 'I'm sorry' note and cease hostilities?

"Der Fuhrer became increasingly convinced that he needed a superweapon that would win the war for him. So, there were multiple secret weapons projects going on in Berlin during the last years of the war, a German A-Bomb among them. Most of the rest were just rockets that went further than existing rockets, or carried a bigger payload. But there are also some crazy projects the Nazis were rumored to be working on.

"And most of them are just that, crazy rumors. But I've been intrigued by those rumors for a long time, so I started to sift through them. None of them could be confirmed. But I realized I could discount some of them as unworkable or not worth the effort, so when I applied the Holmes principle, I was able to work out what the real project was."

"The Holmes principle?"

"Sherlock. When you've eliminated the impossible—"

"Yeah, I know that one. So what was left after Sherlock?"

"Die Glocke."

He drains the last of his drink. Mine's empty too, so I pour another for both of us.

"I don't speak German. What's a Glocke?"

"It means 'bell'. Die Glocke was a giant bell-shaped device, the size of a truck, filled with mercury and who knows what else. And when you turn it on, it taps into an unimaginably powerful source of energy — an energy very few scientists have even guessed at the existence of."

"The strings?"

"That's what Einstein called them. I prefer to think about it like this: imagine the universe is a bubble. Not a soap bubble, floating on the breeze, but an air bubble, floating through the water. This energy is the water. We're surrounded by it, but it's outside our experience. It's vastly powerful, but the bubble keeps it from overrunning our universe. Who knows how some crazy, brilliant Nazi figured out it was there, much less how to tap into it. But doing so was extremely dangerous. Who knows why the bubble didn't simply pop. And who knows why that energy attached itself to people.

"What makes us so special? There aren't any animals flying around with powers. Mundane objects aren't imbued with any special energy. So why us?"

I have a feeling he's not asking me, so much as asking himself on my behalf.

"You have a theory."

"One thing about being a scientist that lay people don't realize, is that a big part of the job is accepting how much you don't know. There's an infinite number of things we don't understand, and a finite number we do. All you can do is try and shine a little more light in the darkness. But there are mysteries we haven't come close to solving and perhaps never will.

"One of those mysteries is consciousness. Why are we able to reason, feel emotion, ask these kinds of questions, when nothing else in the world can?"

I get up from the table. "I'm gonna need some pretty strong weed before we continue this conversation."

He smiles, and motions for me to sit back down. He sips his drink. "Okay, I'll get to the point. We humans — thinking, conscious humans — have an energy nothing else in the world has. And you super-humans have even more of that energy. And it was given to you by Die Glocke."

"So my powers are Nazi powers? I'm a Nazi supersoldier?"

"That was the idea. Except it backfired for the Nazis, since powers manifested all over the world. They created some of the supers who helped win the war for our side. Which brings us back to Einstein's lie. He wanted to insure that was a one-time thing. And for seventy years or so, it was. Until last year."

"Someone built a glocke, or whatever it is?"

"I suspected as much, when we examined that Amberly girl. But now I know it for a fact. I saw it. Die Glocke. Someone built another one."

"Shit. So are more supers cropping up all over the world?"

"It doesn't appear so. Just within a three block radius of—"

"—a warehouse that exploded last year?"

"I wasn't sure how familiar you were with that."

"I was working on it with Finger. Actually, he was working on it, and he let me tag along a few times. So, what does this have to do with Finger? Who killed him?"

"The man who built Die Glocke."

"Hitler?"

I brace myself for that annoyed look Finger always got, but

he laughs. I'm starting to like this guy.

"The new one. That's what was in that warehouse."

"So, that's what exploded?"

"It seems like it. Except we confronted him in a different warehouse, and Die Glocke was there. So either he built a spare, or it survived the explosion. It doesn't really matter, because we have his device now. What we don't have is him. He killed Finger, and then he vanished."

"Vanished, like, ran away? Or vanished, like, vanished."

"The second one. That's his power. His new power, presumably. He seems to enter a gaseous state, and then re-form as a solid. He escaped as a gas, but he's lost his research, and he's wounded. We need to track him down, and we need someone to bring him in who he can't kill."

"Which would be me."

"Which would be you. My bosses don't think you're right for the job, but personally, I think you're the only one who can face this guy. I saw firsthand what he can do."

I drain my glass and pour us both another.

"How do I find him?"

"We're working on that. You just have to be ready once we do."

I take another drink, not sure if I want to ask this next question.

"How did he kill Finger?"

Now it's Mal's turn to take a long drink and think about what he's going to say.

"You don't want to know."

We sit there in silence for a while, drinking our drinks, refilling our drinks, drinking our drinks. Finally, I say the obvious thing.

"Do you want to stay?"

That laugh again.

"That's really not why I'm here."

I raise my glass and try for a coquettish smile.

"It could be."

He smiles, and shakes his head no.

"Lemme guess, you've got a girlfriend."

Now he raises his glass. "Married to the sea."

"You can give the sea the night off for a change. Give a girl a break, I just got out of jail."

My third-most-impressive superpower is my ability to pull my shirt over my head and fling it away in one smooth motion, and since I don't have to wear a bra, the move is pretty unassailable. But when I do it, he just smiles and gently shakes his head like I've done something ridiculous, and takes another sip of his drink. The room seems extra quiet until he sets his drink down and it taps the table.

"I should go."

Damn. This kinda stuff usually works like a charm on guys. Is he gay? I wasn't getting that vibe. But here I am, throwing myself at him, and he's going to politely say good night?

"Seriously?"

"Thanks for the drinks. And be ready. We're going to need you soon."

And he puts on his coat, and walks out. That is one cold fucking shoulder.

BURNS

I stole a motorcycle. Also, I rode a motorcycle. And didn't crash the motorcycle and die. But mostly, I stole a motorcycle. I can not deal. I get home and half expect the Maestro to be waiting for me, fire shooting from his eyes. Or at least the police. But nope, just a quiet suburban street. I drove the most recognizable vehicle in town right into my garage-slash-bedroom and nobody even noticed.

But Dad's going to notice. I mean, even as clueless as he's been all this time, he's gonna notice that I have a bright red motorcycle that matches the one we've seen on the news every few weeks for as long as I can remember.

I have to talk to him. I've already fought with one dad tonight, I might as well just get it all out of the way.

He's in the family room, watching one of those shows whose name is all letters.

"Dad, can I show you something?"

He glances at the screen for a second, then back at me, then sighs as he heaves himself off the couch. I don't say anything, I just lead him into my room, the motorcycle parked right in the center, at the foot of the bed.

"I know you're not my... my biological father."

He looks from the motorcycle to me and back.

"I... yeah, I guess I thought you might have pieced that together by now."

"So why didn't you say anything? I mean, you see what I can do." I sent little arcs of flame from one set of fingers to the other. "You knew I knew something was up. That I didn't know where my powers came from. Why didn't you say anything when this all started?"

"I know. Son. I'm sorry. I just didn't know what to say. I'd been trying not to think about it for so long. And I never found the right time, and I... I didn't want you to think about your mother that way."

"You mean, that she cheated on you. That's how it happened, isn't it."

"Yeah. She did."

He sits down on the edge of my bed, and motions for me to sit next to him. I do, but I give him a little distance. I feel like I'm not so much mad as just finally relieved to be having this talk, but I still feel like I should be mad, so I sit a few feet away and try my best to scowl.

"He saved her life. I guess that doesn't come as a big surprise, it's what he does. A gas main blew up in the building where she was working, and he got there before the firefighters, and pulled the flames away from her just as she was really scared she was going to die. So she was grateful, and emotional, and she was young and pretty, so I'm sure it didn't take much to get him interested, and whatever happened happened.

"I mean, obviously, I wasn't happy about it. In fact, I was furious with her at the time. But at the same time, she wasn't dead. I still loved her, and the thought that I had almost lost her — it seemed like a worthwhile tradeoff. Not my first choice, mind you.

"Don't get me wrong. I was mad for a long time after. At her, at him, even at you. I did leave for a couple of weeks. But then I realized how hard that was on Laura, and how unfair it was to her. And as mad as I was at your mother, I really didn't want it to be over. And, of course, by the time she got sick, it seemed like a small thing in the grand scheme.

"And in the end, you won me over. At first, you were just this thing — this living reminder of what she had done. His baby. And I'll let you in on a secret about babies. Newborn babies? When they're really tiny? They're really pretty awful. They don't do anything. They don't talk to you, they don't smile at you, they're not able to focus their eyes, so they barely know you're there. They just eat, sleep, and poop for the first three months. So you were pretty easy to not like early on.

"Also, I kept expecting you to burst into flames at any moment, or bust into a wall, or fly away. And then none of that happened. You were just a normal baby, and then you were a great little kid. Your first word was 'dada', and after that it was hard to stay mad at you.

"And, honestly? The thing that I think got me in the end? That finally put away all the resentment? You were one, just barely talking, and it was lunchtime, so I opened the fridge, and said, 'okay, kid, what do you want?' And you got this really serious look, and you said, 'I wanna poop!' I laughed harder than I had laughed in a long time. And after that, we were okay."

I couldn't help but laugh at that too. He had never told me that story.

I've spent so many months expecting this conversation to end in shouting and cursing and flames, and I'm actually feeling okay about things.

"You've always been a great dad. I mean, we could have had this conversation six months ago, but other than that..."

I move closer to him and give him a hug. We're not big huggers in our family, but this seems like the time.

REHAB

You ever do that thing where your eyes can't focus on anything? And your brain pushes all the sound to the background? So you can't really pay attention to where you are or what's going around you? I've been having that happen a lot lately. I'm sitting here at the Pink, glass of beer and shot of whiskey lined up in front of me. I always live by a strict rule, that comes in an easy-to-remember poem: beer before liquor / is always great / liquor before beer / is also great. The poem doesn't say this, but beer and liquor at the same time is also pretty nice.

But I'm not feeling it tonight. I keep thinking about Finger. I can imagine a few different ways a guy made of gas could kill you, and none of them sound pleasant. I keep thinking about his family, what a shock it must be to them, how they'll deal, but I don't actually know if he has a family. I guess I didn't know anything about the guy, in the end.

But it still hurts that he's gone. And I can't stand just sitting waiting for someone else's "we're working on it" to bear fruit. That guy's out there, somewhere, but I have no idea where. I remember Mal saying he was wounded, but I was drunk and didn't think to ask how. If I were wounded, and in gaseous form, where would I go? A balloon factory? Okay, stop being stupid. He has to turn solid at some point, I assume. If he's stuck as a gas, what happens? Does he still have to eat? Does he get dispersed in a storm? I have to assume if he can't turn solid, he can't really bother anyone. So let's go back to him being solid again. He's solid, he's hurt, where does he go?

The hospital. I run through some scenarios. He goes to the ER at Mercy, where an anonymous gunshot victim won't stand out. Maybe he materializes at a doctor's office and forces someone to fix him up. If the cops show up, he just disappears again. Which means he's probably in the city — a wounded fugitive is going to stand out more at a suburban HMO, and the cops are a lot less busy, which means a faster response. I assume Finger shot him, but I don't know for sure. Anything could be wrong with the guy. Whatever it is, "wounded" means it's pretty serious. He'd have to know an ER's the best place to go. Of course, if it were me, I'd just go to Jodi—

Shit. Jodi. Does he know about her? Could he? I stand up from the bar before I even finish the thought. I'm sure I'm needlessly panicking, but the only reason I don't fly right through the window and off through the hospital is that the Pink only has one tiny window. I push my way through the crowd, and shove right into Oakley. Shit.

"Shit!"

Sounds like he's not happy to see me either.

"You came back."

I'm sure the delight in his voice is just very well hidden. I try and flash my sweetest smile, hoping that time has healed all wounds.

"Miss me?"

"You broke three of my ribs, you crazy bitch. Just stay away from me."

Crazy bitch. I've certainly been called that before. It pisses me off, mostly because I don't have a strong argument against either half of that equation. I drop the smile.

"Sorry. I lost my shit, a little."

I actually am sorry. I shouldn't have been so mad at him for sleeping around. Hell, I probably would have done the same thing, given half a chance. And even then, I can't lash out like that against someone without powers. I have a tendency to turn from happy drunk to angry drunk on a dime, just another thing I know is a problem but don't ever bother to do anything about.

"Just make sure I'm not around the next time you lose your shit."

He pushes past me, further into the bar. I think about turning around and going after him, but nothing I say right now is going to help. And I have to stop being shitty at my interpersonal relationships so I can go be shitty at detective work. I have to go talk to Jodi.

Except Jodi's not there. Nobody's there, in fact. The lights are all off in the supers wing—no nurse at the desk, no patients in the beds, and most significantly, no doctor. It takes about half an hour of wandering around the hospital before I see a familiar face—a nurse I've seen a few times in the supers wing is working the maternity desk.

"What's going on on the fourth floor?"

Her face registers a flash of that "oh, great, it's you," look I get from so many people.

"Renovations."

She acts like she's too busy to give me a better answer than that, but she's clearly been leafing through an *Us Weekly*, open to a "who wore it better" between a pop singer and a super who has her own reality show. I swing my legs up until I'm sideways, float over the desk, and plot down into the empty chair next to her.

"Bullshit. Where's Jodi?"

"Vacation."

"Oh come on. The girl barely takes time off to sleep."

"Well, so far she's been asleep about two months. If you see her, tell her she's welcome back any time."

If I see her? Holy shit, Jodi's gone. That takes a minute to sink in. Where would she go? Another hospital? I can't imagine her not working. But what if she didn't go on purpose? What if the gas guy got to her?

No, wait, two months means she's been gone a while, long before Finger died. But where would she go? If she ran away, if she's hiding, she could be anywhere. For starters, any hospital in the world would be happy to help her hide out for even a taste of her powers. I try to think of anyone she could have gone to. She mentioned a brother. Who she's not on good terms with, and I know nothing about, not even his name.

I'm at a dead end, as usual. My first instinct is to just go back to the bar, have a few drinks, and hope some sort of lead falls into my lap. But I shake that off and try and think of something I can do that will actually help. I tell myself I'm taking responsibility and doing the right thing, but the truth is I just don't want to run into Oakley again.

Instead, I fly over to her house. It's the only place I can think of to start. Although I don't know what I'm going to find. Maybe she left a note on the kitchen table about where she went and directions on how to get there.

Unsurprisingly, there's nothing on the kitchen table, nothing on the counters, no dishes in the drying rack. Her whole kitchen looks like the fake one they set up in IKEA. Nothing out of place. It doesn't look like she left in a hurry, but at the same time, knowing Jodi it's possible she just never made a mess in the first place.

The bed's unmade, so she's human after all. But I still don't really know what I'm looking for. Did she pack a lot of clothes, to go someplace else? It's hard to tell. Her closet's not packed, but it's not empty, and I don't really know what she had in it before. I can't think of any particular outfit she wore, so I can check to see if it's missing. I only ever remember her wearing scrubs.

I'm about to give up and curse this whole idea as useless, and myself as beyond useless, when I notice her laptop half-buried by the blankets bunched up at the foot of the bed. I fire it up and see that even her desktop is immaculate. I assumed everyone kept all of their crap on their desktop, but she just has the "Macintosh HD" icon. She didn't even give it a cutesy name. The wallpaper is a picture of her out in the country, arm around some friend or other, a green barn with peeling paint in the background, and a pair of silos off in the distance. Kind of the last place I'd expect to see Jodi. Always pegged her as a city girl.

I feel weird going through her files. Not that weird, I guess, since I immediately go through her files. But there's nothing worthwhile. A handful of photos, a disconcerting amount of 80s music, tax stuff, and a shocking lack of "Hey Ree, This Is Where I Went And Why" essays. I close windows in frustration, until I'm back to the picture of the farm. I go back to her photos again. She's on that farm in a few of them. My parents had their share of hideouts; maybe hers do too? The desktop picture's labeled "Eden." Maybe she just thought the place was extra-bucolic, but Eden's also the name of a town out in the country, maybe an hour south of here. Could that be where she's hiding?

It's not much to go on, but it's more than I had an hour ago.

BURNS

I still kept worrying Frank was going to come after me. The thing is, I wasn't even that scared. I'm fireproof! What can he do to me? I mean, if he asked for the motorcycle back, I guess I'd have to give it to him, but beyond that, I didn't have anything left to say to the guy.

So I guess it was a relief when someone came after me and it wasn't him. One day while Dad was at work, this woman came to the door. Short hair, super-serious, dressed like a banker or a lawyer or something. I thought maybe she was from the I.R.S.

"My dad's not home, but if you want me to, like, take a message or something—"

"I'm not looking for your father, I'm looking for you, Charles."

The way she said my name was very flat, like I should have expected her to know who I was. I was getting a little creeped out.

"How do you know my name?"

"Your police file had some basic information. But I'd like to know more."

Oh crap. I assumed the Maestro would come after me himself. It never occurred to me he'd call the police. It's usually the police who call him. Was she going to arrest me? I doubt they'd take my word against his.

"Look, I wasn't trying to steal the motorcycle. I'll give it right back if—"

She looks confused for a split second, then goes back to her all-business expression.

"We're not interested in any motorcycle. We're interested in you. Your powers. There's a very dangerous criminal at large, and we think you can help us apprehend him. We've already talked to your sister, and we were hoping—"

"How do you know about her?" She clearly wasn't talking about Laura. Nobody knows Chloe's my sister besides the Maestro and James Flames, and I'm not sure either of those two would even remember her name. Had this woman been spying on me? Did she work for DOI or something?

I think she sees me tense up, because she puts her hands up a little, and her tone gets slightly less severe.

"It's okay. We've been working with Chloe for a while. She told us about you. Recommended you, in fact."

"Wait... was she working for you when she froze that guy? With the machine? And the cop died?" I know I'm not being very coherent, but she either knows what I'm talking about or she doesn't.

"The officer who died was a colleague of mine. And the man who built that machine is who we want you to help us apprehend. Your sister injured him, but he's still at large, and he's still extremely dangerous. We need both of your help."

"Are you with DOI or something?" If she is, I probably just said the wrong thing. Everyone just assumes the Department of Intelligence is annoyed that their acronym sounds like "doyyyy."

"We're a nongovernmental agency. We go after the bad guys. That's all you need to know for right now."

The bad guys? I'm not sure how seriously to take this, but as this woman seems like the most serious person I've ever met, I decide she's probably not taking things lightly.

"So... what do you want me to do?"

"Before Chloe injured our suspect, we only had two confirmed sightings. One was a break-in at Delspan, which I believe you're familiar with. The other was at a confrontation between the Maestro and the man who attacked you in the hockey arena."

"Yeah, I was there for that too. Chloe said she saw the guy afterwards."

"He wasn't involved, just observing."

"Yeah, I thought that was weird."

"We have a theory. Chloe may have told you about a device he was building. We believe it's designed to imbue people with powers. We believe the man at the hockey arena was given powers by this device, and the man Chloe calls Vaporware was observing his creation in action."

"Okay. But how does that help us catch him?"

"We have his equipment. His only connections to his work are the supers he's created. We think if another fight breaks out, he may come back to observe. I know you inherited your powers from the Maestro, but he doesn't know that. You're an unknown super whose powers manifested around the same time he activated his device. As far as he's concerned, you could be one of his."

"So I'm the bait?"

"You and Chloe. Our plan is to stage a fight between the two of you. We'll have people observing, to see if he shows up to watch, and try and apprehend him if he does."

"But, like, how can you catch him? Can't he just turn into gas again and float away?"

"Our scientists have created a device we think can contain him. And we have you and Chloe. We don't know whether he can be burned while in a gaseous state, but you're certainly welcome to try."

"I have a brother, too. Half-brother. James. He can turn into fire. If Vaporware can be burned, he could probably do it just as well as I could. Should we invite him?"

Invite him. I kick myself for sounding childish, like we're setting up a little kid's birthday party. But if she thinks I sound stupid, she doesn't show it.

"Yes, I think so. The more chances we have to get this guy, the better."

So that's it. I'm using my powers. For real stuff. I'd be lying if I said I wasn't terrified. But this won't be like the hockey game. Other people will have my back. They have a plan. Sort of. But I'm prepared this time. I'm going to ride in on the motorcycle and be the hero. I'm sure Chloe will hate it if I bring the bike, but what the heck. You have to do these things right.

REHAB

It took me for-fucking-ever to find that barn, but I finally spot it on the morning of the ninth fucking day of flying over a mind-numbing array of nearly-identical farmer's fields from sunup to sundown. Thank goodness it's green and not red like every other barn, so I at least know it when I see it. There's a quaint little white farmhouse a few hundred feet away, and I really don't want to barge in on some poor farmer, so I try peeking in the windows. Of course, it immediately hits me that that isn't polite, it's creepy, but too late, I'm already doing it.

No signs of life so far, no lights on, but there is an open window upstairs. Maybe I'll just poke around a bit. Worst case, the farmer comes at me with a shotgun and I get a few more bullet holes in my jacket. Actually, the worst case is Amberly blowing up the house, but I try not to think about that.

I try to float in the bedroom window as stealthily as I can, but as soon as my head's in the window, I'm looking at someone's naked ass, and I'm so startled I nearly cry out. If I wasn't invading someone's privacy before, I sure as shit am now.

I try and back out through the window as gently as I swooped in, but flying backwards has always been weird for me. I hang there a second, just long enough to look at the tangle of arms and legs in the bed and register who I'm looking at. Jodi and Amberly.

I guess I'm not that surprised, although Amberly's a little young for her. I mean, she's 18ish, I think, but I still feel like I should be averting my eyes. I try to stay focused on the door as

I fly over the bed as quietly as I can.

I look for a blanket or something to throw over them, but the only one in the room is under the two of them. Maybe I should just come back later. I'll give them a chance to get dressed, eat breakfast, that sort of thing. But I take a step for the door, and I hear Jodi yelp in surprise behind me. I turn around and try my best to act casual.

"Miss me?"

"Jesus, Ree! What are you doing?"

"Uh, you disappeared, so I was worried about you. And she disappeared, so I was a little bit terrified about that. But mostly I was worried about you. That super burglar you were worried about months ago? He killed Finger. I was worried he'd come after you."

"Oh, shit. Shit, Ree. I'm so sorry."

She makes a move to get out of bed, but stops, and makes a half-hearted effort to cover up her boobs.

"Look, can you give me a minute? And we can talk about everything?"

"I'll be downstairs. But I'm not leaving until we've worked some shit out."

I close the bedroom door behind me. Always weird seeing your friends naked.

At least the kitchen's well stocked. I put on some coffee and wish I had a slug of whiskey to pour into mine. This is not going to be a fun conversation.

She knows it too, as she sits down without a word.

"Okay, for starters, I'm honestly really happy you found someone. I mean, after punishing yourself with all those long hospital shifts, it's about time you got laid. Seriously, good for you. But did you have to pick the most dangerous girl on Earth?"

"She's been fine. Ever since we came out here. Things are just normal. She's mostly been normal."

Jesus, listen to her. "You've seen what this girl can do. You saw what she did to Finger. That could be you. Any minute, she could explode and kill you. We don't even know what sets her off. Stress? Maybe? But who knows for sure. And when it happens, there's a very good chance you'll die. She won't intend to do it, she probably won't even know she's doing it. But it's only a matter of time."

I see tears in her eyes, as she knows I'm right. She's probably been telling herself all the same stuff and just making herself not listen. I know it's shitty, but she has to hear it.

"You're in love with her, aren't you?"

"I... maybe. I don't know. But there's more to it than that. I want to... I have to try and fix her. It's awful. I know I shouldn't."

"What do you mean? Of course you should. I mean, can you?"

"No. Probably not. But that's why I can't stop thinking about it. I can fix everybody else, why not her?"

"Look, nobody's ever dealt with anything like this girl. It's not just you."

"You don't understand. This is a problem I have."

As she says this, she looks about ten years older. I see deep lines in her face, and the pained expression she almost always has looks positively cheerful compared to the one she has now. She takes a minute to collect herself before she speaks again. Whatever she's building up to clearly isn't that easy for her to talk about.

"My powers kicked in pretty early. A little at a time, but by middle school I had a pretty good handle on them. When I was in 4th grade, this girl kept spreading lies about my friends. Just typical 10-year-old's gossip. I made her nose grow like Pinocchio. She was so freaked out. Just absolutely lost it.

"That was when my parents gave me The Talk. The one about how people were always going to resent my powers, and to keep a low profile. But that didn't even hit me as much as seeing how upset that girl was. She had been spreading gossip to make herself feel powerful, important, whatever. And I just made her feel like nothing. I had absolute power over her. Forget about her nose. I could have given her four extra fingers, or made them all fall off. I could have stopped her heart with a thought. I can still do that. To everyone I meet. Every single person. Except you, and maybe Amberly. Everywhere I go, I have a gun pointed at everyone's head, at all times, and I just have to trust myself not to pull the trigger.

"It sounds corny, but that's when I decided to use my powers for good. I didn't want to hurt people the way I hurt that girl. So I started fixing people. People I knew, strangers, didn't matter. Anyone who had something wrong, I fixed it. I mean, there are people out there whose cancer was cured because they were waiting at the same bus stop as I was.

"That went on through high school. Until junior year, there was a guy in my class, Greg, with cerebral palsy. That's caused by an undeveloped region of the brain. The one part of the body I hadn't messed with. The more you study medicine, the more you realize we've gotten really good at understanding the body, and we really have no idea how the brain works. I would look at this kid's brain once in a while, just trying to see if I could see what was wrong. I never quite got it, and that always nagged at me. I really, really wanted to figure out what to do. Partly to help Greg, but part of it was just that I hated that I couldn't, you know?

"So Greg had poor motor control, as you'd expect, and he had seizures occasionally, which not everyone with CP gets, but he did. And one day he must have forgotten to take his meds, and he had one in class. His brain lit up. It was like a neon sign, with a letter burned out. I could see exactly where the neurons weren't firing. I knew how to fix him.

"So, the next day, I tried. Sometimes I'd fix people without even letting them know. Pretty sure I prevented my dad from having a heart attack later in life and he never had any idea. But I told Greg. I showed him what I could do. I changed the skin on my hand to dark brown and back, and that was enough to impress him. I told him I wanted to try and fix him. I told him it could be dangerous, and he said he understood, but really, neither of us understood.

"Fixing a wound? Growing back a finger, or an arm? You're really just hitting copy-paste on the cells. You just make more skin, more bone, more muscle, until you've built a body part. Organs are a little trickier, but the heart's made of one thing: heart cells. Someone has a hole in their heart? You make more heart cells and fill the hole. It's not that complicated.

"The brain's different. It's like every cell does its own thing. I also know now — I didn't then — that neurons are constantly sending electrical impulses in an incredibly complicated pattern we can't begin to understand. But 16-year-old me thought she understood everything."

She stops, and I have a sinking feeling I know where this story's going.

"You didn't fix him."

A tear runs down her cheek, but she keeps going, voice breaking a little.

"I broke him. I broke his brain. I knew where the dead zone was, I was just trying to fix those cells, but something happened. Some connection was severed. And everything just stopped working."

"He died?" I didn't want to say 'you killed him,' even though I was sure that's where this was going.

"Not for a long time. He went into a coma, and he never came out. It honestly might have been better if I had killed him. His poor parents. Before I came along, they just had to worry about him getting up stairs, or whether it'd be hard for him to find a girlfriend. Now they had to watch their son, still alive, alive for years, but damaged beyond repair. Because of me. I've had to live with that too, but for them it had to be so much worse."

"So... that's why you work around the clock? To try and make it up—"

"No. Setting up the supers wing was the deal they made for me when I sent my parents to jail. They can keep an eye on me, I can do what I do, Mom and Dad can't get to me. Penance and witness protection all in one. My name's not really Jodi."

I want to ask her more about so many things. What did her parents do? What are their powers? What's her real name? But Amberly's standing in the doorway. Wearing a shirt, at least. That hockey jersey she had on last time I saw her. I wonder if Jodi even got her any more clothes of her own. I'm also starting to doubt she's 18. She looks like a kid, apart from the scar down her face, which still looks as fresh as it did the first time I saw her.

"Look, thanks for, like, checking up on us and stuff, but we're really okay here."

"So far."

"Yeah, so far. Isn't that a good thing? I'm relaxed, I'm happy, nothing's setting off my powers. Isn't that a good thing?"

"So far."

She looks exasperated, and I'm sure she'll be harder to convince than Jodi, but I can't just leave her here and hope for the best.

"You know how dangerous you are. You're probably even more dangerous than that. Look, give Jodi and I a few minutes to talk. We need to figure out what to do next."

I don't really feel right talking about what to do with Amberly when she's in the room, but we can't really tell her to go upstairs and cover her ears, so we put her in that awkward position of Mommy and Daddy deciding your fate right in front of you.

"You can't just stay here."

"We can stay here! We're not near anything, she can't hurt anyone." Jodi's starting to sound less sure. I just need to stay firm, wear her down.

"She can hurt you."

"She hasn't so far."

"That just means she's due! You can't fix yourself if she blows you up!"

Amberly has been looking back and forth at us like she's watching tennis, but she finally speaks up.

"I've only gone off once since we've been here. I feel like maybe the country... and the quiet..."

She trails off, and looks over at the TV. It's been playing

quietly in the background the whole time, but the volume jumps up for the music they play when they interrupt with a news bulletin. Something about how they've captured a super. A super who killed a cop. They're holding him downtown. Jodi and I have been half paying attention, but Amberly's transfixed. It just starts to flicker in the back of my mind that that cop might be Finger, when they flash a picture of the suspect. Amberly stands bolt upright, still staring at the screen, and says one word:

"HIM"

The screen goes bright white, and I see concern and regret and sheer terror on Jodi's face in the split second before the room explodes.

BURNS

I realize we're trying to catch a murderer and it's super-serious, but this is actually pretty fun. Chloe keeps walling off a section of Washington St. downtown with ice, and James and I keep busting through the walls. They picked a great location, since one side of the block's pretty empty, but this end of the block is a hotel, which means lots of people come to see what's happening. This is only going to work if we draw a crowd, and so far we've got a pretty decent one, pushed up against police barricades to get a glimpse of the action.

The motorcycle is parked around the corner, and we have a change of clothes for James on either end of the block for when he reverts to solid form; a long, heavy winter coat he can slip into easily. And that scientist guy who Chloe worked with before — Malcolm something — is here, trying to blend in with the crowd, hoping nobody notices his device. He built this weird vacuum cleaner-looking thing that's supposed to be able to suck up Vaporware in gaseous form. He said creating one-way suction, where air keeps going in and nothing comes out is impossible, so it took him a few weeks to figure out how to do it. Showoff.

Still, I get to show off too. I burn a circle in one of Chloe's walls, which she quickly patches up. I realize pretty early on I could just melt either side, where it connects to the buildings, and it would just topple over. But there's probably an even chance of it crushing me or her, and I don't want to do either, obviously. She also busted open a fire hydrant, so there's lots of

212

water to freeze. Just getting the fire department or whoever to shut off the water would probably hamper things for her too.

But we're not here to stop her, we're here to make a spectacle, and that's where the fun comes in. Next time I make a hole in the wall, she sends a bunch of snowballs flying through. I make a show of zapping them in mid-air with little jets of flame. I'm actually impressed I'm able to hit them in mid-air. I don't have the coordination to, say, get a basketball into a basket reliably. But hitting a snowball in mid-air? I guess that just plays to my natural abilities.

The snowballs stop, the wall seals itself up, and I assume she's turning around to pretend to fight off James. I wonder what he's doing over there — I feel like he could just walk through the wall and turn it into a puddle if he wanted to. It's funny, I feel like if we were in a real fight, I could put Chloe in the hospital pretty quickly. But at the same time, I feel like she has the better power. I mean, a giant wall of ice? How cool is that? No pun intended.

So, inappropriate as it is, I'm enjoying myself. At least, until I hear that voice behind me.

"I see you're having fun playing superhero. Take a seat, kid, there's a grownup here."

"Fuck off."

I guess I'm not surprised to see him. Our whole plan was to create a spectacle. I guess we couldn't expect Vaporware to take an interest and the city's protector to ignore us. But besides him just being a dick and me not wanting to deal with him right now, I'm seriously worried he's going to screw up our plans. Chloe's playing supervillain for the sake of putting on a show, but Frank doesn't know that. What if he tries to stop her?

The first thing I do is stop shooting fire. Why give him ammo? Beyond that, I don't know what to say to the guy. But he's already looking past me at the wall of ice.

"Damn, kid. Is that your sister causing all this trouble? Little sibling rivalry between you two?"

"Not exactly."

Crap. Crap crap crap. He's going to mess this whole thing up. Can I explain the plan to him? Would he even care? It's supposed to be a secret, and for all I know Vaporware is already in the crowd behind us. A crowd that's obviously thrilled to see the Maestro, and wondering why I'm talking back to him, and therefore hanging on our every word.

"I can handle this. Stay out of it. This has nothing to do with you."

"Handle it? There's a giant wall of ice blocking the street. If you had the slightest idea how to use your powers, this would have been a puddle the minute you got here."

"I'm not trying to melt it, I'm—"

Crap. What do I tell him? My instinct is to shoot fire into his smug face, but he'd just swat it away. Or torch the whole damn wall, just to show him I can. But he could do who knows what with that fire. I can't risk him burning Chloe, and if he scares off Vaporware, we might not get another chance at the guy. Assuming he's even here.

I need to talk to that scientist guy. But he's on the opposite side, James' side. I don't want to do something rash and screw this up for everyone else. I have to at least talk to Chloe. But at this point I haven't shot any fire her way in a few minutes; she's behind a glacier. I could shoot fire and melt through it easily but any fire I make, the Maestro can do who knows what with.

But of course, he doesn't need me to start a fire. He's already past me, and his hand's in his jacket pocket. The gold lighter. He's going to melt the wall, and then do who knows what to Chloe, and then probably toss James around like a frisbee just to annoy him.

The crowd's standing back, but they're pretty loud, so I might have a chance to sneak up on him. My only chance is if I can surprise him. I edge around to the side of him, just enough to see the glint of gold in his hand. I shoot a quick burst of flame at the lighter. Maybe if I hit it just right, I can make it too hot to touch.

"Fuck! What the hell is wrong with you, kid? God damn it!"

He's holding his hand and hopping up and down. It never, ever occurred to me that he isn't fireproof. Maybe that skipped a generation or something. I run past him and kick the gold lighter, away from him, away from the crowd, towards the ice. It slides along in front of me as I run towards the wall. I hear him cursing me and I don't look back to see if he's running after me. I can't shoot any more fire, but I can still make it through the wall.

When I was first starting out, I'd do this thing where I'd build up to shooting a flame. I could feel myself getting warmer for a few seconds before the fire would start, like the buildup before a sneeze. I try doing that again, but not getting to the sneeze. I just try and heat up my whole body, not quite hot enough to ignite. I press myself against the ice.

It's at least a foot thick, so it starts to melt, but it's slow going. I can see Frank limping towards me, looking mighty pissed off. I forgot he still can't run, so I've got a minute. I hope I can get through this fast enough. I've only melted about three inches when he's close enough to start shouting at me.

"Why do you keep doing this shit to me? What'd I do to you? I tried to help you! I wanted us to work together! Father and son and all that shit."

All that shit. I felt my anger rising. I tried to channel it into more heat, more melted ice. There was a puddle spreading at my feet, and my clothes were wet. But I was still only about halfway through.

"You're not my father. You never were. So don't start pretending you care now."

I try to sound angrier than I really am. I know I should feel more of a connection to this guy, or like it's more of a big deal that he's my "real" father or whatever. But even when we were meeting regularly and he wasn't being a jerk, I never really felt much. Just curiosity. So that's where my powers come from. This guy. But I'd rather he kept talking if it slowed him down even a little, so I keep it up.

"You're second-rate. That's why we all can't wait until you retire. Maybe we'll get somebody to replace you who's actually good at his job. Look at you. Take your lighter away and you're a sad old man."

Okay, maybe I'm a little emotional.

Finally the ice is thin enough that I can put my weight against it and it cracks. I'm through. Chloe has her back turned, she's patching up holes in the wall as fast as James can make them, hair swishing this way and that as she works. But she must hear the ice crack, because she turns around, and as soon as she sees me, I can tell she knows something's wrong.

"Maestro's here."

"Fuck."

She runs towards me, but pushes me out of the way to

get to the hole in her ice wall. Over her shoulder, I can see her shooting ice from her hands and hear a shout from the other side. I shout to James to stay back. To turn back into himself. A second later, he's shivering, naked, on this side of the ice wall.

"The Maestro. We don't want to give him any fire to work with."

"Fuck that shit." I'm sure James wants Frank tossing him around even less than I do. But I don't think he has much to worry about. I turn back to the hole, and see Frank on the ground, encased in ice from the neck down, Chloe standing over him, glowering. He keeps flexing his arms and cracking the ice, but Chloe just adds another layer and he stays immobile.

"God damn it! You little bitch!"

"I can freeze your mouth, too."

That shuts him up.

The crowd is torn between anger and fear, some people trying to run away from the Ice Queen who just beat the city's protector, and some wanting a closer look at her. It takes me a second to remember I'm supposed to be fighting her, keeping them safe from her supposed menace. If they realize it's all an act, what happens? We probably lose any shot we had at finding Vaporware, but what about the crowd itself? If they decide we're both up to something, and have the Maestro in a block of ice, would they decide to attack?

No sooner does this thought cross my head when I hear a high-pitched voice shout, "Unhand him! Or face the blinding light of justice!"

Unhand him? Who the heck talks like that? I get my answer almost immediately as a flash of light from the crowd momentarily blinds me. Glimmer. What she lacks in powers, she makes up for in self-promotion. Making yourself light up isn't all that helpful to crimefighting, but that's never stopped her from trying, at least as long as there's a photographer handy.

For a second, everything's black and I see stars. I'm tempted to shoot a burst of flame, but I don't want to burn anyone in the crowd, and I do want to burn Glimmer but probably shouldn't. My vision starts to creep back in slowly. I can just see a small circle of light come into focus, which slowly starts to widen. And it widens around a face in the crowd. A face I've seen before.

"Chloe." I try my best to whisper. "It's him."

She doesn't look at me, just stares blankly towards the crowd. I watch her eyes start to focus. Her glasses frost over. I expect her to say something, but before I know what's happened she flings her hands out, and a scream rises up from the crowd.

My vision has cleared, and I see a giant block of ice where Vaporware was standing, the blurry silhouette of a man inside of it. People in the crowd are shoving each other, trying to get away. When she was shooting ice at me, they were happy to gawk. But now she's shooting at them, and you can feel the rising panic.

People are running every which way, yelling, sirens are blaring, but all I can focus on is the block of ice. The figure inside dissolves away to nothing. He's turned into gas. I swear I hear the ice crack. Is it just settling? Is that something big blocks of ice do? I'm afraid to ask Chloe, knowing she doesn't have any more answers than I do: "Is he still in there?"

"I don't know. Not if there's a crack in the ice."

"Can he break through the ice?"

"I don't know. I don't know."

I hear panic creep into her voice. We've got him. We're so

close. And if one tiny thing goes wrong, he'll get away and we'll probably never get another shot.

"Get the guy. The scientist. I think I can pin him down."

She starts adding another layer of ice. I don't stick around to watch. I run to get Malcolm, but he's already trying to wedge his device through the hole in the ice wall. This time I don't worry about the Maestro, who's still on the ground, his legs encased in ice, muttering curses. I put a hand on either side of the hole in the ice, and within a few seconds water's pooling on the ground and the vacuum cleaner thing slides right through.

I help him carry the device over to Chloe. The block of ice is the size of a car now.

"I don't think it cracked. I think he's still in there." She's not looking at us, her whole attention is on the hollowed-out space in the middle of the ice, hoping it's not as empty as it looks. Malcolm holds the nozzle to his vacuum cleaner thing up to the ice, but he isn't really sure what to do with it.

"I got this." Thank goodness he made it out of metal and not plastic. I warm up the nozzle until it glows faintly. At that temperature, it slides through the ice like it's not even there. He flicks a switch and it starts humming before I've finished breaking through to the hollow center. The ice starts to groan and turn white where it's starting to strain against the suction. I can hear it splinter and crack.

"It's breaking! He's busting out!"

"No, no, I don't think so." The scientist is right behind me, one hand still on the on/off switch. "We're creating a vacuum inside the ice. The pressure's breaking it apart."

"But what if he escapes when the ice breaks!"

"If the suction is powerful enough to break the ice, he

didn't escape. I think we got him."

He peers at the device. Incomprehensible LED lights flicker on one side of it. I guess it means something to him.

"It's not just air in here. We trapped something. Someone, I mean. At least, that's what it looks like." He looks up at the three of us, me not wanting to let go of the nozzle, James holding his long coat around himself, shivering, Chloe just staring at the device, shaking a little, like she still wasn't convinced we got him. "You three did great."

"Chloe." I squeeze her arm. "You were terrific." She breaks into a smile. I start to smile too, and I start to lean in closer. I catch myself, and let go of her arm. I'm still not sure how I'm supposed to act around her, now that she's my sister. Her smile drops. I guess she doesn't really know either.

Still, we made a good team. Our sort-of family group. Catching bad guys together. We're real superheroes now. And the fact that we made Frank look like an idiot — well, I'm not going to pretend that wasn't the icing on the cake.

REHAB

I come to and don't understand where I am. I remember being in a house, but now I'm outside, in a storm. I have to look around for a full minute before I realize I'm lying on a pile of kindling that used to be a couch, and I'm outside because the house isn't there anymore.

A chunk of the coffee table is covering my legs, and sitting on the tabletop is an arm. I nearly black out again when I realize that a minute ago it belonged to Jodi.

I frantically search the rubble until I find the rest of her under a section of wall. Blood everywhere. Legs crushed, one barely attached. Stump of her arm gushing blood. I give silent thanks that my parents forced me to do EMT training at a ridiculously young age. Her shirt's in tatters, so it's easy to tear strips and make a tourniquet for her arm. And the worse leg. I stop short of doing the other leg — I'm not sure restricting that much circulation is helping anything, and I can't waste any time.

I don't know if any of it is going to help. The only person who can save Jodi is bleeding to death in my arms, if she's even still alive. But I fly for the hospital, because I don't know what else to do. The ground is a blur below me, as I fly as fast as I've ever gone. It's not until I'm a good ways up in the air that I notice the fire. Below me, and behind me, there's a gash cut across the neat squares of farmland. Crops are burning, trees are burning, and as I speed away from it, I realize the fire's drawing a straight line, pointing back towards the farmhouse. And ahead towards the city.

I start to hear more than the usual chatter in my earpiece. A farmhouse hit by a tornado. A building collapse in one of the Southtowns. A freak storm south of the city.

I try to focus all of my thoughts and energy on Jodi, on getting her help, on getting to the hospital. But I can't shut out the voice in the back of my mind — it has to be her. Amberly's still going off. And she's heading for the city. She's heading for him.

I barely slow down when I get to the hospital. I fly backwards through a window, right into the floor where she worked. The lights are off, and the halls are empty. I remember too late they've shut it down without her.

"SOMEBODY HELP!!!!!"

My screams echo through the empty halls. I keep flying, down hallways, through double doors, down hallways, until I see people in scrubs. I push a guy off his gurney—he didn't look like he was in that bad shape—and drop Jodi onto the mattress, blood already soaking into the sheet. I grab the first person I see in blue by the shoulders.

"Save her. Please."

I want to stay. I want to not leave her side until I know she's okay. But I can't. The word "Please" has barely left my lips when I'm flying again, careening down the hallway, knocking over monitors, fumbling for daylight, crashing through a window, hurtling up, up, high enough to get a view of the city.

There's no question where she is or where she's going. There's a straight line cutting across the landscape, smoldering all the way back to the farm. I fly towards the front of the line and even from miles away, it's like flying through a thunderstorm, the air crackling with electricity, the wind pushing me to one side or the other as I try and stay on target.

It only takes me about two minutes to get to her, but every second of it is full of mounting dread. I hear Dr. Science in my head. My energy is like a faucet. Hers is like a fire hose, that we can't control. That we can't shut off. I see a cloud of dust approaching and I swoop in lower to meet it head on. I brace myself for the worst.

But it's even worse than that. I thought there was an outside chance I could reason with Amberly, or at least fly her away from people and wait for the storm to subside so I could talk to her like a human being. But I'm not sure what I'm face to face with is still human. Amberly's body floats just off the ground, her bare feet brushing the tops of the grass. Her head lolls to one side, her arms hang limp. Her Anger jersey is a smoldering rag hanging off her limp body. And the scar. The scar is glowing like the inside of a volcano.

I barely have time to take it in, because she's still moving, inexorably, towards the city, and fast. Behind her I can see a suburban house in ruins, one side caved in, fire in the windows. The street in front has a furrow in it like someone had run a giant plow through it. As she floats towards me, I see streetlights twist around and fold in half; windows shatter from blocks away; fire hydrants explode into sprays of water that turn to steam; in the distance are people running for their lives.

I fly at her, hoping to knock her down, or at least slow her down. But I can't get near her. It's like a bubble surrounding her, and I just bounce off and deflect to the side. I tumble onto the grass and look up in time to see her float through the wall of a house like it wasn't there, the wood turning to matchsticks as she passes, smoke detectors going off, then a crash as she emerges from the other side.

I try to fly at her again, just as my earpiece blares an evacuation notice for Woodlawn, Blasdell, Lackawanna — all the towns between us and downtown Buffalo. The voice cuts out half a second before I get to Amberly. I'm thrown aside again, and feel a melted lump of plastic fall out of my ear.

And she's still moving. I fly above her, watching the destruction at a remove. Cars flipping over, stoplights exploding into sparks, a truck crashed into the furrow she left in the pavement, the ground cracking open every time she gets too close to a water main, and me helpless to stop any of it.

I try to think what Mom and Dad would do. But I'm not sure they'd be any less lost in my place. Mom was great against guns, knives, fists... but this? Dad could fly at her, same as me. Maybe his strength would get him closer, but that's no good to his weakling daughter. And I can't ignore what happened when they did tangle with an out-of-control super who made himself explode. They died. Along with thirty thousand New Yorkers. I've always been pretty convinced I can't die, but right now, for the first time in my life, I'm not so sure.

I start grasping at straws. She's going to skirt the lakeshore. Maybe she'll cut across the water? And conveniently drown? Even if she floats across the surface, at least she won't be hurting anything. She's also going to pass close to the steel mill. If only the smelter were still running, maybe I could push her in.

I wonder, can I at least nudge her in some direction? I fly up high this time, well away from her, so I can build up a good head of steam. I hurtle towards the center of the storm, parallel to the path of destruction stretching out behind her, straight for her, closer, closer—then the world spins around and I find myself lodged in the windshield of an SUV. I think I got closer to her that time. Maybe I just need to go faster.

Or maybe I just need more horsepower. I push aside the windshield fragments and slide into the driver's seat. I hope my hotwiring skills have held up since my joyriding days, but there's no need, as the keys are sitting in the cupholder. Oh, trusting suburbanites. Didn't teenage me teach you anything? The engine roars and I speed away from her, behind her. Then I spin the car around and floor it. I manage to find a clear stretch of road that isn't torn up, but I can see smoke, fire, and rubble on both sides of me, red lights flashing in my peripheral vision. I'm up to 80, then 90, then 100. She's coming up fast, and sparks start flying from the dashboard like I'm on Star Trek, but I keep the pedal to the floor. I hear the gas tank ignite behind me, and the explosion pushes me forward, closer, faster, and then the car's on top of her and she's down.

There's a moment of silence. Well, not silence. Car alarms, police sirens, buildings collapsing. But it feels quiet. The rampage has stopped.

And then she's up again, moving forward. Slowly. Surely. Unstoppably. I pry myself out of the wreckage and keep going. The car's a pile of confetti, my clothes are torn to ribbons, but I got her. For a second, at least, I got her to stop. I let the remains of my leather jacket fall of in pieces and I'm airborne again. Now. How do I get her to stop for more than a second? Hit her with something bigger. A semi truck? Can I crash an airplane into her? Would NASA let me borrow the space shuttle?

Then I see it. The steel mill. The big one. It hasn't had any molten metal active for years, but it's a giant, decrepit building. Can I bring it down on her head? Would that be enough to stop her? I circle around, looking for another car I can use, but none of the ones strewn around the rubble are upright. And the building's a concrete monolith. I doubt a high-speed collision with a Chevy would do more than scratch the paint off the building.

The chain link fence around the yard breaks into fragments as she floats through it. If I'm going to do something, I have to do it fast. Finally, I see just the thing—a delivery truck. Okay, just the thing would be a tank, but this is the best I'm going to do. It's an old truck, thankfully, which means it's still hotwireable. I glance up to see her put a hole in the side of the building, and then I touch wires together, sparks fly, and the engine roars to life.

I aim for the hole in the building, hoping the truck will fit through. Hitting the outer wall isn't going to do anything, but maybe if I can knock down a support pillar, I can bring the roof down on us. The truck doesn't accelerate as well as the SUV, but I'm up to 70 by the time I get to the building. I hear a screech of metal as the jagged opening rips off my side mirrors and scratches one side of the truck, but I keep my foot down. I can see her, across the cavernous room. Sparks fly from equipment that's been dormant for decades, lighting the room here and there in flashes, but there's no mistaking Amberly—inside the dark room, she has an unearthly glow, and there are smoldering embers coming from her clothes. Or maybe from her body. I pump the gas pedal and head straight for it.

There's a large pillar right in front of her, and if she tries to pass through it, she might end up doing the work for me. But it's too late to slow down now. I hit her from behind, and the truck smashes her into the pillar before both practically dissolve, and sure enough, the ceiling collapses onto our heads.

For a second, it's quiet. I'm in pitch darkness, but I can

sense the slab of broken concrete pinning me down. I'm under who knows how much rubble, but so is she. I hold out hope that that's it. She's trapped, or better yet, she's dead. I've spent months trying to keep Amberly alive, and now I want her dead more than I've ever wanted anything in my life. If this didn't stop her, I'm terrified of what happens next.

And it's only a few more seconds before the thing I'm terrified of happens. I feel the rubble shake, I hear slabs of concrete scraping against each other, and there's no mistaking what's happening. She's getting up. The sound starts to recede into the distance. She's on the move. And I'm stuck here under ten tons of steel mill.

It felt like an eternity before I could hear the sirens, but in reality it was probably about ten minutes. But those ten minutes were full of visions of the destruction that was in store. Amberly could lay waste to the city. And once she had, then what? I had no doubt other, more competent supers were already flying in to try and stop her, but did they have any idea what they were dealing with?

Now there were emergency responders outside, but did anyone have any idea I was under here? Would anyone look at the pile of rubble the building had been reduced to and think anyone would be alive?

I scream until I'm out of breath, but I doubt they can hear me. I try and move. Not that I can just climb out from under, but maybe I can wriggle a bit closer to light and fresh air? Close enough that they can hear me? But I'm pretty stuck. Then I try and fly. Up. Down. Forewards. Sideways. I always forget that my powers are much stronger than my muscles. Eventually, I push hard enough in some direction that the rubble shifts, just a little bit. This isn't going to help me get out, but maybe I can at least get someone to notice.

I keep pushing. Changing direction, making small rumbles here and there, pausing to hear if anyone's out there. Finally, I hear a faint voice: "something something alive something."

"I'm alive!" I shout as loud as I can. "ALIVE!!! ALIVE!!!"

Nothing. I try and fly again, shift the rubble around, but I can't get any movement going in any direction. I listen again, and for a minute there's nothing, but then the sound is inescapable. Concrete scraping against concrete. They're digging me out.

I hear a dull thud, and I think they've pulled a slab of ceiling off the pile I'm under. I can hear the voice again, less faint. "Can you hear me? Are you okay?"

I take as deep a breath as I can in close quarters, and try and project it all toward the sound of the voice. "I'm indestructible! Get me out! I need to stop her!"

I swear I hear the voice saying, "It's a her?", but that's soon drowned out by concrete moving. This goes on for a while, and eventually I can hear the sound of engines along with it. Finally I see a sliver of daylight. Then more. Then a slab of concrete slides away. They brought a crane! I don't know how emergency responders could get a crane here that fast, but I make a vow to buy them all drinks for the rest of their lives.

Another chunk of rubble lifts up, and suddenly I can move and I'm airborne, and I'm about to speed toward Amberly, hoping she hasn't gotten to the city yet, when I glance back for a second

It isn't a crane.

It's an old, old man. Frail, leaning on a walker. White, with skin so pale it's almost translucent apart from the liver spots

Wisps of white hair. Just staring blankly ahead, like he's not sure where he is. He has to be in his 80s, at least. But there's no mistaking him. Vulcan. Before the Maestro, before my parents, he was the city's hero, and he was the real deal, to hear my dad tell it. Could move things with his mind. Retired when he turned 50, after getting hurt pretty badly, and my parents took over. A chunk of rubble clatters to the ground and his eyes get their focus back. A few rescue workers look on in awe. I can't help but do the same.

"You're... you've still got it!"

He nods his head imperceptibly. "Yep."

"I don't know how to thank you."

"It's the job. Now go do yours."

"Yes, sir."

I'm not sure I've ever called anyone "sir" before, but he seems like the one guy you make an exception for. I take one last look, and I'm gone, hurtling towards the city, following the straight line of destruction, hoping against hope it's not too late.

BURNS

So, we won. We got the bad guy. I'm not sure what I expected. Medals? Champagne? Thanks of a grateful nation? I guess none of those things. But the last thing I expect is to get to the police station and have no one notice us or care.

The place is bedlam. Phones ringing, people shouting, sirens going off from every direction. When we were outside it was bedlam, but it was directed at us — TV cameras, questions from reporters, as many of them about the Maestro as the guy we caught. Most of it was directed at Chloe, and she didn't say a word, so I felt like I had to be the one to speak up. But getting six questions at once was pretty overwhelming. I said something about this being a dangerous guy and that we got him, and I tried to make it clear that Chloe was on our side, and she only created a disturbance to attract Vaporware. (Except I called her Ice Queen. I figured we probably shouldn't give out our real names.)

But that just led to more questions. Why did she freeze the Maestro? What did he and I fight about? I quickly realized why she had kept her mouth shut, so I tried to do the same until we got into the police station.

Now that we're here, though, everyone's in a panic about something else. Someone says something about a tornado heading for downtown. A female cop is shouting into two phones at once, saying evacuate downtown, evacuate the North-towns, just get everybody out of its path. Every second or two, I'm jostled aside by a cop or EMT or someone who's job I don't recognize, running into or out of the building in a hurry. I look to the scientist guy for guidance, but he seems as overwhelmed as I am. Chloe's still next to me, and I only just realize she's been holding my hand the whole time.

One of the cops spots Mal and makes a beeline for us. She seems to be the only person here who isn't panicked, but I'm guessing she just hides it well. Even standing still, I've been on the verge of getting knocked over every other second, but she walks straight through the crowd as if it's an empty room.

"We have a problem." This is directed right past me and to Malcolm. "Something's headed this way, and it, whatever it is, is incredibly powerful. It's leaving a trail of destruction in its wake. It's not safe here."

The scientist blinks a few times, like he's doing math in his head, or trying to remember something. "Has anyone checked for string energy? Far more than the usual amount? I think I know who this is, and it might not be safe anywhere. In the short term, we have to get this guy" — he gestures to the vacuum cleaner — "somewhere for safekeeping. And these kids aren't equipped to handle this. We shouldn't put them in harm's way again."

"Agreed. We get to safety, regroup, and see what assets we can call in."

They both head for the door, assuming, I guess, that we'd just follow them around. I look over at Chloe and James, not sure what to think. Chloe mouths the words "what the fuck?," but we all follow them. I don't like being talked about like I'm not in the room, or for them to decide what we can and can't handle. But I don't know what else to do.

We follow the adults around the corner towards where

Malcolm's car and my motorcycle are parked. The wind is whipping around and the light's all weird like there's a storm coming. We stop at the corner where cars are getting off the Skyway—an elevated highway that runs past downtown and along the river. We're right at the part where it goes down to level ground. I look up, past the cars, past the highway, and that's when I see the storm.

Sometimes you see a storm coming, and it's a bank of black clouds that fills the whole sky. But overhead were light, gray, harmless-seeming clouds, like any other day in Buffalo. The storm was coming from the ground. A massive cloud of dust was being kicked up by something — or someone — and it was heading our way. This is what they were running away from. The five of us just stand and stare, open-mouthed. James lets out a low moan. Chloe grabs my arm. We just stay there for a minute, transfixed, and I swear I can see the cloud coming closer.

"What do we do?" I'm not even sure whether I said that out loud or not, but the scientist answers.

"I don't think there's anything we can do but pray. She's extraordinarily dangerous. I'd need a lot more information to figure out how anyone can stop her. We have to get clear, and hope this isn't the end of the world."

End of the world? He doesn't know how to stop her? She?

That's when it hits me. It's a super. A super who's out of control. It's the World Trade Center all over again. No one knew how to stop that either. All those people died. Some of them super. Titan. Hydra. Mercury. Gravesend. Everybody knew those names. No one would know ours.

I want to say something. Do something. Come up with a plan. Fight. Run away. Something. But I'm rooted to the spot shaking all over. All I can do is look at the storm, so that's what I do. Until I see something. A spurt of dust spits out of the side of the cloud, like someone shot a bullet through it. The bullet streaks away from the storm and towards us. It's not just dust, it's something solid. The cloud is shooting at us.

We're still standing and staring as the bullet gets closer, trailing dust behind it like a comet.

"What do we do?" The question hangs there in the air for a minute. "Can you freeze it?"

"I don't know." Her voice is shaking just as much as mine must be. "Can you burn it? Knock it out of the sky? Whatever it is?"

"I don't know. But I can try."

The scientist puts his hands on both of our shoulders. "You can't do this. You're kids. We have to get you to safety and bring in more experienced supers to handle this."

"They're not here. We are. We have to do something. Or else what are these powers for?" I ignite my hand to try and underscore the point. Chloe gives me a look I can't place. Bemused? Astonished? I think maybe it's admiration.

"We have to try." She raises her hand. It's encased in ice.

Next to her, James Flames is shaking his head. "Look... I'm with these guys." He gestures towards the adults. "I don't know what that thing is, and I don't wanna fuck with it. You can do what you want, bro. I'm getting the fuck out of here."

I guess I'm not that surprised. In fact, I'm worried he's right. But the bullet is getting closer. And I don't just want to run away. I want to at least see what it is. See if it can be stopped. The cloud is an amorphous nightmare, that I can't imagine trying to stop. But this? This is a thing. This, I can at least try and fight.

Then, maybe, probably, run away.

The cop seems to be with me too. "Take the prisoner to the Falls for safety. I'll stay here just to gather information, and then join you as soon as I can."

But Mal shakes his head. "Do you see where she's heading? Directly for the Falls. That might be her target for all we know. I have to go east. Maybe all the way to New York."

She nods, and he picks up the vacuum cleaner and takes a few steps towards his car. But I see his eyes go wide as he looks back towards the bullet. It takes me a second to see it too. It's a person.

Is this the super they were talking about before? I actually breathe a sigh of relief. A person, we can handle. Freeze her in ice. Burn her up. I guess those are our only two options, but they're good ones. I brace myself as she comes closer. The brown blur across the sky starts to have a more definitive human shape, streaking towards us like a comet. I brace myself, and get ready to shoot fire. But the comet doesn't slow down at all. It goes hurtling just over our heads and we all hit the ground before a deafening crash sounds somewhere behind us.

I turn around, and there's a dent in the side of the police station, a pile of broken bricks and plaster dust on the ground and a body lying in the street, just a tangle of arms and legs. She straightens herself out and gets to her feet, still a bit wobbly. It takes me a minute before I realize I know who this is.

Rehab.

She looks like hell. She shaved her head completely, or her hair all got burned off or something by the tornado. Her clothes are in tatters. She's the one who told me to get a bulletproof wardrobe, so hers must be pretty tough, but right now she looks like got run over by a lawnmower. But if she's fazed by whatever happened to her, never mind crashing into a building at high speed, she doesn't show it.

The second she's upright, she starts yelling. "You have to evacuate! Get everyone out of the police station now!" A few cops have already come around the corner, guns drawn. They're not sure what to make of it. All four of us are already sprinting towards her from the other direction. She yells at the cops again. "She's coming here! She's destroying everything in her path! Get everyone out!!!" Then she notices us. She looks past me and Chloe and her eyes focus on the scientist.

"Mal. Holy shit, Mal. It's her. Amberly. She going off. I can't stop her. I'm not sure anything can. We have to get everyone out of here."

"They've already evacuated most of downtown. They're clearing out the Northtowns next."

"No, I mean here. The police station. She's coming here. They captured a super today. That's who she's after."

Mal holds the vacuum cleaner tighter. "We captured the super. I've got him in here. In gaseous form. He's the one that built Die Glocke. He gave her those powers."

"Well she's not happy about it. I don't know what happens when she catches him, but it won't be anything good."

She's interrupted by a low rumble. We all look up the street, where you can see the Skyway rising off into the distance. Except it's rising up into a cloud of grey fog. Another crash, and another cloud of dust rises. The roadway is collapsing. And whatever's knocking it down is getting closer.

REHAB

I was 12 before I really understood what my parents did for a living. I mean, I knew they were superheroes. I went flying with my dad; I had seen mom stab herself and heal over in two minutes just for laughs. And I knew that they patrolled the city, but I guess my little-girl mind still imagined that as getting kittens out of trees, and the occasional pompous "Take that, you villain!" speech. It really wasn't until I was kidnapped that I realized what the job was really like.

I have to give the kidnappers credit; they really got me. I was walking home from the basketball courts, and there was a homeless guy panhandling on the sidewalk, wrapped in a blanket. It struck me as a tiny bit odd that he was on the side of the parked cars and not against the building, which was the usual spot, but I followed my usual instinct, which is to give him a little distance, not make eye contact, and keep moving.

But when I got close, he stopped muttering, "change, change, anybody got change," and looked me in the eyes, and flashed this big smile, and said loudly, "you look like the girl I'm going to marry!"

It was such an odd thing to say, and it caught me off guard enough that I stopped for a second. And in that one second, someone walking right behind me threw a hood over my head. Everything went black, and in that first moment of disorientation, the homeless guy slapped handcuffs on me — he must have been hiding them under the blanket. My instinct, of course, was to fly away, but they clearly did their homework, because the handcuffs were chained to something and I only got a few feet up. I heard an engine roar, and I felt myself being pulled — the chain was attached to the van the homeless guy had been sitting in front of. They drove away and I had no choice but to fly after them, bumping into streetlights and who knows what else. The chain kept pulling and pulling, and they just reeled me in like a fish, into the back door, and then I heard it roll shut, somebody put duct tape over my mouth, and that was it for a while.

We drove on, I still don't know where, but in my head they took me someplace in Jersey. I picture a low, decrepit brick building out in the swamps, near the "leave the gun, take the cannoli" spot from *The Godfather*, but really, it could have been anywhere.

I was there for a couple days. They kept me chained to the wall, like a medieval dungeon, except it was obviously just some empty warehouse somewhere. They mostly kept to the office room where I couldn't see them. I know I should have been scared, but it was mostly really boring. What were they going to do, torture me? They couldn't hurt me at all. Nobody tried to rape me or anything — I think they were too scared that if they let me down from the wall, I'd just fly away. They might have thought I was super-strong, who knows.

Nobody really said anything to me, they'd just bring me fast food and otherwise ignore me. I have no idea what their plan was or what demands they made, just that somehow Mom and Dad found them. I had seen them mad, at me, at each other, at plenty of people. But not mad like this.

I was daydreaming, hanging from the wall, when I heard voices from outside. I thought that was strange, since none of the kidnappers had gone anywhere that day. Then there was a loud bang as the door flew off the hinges. It was Dad. It was a thick, steel door, and he knocked it clean off the hinges with one punch. That was Dad. Mom came in ahead of him. I was surprised he waited, but as soon as the shooting started, I realized she was his shield. He wasn't bulletproof, not by a long shot.

Of course, she wasn't either. She healed fast, but not until after she had gotten hurt. They shot her so many times. So many times. I just remember screaming and screaming, watching all the bullets go into her, blood soaking through her shirt, but she didn't stop coming. You could see the bullets knocking her back, but she'd lurch forward, step by step, until she was right up close to one of the guys. He shot her right in the eye, her head whipped around, and for a second, I saw her face. The eye was just gone, a gaping black hole with blood gushing out.

Then she turned back to him. She had these two knives, that were really long and super-sharp. She told me later she liked them because they never ran out of bullets. One of the knives flashed and she sliced his gun hand clean off. By the time that registered with me, the other knife was in his throat. By the time that registered, he was on the floor in a pool of blood and she was on to the next guy. The next time she turned in my direction, her eye was already starting to re-form, but she only glanced at me and went back to work.

Once she had killed a few of the guys, Dad came flying. Two guys were standing on either side of me, one with his gun pointed at me like he was taking me hostage, but really, what was he going to do? The bullets would just bounce off. He must have known that but was just out of ideas.

When Dad came flying across the room, he just smashed

into one of the guys and smooshed him into the concrete wall. Who knows how many of that guy's bones broke or whether he was still alive, but he hit the floor in a heap like he probably wasn't. Then Dad punched the other guy in the face.

I'm sure you've seen boxing, or a bar fight, or whatever, and you know how hard guys can hit. You have no idea how hard a guy who can throw a car hits when he's mad. I didn't realize that Dad had been pulling his punches my whole life until that guy. He punched him square in the nose, and his fist just kept going. Whatever bones were in the front part of his skull just turned into powder, and Dad's fist went through his head like he had punched a watermelon and gotten his hand stuck inside.

He shook his arm until the guy's head fell off his fist, and he pulled his hand away, covered in blood and brains. I just stared at the body, the crushed-in skull that used to belong to a person, until I stopped screaming. By that time, Mom was there, soaked in blood, hers and other people's, but healed up again.

So that was Take Your Daughter To Work Day. That's what my parents did at their jobs, and that's what they were raising me to do, right up until they died.

BURNS

"Whatever we're going to do, we have to decide now. This is it."

Mal is clutching the vacuum cleaner to his chest, which I'm starting to think might be the most dangerous thing anyone's ever done. The cop tries to take charge. "We have to get the prisoner away from here. Maybe we can outrun her."

Rehab isn't having it. She pries the vacuum away from Mal, and gives him a little shove when he tries to hold on. "She's after him. Anywhere you take him, she'll follow, and destroy everything in between. But there might be one place she can't follow."

And then she's airborne. Ten feet up, then twenty, then fifty. As she recedes towards the clouds, I look back at the Skyway as I hear another segment collapse. More dust floods the air. What looked like a storm from a distance is just the dust and debris rising, from whatever this is, destroying everything in her path. There's nothing left of the Skyway but the onramp, and before I have time to move or think or do anything, the two opposing lanes fall away like Moses is parting them, and I see what we're up against.

Chunks of concrete roll away like they're styrofoam, and something rises up out of the rubble. I only know it's a girl because somebody said "her" before. In fact, it's hard to even tell it's a person. She's just a limp body, slowly floating towards us, more like a balloon caught in the breeze than something that just left the trail of destruction I can see behind her. But as she gets closer, I feel my skin crawl as I get a better look at the cause of all of this.

Her skin is charred and blackened like newspaper curled up in a fire. Where her eyes should be are just two points of pure flame. And there's a line running down her face that's too bright to look directly at. It's like someone hit pause as she was spontaneously combusting.

One thing seems obvious. Hitting her with fire isn't going to do anything. Ice, maybe. I look at Chloe and she's clearly every bit as terrified as I am. I start to ask her if she wants to try freezing this thing, but I can't form the words. A little bit of ice isn't going to stop someone who just walked through the Skyway like it wasn't there.

"We have to get out of here."

She nods mutely, and I grab her by the hand and we run. The motorcycle is a block in the other direction. Away. Away from her. We can speed away from this, stay out of the path of destruction, let some other supers — real supers, grown-up supers — deal with this. I jump on the bike and feel Chloe put her arms around me. The engine roars to life, and I'm ready to speed away from this and not look back, when something catches my eye. She stopped.

My brain is screaming at me to ride away, to stay safe, to keep Chloe safe, to get as far away from this as I can. But I don't rev the engine. I have to see what happens next.

Whoever, or whatever she is, she's stopped. She's looking up. Up to where Rehab must be, above the cloud cover. For a minute, she floats there in the middle of Delaware Avenue, staring at the sky, car alarms and police sirens blaring in the distance.

And then it hits me. A shock wave knocks over the bike and sends us sprawling across the empty street. On both sides of the avenue, windows shatter, trees burst into flames, the blacktop disintegrates, and steam sends a manhole cover shooting into the air. But I don't think she was aiming at any of that stuff. The whole block just got caught in a blast she sent straight up, because a moment later, I see a black speck in the sky. Rehab, plummeting like a stone.

"What do we do?" I'm really just talking to myself out loud, but Chloe answers.

"We run."

"What about her?" The figure in the sky is close enough I can make out a human shape. Falling, not flying. "We should help."

"She's indestructible. She'll be fine. And what can we do against that? This is out of our league. The best thing we can do is get someplace safe."

I know she's right, and I tip the motorcycle upright and throw one leg over. But I still look back. I want to see how this plays out, even if that might be a suicidal impulse. I look up at Rehab falling, and I see a second shape, plummeting just as fast. The vacuum. Vaporware. While she's falling straight back towards the burned girl, the metal canister is sailing over our heads, until it smashes to bits further down the street. Chloe cries out when it hits.

"Dammit, we just caught that guy!"

She jumps onto the back of the motorcycle and I take off down the block, towards the remnants of the canister, and away from the destruction. Chloe's onto something. We can't face down an unstoppable monster, but we can get Vaporware. We've already done that once today.

But as I speed past the wreckage, I realize two things. Vaporware's a gas, he's probably long gone. And that blast wasn't aimed at Rehab. It was aimed at him. Which means she's heading this way.

I feel the ground rumble under my wheels, and what sounds like blacktop being torn up behind me. To be completely honest, I'm scared to death riding this motorcycle at the best of times, but now, with the ground shaking and my heart pounding in my chest, I don't really know how I'm even upright. But I speed away, to the end of the street, making an arc around Niagara Square (which, despite the name, is a traffic circle at the center of downtown).

I'm about to spin out of the circle, back onto Delaware Ave, and away towards safety, if there's any such thing. But the motorcycle's engine dies and we skid to a stop just in time for it to start raining broken glass. Windows are shattering in the buildings all along the square. As fast as I tried to go, it wasn't fast enough. She's floating across the square, trees catching fire, only the big bronze statue of Titan and Hydra unaffected.

For the first time since she came floating through the ruins of the Skyway, her feet touch the ground. She stands, motionless as a statue, and an unearthly rumbling sound, a bass note three octaves below anything you've ever heard starts to resonate through the square.

The wind starts to pick up. That's not unusual this time of year, but it only takes a minute to realize this is anything but usual. The wind's speeding past in a perfect circle, with the burned girl at the eye of the storm. Dust and grass and broken glass and bits of trash get swept up until the circle looks practically solid. I realize that Vaporware must be getting swept up in it too.

Or maybe he isn't, because the wind shifts, and now it's blowing towards her. I feel a pop can blow into the back of my head and keep going. To my left, the spray from a broken fire hydrant is getting sucked into the vortex. I stare at it transfixed, half expecting to see people and animals suspended in the wind like the beginning of *The Wizard Of Oz*.

Chloe snaps me out of it. She grabs my arm and mouths the word "run." It's too loud to hear each other. And I realize too late that it's too late to run.

At first, we can push against the wind, and take slow steps away. But then it takes all my strength just to not get knocked down. I hold up for a minute, not sure what to do next, when I see Chloe stumble and then vanish from sight as she's carried away by the wind.

I'm not sure I can push myself forward, but now I'm not sure I want to. I can't just let her go. Even if it means getting sucked into certain death myself. I have to try and save her.

I only have to relax my muscles for a second, and I'm flying backwards, into the whirlwind. Everything's a blur as I get sucked into the dense vortex, and I feel myself get nicked in a thousand places by dirt and debris as I'm hurled through the air.

I don't have time to think as I'm flung through the air, the world spinning in front of me. I squeeze my eyes shut as dust and debris pelt my face. I fly through the air for what seems like forever, getting hit by airborne junk, no idea where I'm going or which way is up. Finally I feel a sharp pain as I hit something solid. I feel something snap in my back – probably a couple of ribs. I look around frantically, but don't see Chloe anywhere.

I'm too stunned to feel more than shock, although I'm sure it will catch up to me pretty soon. I'm lying on the ground, and looming over me is what I hit. The bronze statue. Hydra. Titan. Those two were heroes. They would have stopped the destruction while it was still in the Southtowns. By comparison, I'm just a scared kid who doesn't know what he's doing. In this or any other situation. Heck, even the statue's better at this than I am. It's the one thing strong enough to stand up to the whirlwind. The statue's half-protruding from it, wind whipping against Titan's face and him just sitting there, taking it. If Hydra had just been sucked into oblivion, would he keep going? He probably would. But I'm not him.

The noise sounds like the end of the world. I'm pretty sure that's exactly what it is. I brace myself for whatever's coming. Chloe's gone, and I'm next. I close my eyes, waiting for the end. But through the noise, faintly, I can hear a scream.

It's not a cry of pain, it's a woman's voice, trying to form words. Rehab. I struggle to sit up so I can lean closer to the whirlwind as I strain to hear her.

"Melt it!"

It takes me a minute to realize what she means. Melt it. The statue. Her parents. I shoot a stream of fire from both hands. I can barely shoot it straight, the wind is so strong. And the metal's solid. It's not melting.

I slip out of my jacket. I light up my whole torso, shooting a pillar of flame now. I can't tell if it's working or not, but I have to keep trying. I can't tell if the heated air is making the flame look wavy, or whether the whirlwind is blowing it off course, but I'm missing the statue. I turn my body to adjust, and try and keep the flame on target. I'm hitting one spot consistently, but I still can't tell if it's having enough of an effect.

Then the fire starts to spread. I'm not doing anything

differently, but instead of hitting one spot, the fire gradually creeps across the surface until every exposed surface is enveloped, and peals of flame are being sucked into the vortex. I look over my shoulder and see the Maestro, down on one knee, arms outstretched, doing his thing. He nods. I nod back. I still don't like the guy, but I have to give him credit, he's still here. Still fighting.

At first, it's hard to see any change in the statue through the flames. But slowly, surely, the shape starts to change. It's softening, melting. I keep the fire going full blast. The Maestro keeps it on target. I start to see the whirlwind glow, as golden liquid pours into it. Eventually, the gritty black wind gets shinier, and brighter, until my whole field of vision is a storm of liquid metal spinning by.

Now it's Chloe's turn. Except I don't know where she is, or if she's even alive. All I can do is hope she can hear me. "Freeze it! Get ready!"

No response. Please be alive. Please be alive.

I cut off the flames, and Frank is smart enough to see that and let them extinguish. I watch the swirling mass of molten metal for a few moments. Probably only a few seconds, but it feels like ages, watching patterns of light and dark as streams of liquid bronze spin around the vortex.

Finally, I hear a crack. And then another. There are snaps all around like twigs breaking, and I realize it's the bronze, hardening quickly. The streams of metal slow down, and stop, and the wind dies down with it. A coating of frost creeps across what's now a hard shell, a scarred, misshapen lump. I edge around the remains of the statue until I see Chloe. Alive. Her glasses are gone, her forehead's bleeding, and her left arm's hanging limply at her side, but she's alive.

"Now my arm's broken, you jerk!"

I'm so relieved I burst out laughing and start crying at the same time.

But it's quiet. The wind has stopped. The air has stopped humming. There are no cars driving by, no people talking, no birds. Just silence. Either I'm dead, or we stopped her and it's all over. Relief hits me either way, but so does a stabbing pain in my back. And a thousand other smaller pains pretty much everywhere. Definitely not dead. Woozy, though.

I limp over to Chloe and give her a one-armed hug, trying to avoid her bad arm. We're both a mess, I can't see through the tears, but I also can't stop laughing. "We did it. We're alive. We did it."

"Next time? We're taking my suggestion and running away."

I laugh again, and brush the tears from my eyes.

"We need to get you to a hospital." I feel another sharp pain in my back. "And me. Mostly me."

"The hospitals are probably overflowing right now. Just take me home. I'll be fine."

She winces as she holds her arm straight, and ice starts to form around her arm, thicker and thicker until she's got a solid-looking cast. We both still need to see a doctor sooner or later, but for now, I think we're okay.

I look around the circle and realize I don't know what happens now. Do the police show up? Do we wait around for them? It's eerily quiet. No cars, no people, just debris all over the streets. Broken glass, trash, fallen branches, the odd telephone pole. And a glint of something red. Half buried under a tree limb is the Maestro's motorcycle. My motorcycle.

I limp over, and to my shock, it's still in one piece, ever after the vortex, and getting hit by a tree, and everything. The front fender's missing, and the left tailpipe has a big dent, but it's basically okay. The tires aren't even flat. I guess it makes sense the Maestro's ride would be super tough.

That reminds me. I turn around, and he's coming around the bronze lump, as Chloe cradles her arm and backs away from him.

"So... I don't know what the hell that was, but damn. You kids were great. I'm real proud of both of you."

I push the motorcycle over to Chloe. I see the look on her face and figure I should say something before she encases him in ice. Again.

"I don't care."

He looks shocked, and disappointed, and tired, and all he can manage is a confused, "Hey..."

"Look. Thanks for your help. That was legitimately great. You helped save the city, like you always do. But I don't need to talk to you about it. Neither of us do. Go do your thing. Save people, whatever. But I don't want to be involved. Neither does she. Leave us out of it."

I get on the bike. Against all odds, the motor starts.

"Look, kid, we've had a rough couple of days. I got off on the wrong foot with both of you, and things just got out of hand. Can we start over? Bygones and all that?"

I feel a sting of cold as my sister gets on behind me and her ice cast presses against my side.

"Come on..." he offers, lamely. "We really worked together! As a family!"

Chloe turns her head and says it before I get the chance: "I already have a family."

I turn the throttle, and we speed away.

REHAB

I killed her. I promised myself I'd protect that girl, and instead I held her burned, broken body into a stream of molten metal until it enveloped her. I watched the metal cool, and I waited, for hours, making sure she didn't move, she didn't breathe, her powers were gone. Not that I had a choice — I was half encased in solid bronze. It took them two days to get me out.

I didn't think I'd ever kill anyone. And I really didn't think I'd be so okay with it. But in that moment, it was easy. I just did what had to be done. And whatever it was that cut that path of destruction, it wasn't Amberly. That poor girl was long gone. Just another person that fate shit all over. I feel bad for everything that happened to her. But I didn't feel bad for a second about what I did. I didn't even need a drink afterwards.

It was a rough winter for the city. Lots of snow, falling on lots of rubble. But people came together, like they always do when there's a disaster. People opened up their homes to the families whose houses had been destroyed. The President showed up and talked about rebuilding. And now, it's spring, and they're rebuilding. Everyone had said for years the Skyway was an eyesore that blocked off the waterfront, so now it's going to be a wide, tree-lined boulevard, with easy access to the lakeshore. The old, ugly-as-sin police headquarters is being replaced by a sleek, modern, steel-and-glass number. (Of course, the only part that was undamaged enough to keep was the cells below the basement, so I'm sure I'll end up back in my old room eventually.) That steel mill that collapsed on top of me? They're building a huge solar panel factory on the site. Lots of jobs. Money coming into the city. Buffalo's finally getting dragged into the 21st century.

But the most surprising thing is, the Maestro finally retired, and we've got a new protector. I thought it was a pretty lousy choice at first—an impulsive, unreliable alkie with very little experience. Seems like a recipe for disaster. I actually said no the first time they offered, but then I figured, shit, what else am I gonna do with my life? Work in an office?

I still think it's hilarious what got me back into the public's good graces. After Amberly blasted me out of the sky, I knocked over a cop who was fleeing the police station. I did it on purpose, to get her gun. Complete dick move, and it didn't help anything at all. The bullets melted before they got to Amberly. But a security camera caught me in midair, knocking her over. On any other day, that photo would be someone's "Exhibit F," but the funny thing is, somebody looked at the picture and decided I'm pushing her out of the way of one of Amberly's blasts or something. So it was on page one of the paper with the headline "Rehab to the Rescue." They had me saving a cop from certain death, and for whatever reason the cop herself didn't contradict that. Print the legend, I guess.

I'm the reason Amberly was running around on the loose, I failed to stop her again and again, I never found out what happened to that arsonist guy, and in the end I murdered a teenage girl with my bare hands. But as far as anyone's concerned, I'm the hero. Go figure.

But since they all think that, I decided I'm going to at least try to live up to it. I moved into my parents' house. The mansion. With the alarms, and secret rooms, and all the superhero bullshit. I didn't bring anything from my old place. Especially not the booze. I'm not saying I'm stone cold sober now or anything, but I don't drink at home. I try not to overdo it when I'm out. I act like I could get called into action at any time, and that's usually not far from the truth.

As exciting as the superhero life looks from the outside, it's a fucking job. I saw my parents deal with that, but there were two of them, and they were in New York where there are a bunch of supers to share the load. Whereas I get every single call. The police call me with nickel-and-dime stuff, and the Falls calls me with big stuff. I know a little more about Dr. Science and what he actually does and who he works for, but honestly not that much.

But I get to be one of the good guys. I get to feel like I'm helping. I mean, a lot of it is just stopping some idiot from shooting some other idiot, or getting some drunks to calm the fuck down. And occasionally, I have to keep another super in line—no one as bad as Amberly, thank goodness, but those are usually the tough cases. Once in a while I save a kid from drowning or pull someone out of a burning house, and feel like I'm actually making a little bit of a difference.

And when I'm not doing that, believe it or not, I'm gardening. Gardening bordering on farming. I used a little of my parents' money and bought the whole block I used to live on. It was depressingly cheap. You couldn't get a parking space in New York for what that whole block cost. There were only two families left on the street, and I found them nicer places. I know firsthand what a shitty place that is to live in, and I felt bad. Then I knocked the few remaining houses down apart from mine, and turned the whole block into a community garden. And when say I set up a community garden, I mean I found someone else who wanted to set up a community garden and let them do it.

Which was a stupid, stupid idea. The soil's polluted, we get three hours of sunshine a year, and the growing season's about two weeks. But I'm stubbornly insisting it can work. As it is, I've got a bunch of people in the neighborhood helping out. People who have never held jobs and have nothing but time on their hands and are just happy to do something somebody thinks is worthwhile. People who work for minimum wage doing pure drudgery who are glad to take a break from that and feel like something they do has a purpose. The local middle school is even sending kids over to help pull weeds and shovel dirt and whatever else. As long as I don't have to watch the little brats personally, I'm all for it.

It's a naive, probably-doomed effort, as far as producing any amount of food goes. But there are times when I feel like I'm doing more good with this than flying around getting shot at. I'm actually getting to know the neighbors I used to spend so much time ignoring. After slumming it in this neighborhood for so long, it feels good to make this shithole a little less shitty.

I'm also not protecting the city alone. Those kids who helped me stop Amberly, well, let's say no one expected them to go back to algebra class after that. The sister acts like she's too cool for any of this, and has better things to do. But I can tell deep down she knows how powerful she is and she loves it. And the brother? He's come a long way since I saw him in that jail cell. I mean, he's still an overeager kid who desperately wants to be taken seriously, which makes him impossible to take seriously. And he's going to break his neck falling off that motorcycle one of these days. But at least he's not scared of his own shadow anymore.

So we meet up at the mansion once a week to talk about superhero stuff, although it ends up being me telling them stories of drunken escapades, or my parents being heroic, or what New York is like. I have to admit, thought, it's nice to be able to call one or both of them in when I'm in trouble. I finally got a phone and have managed to keep it in one piece. Surprisingly much easier to do when you're sober.

I have to be honest, it's weird being the grown-up with those two. Especially when they're both way more responsible and levelheaded than I am. Chloe is, anyway. I'm pretty sure she's about six weeks away from being able to take over for me, so it's good to know I can retire soon.

Even with everything else going on, I found time to visit Jodi every day for weeks after Amberly's rampage. Every time I saw her, she was eating. She said it took loads of energy to regrow her arm, plus the leg they had to amputate. And she couldn't even start that until she fixed who knows how many things internally. I'm not a doctor or anything, but it's obvious anyone else would be dead several times over. So I tried to see her as often as I could because I came so close to not being able to.

Except one time, I got there and the bed was empty. So was the room — no flowers, no empty wrappers, no sign of her stuff. I walked back out into the hall and ran headlong into a nurse. I almost knocked her down, but she grabbed onto me for support and we both righted ourselves. Awkward. She was Indian, young, dark skin, big eyes, pixie haircut. I hadn't seen her on the floor before. She mumbled an apology and tried to speed down the hallway, but I called after her.

"Do you know what happened to the patient in this room? She used to work here."

She looked torn between answering and hurrying on her way, before shaking her head no and mumbling a few words. "Don't know. Sorry."

I got a sinking feeling in the pit of my stomach. Did I lose Jodi again? I had hoped she'd say something before she was discharged. Maybe they just let her go on short notice and she was at home. I still felt like I should check up on her. I reached for my phone, but there was a piece of paper in my pocket that hadn't been there a minute ago. I unfolded it, and in neatly printed letters it said,

I'LL BE FINE

I ran after her, but when I got to the end of the hallway and the nurses' station, no one was there.

I don't blame her. Not for Amberly, and how it all went wrong. Not for keeping secrets. Not for leaving. I get all of it, and I don't blame her. But I miss her.

We finally get a warm day, so I drop by the garden, and to my surprise, Oakley's crouched down, inspecting some budding tomatoes I have high hopes for.

"I heard you were a farmer now, but I didn't believe it until I saw these tomatoes." He lifts up some leaves and reveals a misshapen yellow blob. "I still don't believe it!"

"Don't look at me, a bunch of school kids had to plant hose for community service."

"You're really cleaning up the town, from what I hear."

"It's just one block. Just my stupid pet project."

"That's not what they say on the news. I read in the paper they call you Rehab because you're gonna rehab the whole city."

"Yeah, I don't know who told them that. It's weird to be getting good PR all of a sudden."

"You saved the city. That wins you a lot of points with people."

I shake my head. "Just between you and me, I didn't save shit. Half the city's destroyed, and in the end it might have played out exactly the same way if I wasn't there." I honestly don't know if that's true or not. She might have just burned herself out once she swallowed up Vaporware. I guess there's no way of knowing. But Oakley's not having it.

"Well, all I know is what I see on TV, and they say you're hot shit. And I get to tell people I got you into bed before you was anybody, so don't screw that up for me!"

"You're such an asshole." Same as always, but I can't keep myself from smiling as I say it. Same as always.

"I guess we can't go into the house." He nods to my old safehouse, the front porch now sagging with bags of fertilizer and milk crates full of bulbs to be planted. We can hear a bunch of teenage kids talking and laughing as they wash the dirt off their hands in my old kitchen sink.

"You wanna go back to my place?"

He gives me that sly look I've seen so many times before. Works every time. But maybe not this time. I've been down this road enough times to know where it's going to lead. I smile at him, but I take a step backwards, onto the sidewalk.

"You know what? I'm good."

I take off, and I close my eyes and just enjoy the feeling of the wind on my face. I head up towards the clouds, and then I keep going.

I'm good.

For a minute there, I start to believe it.

Thanks to everyone who took a chance on a first-time novelist whose best known work is a miniature golf course in book form.

Thanks to everyone who read the book in progress and helped nudge the story in the right direction — Anna Klobnak, Dustin Koski, Randall Lotowycz, Sailor Pancakes, Hannah Rae, and especially Doug Woycechowsky, whose time, insight, encouragement, and friendship were invaluable in getting this book finished.

Special thanks to my parents, for instilling in me a love of books from a young age, not complaining too much when I was up past my bedtime reading under the covers, and for their thoughtful feedback on this book. Sorry for all the cursing.

And thanks to my wife Lorraine and my kids, Stevie and Jude, for being a wonderful family, and for five or six years of not rolling their eyes every time I talked about the book I was *almost* finished with...

ABOUT THE AUTHOR

Mike Vago is the creator of two interactive books for kids, *Train* and *Rocket*, and two interactive books for all ages, *The Miniature Book of Miniature Golf* and *The Pocket Book of Pocket Billiards*. He is also a regular contributor to *The A.V. Club*. He tells people he lives in New York City, but he really lives in New Jersey.

95711965R00152

Made in the USA
Lexington, KY
11 August 2018